# NANNY WANTED

## IONA ROSE

SOME BOOKS

# AUTHOR'S NOTE

Hey there!

Thank you for choosing my book. I sure hope that you love it. I'd hate to part ways once you're done though. So how about we stay in touch?

My newsletter is a great way to discover more about me and my books. Where you'll find frequent exclusive giveaways, sneak previews of new releases and be first to see new cover reveals.

And as a HUGE thank you for joining, you'll receive a FREE book on me!

With love,

Iona

Get Your FREE Book Here

Get Your FREE Book Here

APPRECIATIONS

Thank You
To

Leanore Elliott
Brittany Urbaniak

ELLA

*A*loud banging at the front door woke me up from my sleep. I bolted upright in a terrible panic, my head whirling around towards the sound.

The landlord!

That was my first thought. He had come to kick me out of my apartment. Heart pounding, I stared into the darkness. My chest rose up and down. I glanced at my bedside table clock.

*Four freaking am!*

No way was it the landlord. Surely, they're not allowed to harass their tenants like this by law. I waited, hunched inside my duvet. Silence. Jesus, it had just been another nightmare. A nightmare so real, I had believed it was a banging on my door.

I fell back onto my bed with a sigh. This was no way to live. My life was in shambles. No wonder I was getting night-mares every night. The rent had been due two days ago and I had no money. My life which had been so orderly, now seemed like it belonged to someone else.

Fuck Stan. He had played his games, messed up my brain, and caused trouble at my workplace. Then I had to get a restraining order on him, but it was too late. I'd been fired from my last position in the real estate company I worked for. Which would have been understandable given the poor state of the economy, except I had been one of only three people laid off out of a hundred and ten.

And the other two were ladies in their sixties, and one of them had already mentioned wanting to leave.

There seemed to be no point in trying to sleep when clearly, my brain was done with any thoughts of sleep. I swung my legs off the bed and padded to my minuscule kitchen to make some coffee.

In my tiny living room, I opened my laptop and checked my email for job offers. Given the number of interviews I'd done, surely there had to be an invitation somewhere. None. Zilch. My heart pounded hard against my chest as the implications of this sunk in.

I would be kicked out of my apartment. I'd be homeless. Sweat gathered under my armpits. I wanted to kick something, but I restrained myself. The last time I'd given in to the urge to hit something two years ago, I'd ended up with a broken toe after kicking a brick wall.

*Think, Ella. Think.*

There must be something else I could do besides sell real estate. I thought of my dream to be a fashion designer. Then I shoved it out of my mind. Fashion design was for people who were born wealthy, not people like me who needed to work at real jobs to feed, clothe, and put a roof over myself.

I opened a browser and typed in 'available jobs in South Carolina.' I clucked my tongue at the results pages. Most were domestic cleaning type jobs, which I was starting to consider. If the pay was good enough why not? I wasn't too proud to be cleaning homes for a living. Then in the sea of domestic help needed ads, a different type of advert caught my eye.

*Nanny urgently needed.*
*Excellent pay and benefits.*

Hmmm... interesting. What could be difficult about watching a child or children? I was good with children.

My sister, Angela's three children loved me. I was their favorite Aunty. Not that there were any other contenders. Still, I felt certain I would have been their favorite aunt if we had more sisters.

My interest was further piqued as I read the job description.

The child that needed minding was five years old, just like my niece Charlotte. True, I had rarely seen my sister's family during the last two years, but I facetimed or Skyped Angela a lot and always got to speak to the children every time too.

However, I was aware, this probably wasn't enough to get to know the ins and outs of being a nanny to them. If I were being honest, I had no idea what five-year-old girls were like, but there were lots of books I could read on the subject and I was once a little girl. I made a decision there and then to apply for the position. It would be a stopgap until I got something better in real estate.

I poised my fingers over the keyboard as I thought of what to say. Then I wrote an email to the contact email given. When I read it through, I realized that even I wouldn't hire me. So, I exaggerated my experience somewhat. Okay, maybe I went overboard and did more than a bit of embellishing. I couldn't help it. As my grandma used to say, *you can't polish a turd*. As I re-read my email, I felt an almost desperate desire to hire myself before someone else snapped me up.

*Good.* I hit send. They were all white lies anyway.

## ELLA

*T*wo hours later, I got an email requesting me to attend an interview. The wording gave no clue about the potential employer, other than a name. Luke Meyers and a work email address. Excitedly, I quickly penned back a reply. The following day would be awesome.

Just as I hit send, my cell phone vibrated from the table. I reached for it and smiled when I saw the caller. My best friend, Ruby.

"Don't tell me the slave driver has left," I said referring to Ruby's boss, a workaholic woman who owned the beauty salon where she worked.

Her laughter crackled through the phone. "No chance. I'm between clients."

Ruby was a makeup artist and one of the few people I knew who really loved her job. And she was really good at it. When I got married, I was having her do my face.

"Anything new?" she asked, referring to my jobless situation.

I sighed deeply. "None. Not one. Anyway, I might have found a temporary situation." I told her about the nanny position I had applied for.

"God Ella, what do you know about kids? I want to be supportive and all, but a nanny?" She ended the question with a laugh.

I threw my shoulders back. "I'll have you know that I do have experience with my sister's kids."

Ruby went silent for a few seconds. "Is that all of your experience? Watching your sister's kids whom you see once a year?"

"Well, I kinda made up some stuff," I admitted.

"You didn't!" she gasped.

"I did, but I figure it isn't exactly rocket science. I mean, I saw Mary Poppins and there must be a bunch of books on the subject. I'm going to read until my eyes bleed."

"I don't know. I still think you should wait for a more suitable job," she said doubtfully.

"At this point, Rubes, I'll take anything. Rent was due two days ago, and my bank account is crying."

"Hey, stop being so proud and let me lend you some money," she offered softly. "It's not a big deal and I do have plenty."

Ruby was a saver, unlike me. I spent it as quickly as I made it, but this experience of being so close to homelessness had taught me a big fat lesson. After this, I intended to start religiously saving at least twenty percent of what I earned. But first, I needed to start earning. "No, it's okay. That's another slippery slope I don't want to get on. I'll be fine." I refused to take advantage of my best friend's kindness.

We chatted some more, then Ruby had to go in a hurry. Her boss had passed by and gave her the beginnings of the evil eye. I laughed as I disconnected the call. Just by being herself, Ruby always managed to cheer me up even when my circumstances were dire like they were now.

I spent a couple of minutes trying to figure out what nannies wore. In my mind, I thought of nannies in nurse like blue uniforms, but since I owned nothing like that, I decided to be myself. With that problem solved, I went online and started my research on Reddit. I found a nanny sub-Reddit and began my introduction to being a nanny there.

Okay, there did appear to be the existence of kids from hell and parents from deeper hell, but generally, I felt I could handle it. I downloaded a PDF and a book on being a super nanny and waded through both. I actually learned a lot from the book and started to feel really confident about my decision.

# ELLA

The following day found me in an Uber on Cotton Hollow Street, which turned out to be a suburb for the rich. It wasn't far from the city but it seemed like a different world. Tree lined winding streets and houses set so far back, that you only got a peek of them through the gigantic trees.

I swallowed hard when the car came to a stop in front of a pair of massive gates. Before I could get out and press the intercom, the gates swung open noiselessly.

As the car drove through, I looked around at a house surrounded by old mature trees and a lawn which would not look out of place in a golf course. I sat unmoving as I debated whether to go ahead with my scatter-brained idea of pretending to be an experienced nanny.

The longer the drive extended, the more I became convinced that this had been a stupid idea. The worst I'd ever had. I wanted to tell the Uber driver to turn around, but the thought of facing the landlord with no money kept my mouth shut. I blinked rapidly and stared ahead at the mansion.

"Planning to get out any time this year?" the driver asked sarcastically.

The car had come to a stop. Before I could formulate a reply, one of the huge, double doors swung open, and the most gorgeous man I'd ever laid eyes on stepped out. The first thing I noticed was his height. Definitely over six feet. He wore a white t-shirt that clung to him and showed off his abs.

"Fuck," I said, apparently not quite under my breath, judging from the chuckle coming from the driver's seat.

I took a deep breath. *Showtime!* I opened the door and slipped out.

Running hands down my dress, I plastered a big ass smile on my face and sashayed up those steps. "Hi," I said, and struck out my hand.

Then my eyes met his and all rational thought left my brain. I was a step away from drooling. His eyes were so blue that they reminded me of a perfect summer sky. My gaze took in his chiseled, classically handsome face before dropping to his perfect body. With my height, I didn't have to lower my gaze too far down before settling on the bulge in front of his jeans.

And for some weird, totally incomprehensible reason, I started thinking like a nymphomaniac would. I imagined my hand stroking his package, as it grew larger and larger.

He cleared his throat.

Startled, I looked up and met his slightly amused look. My face burned with shame and embarrassment. This could be my boss for crying out loud. What am I thinking? God, what must he think of me? If I were him, I'd think I was a perv who couldn't be trusted with my precious daughter. I just lost the job before I got it.

I knew what the problem was. I wasn't a nympho/slut. I was just nervous as hell. So jittery I was behaving in a way that was alien even to me. I got myself ready for him to tell me to call my Uber back, the interview was over.

Then he spoke in a totally dark and delicious voice, "Miss Cooper."

God, even his voice was hot. I swallowed excess saliva and tried to smile confidently. "That's me."

"Luke Meyers. Come on in," he said as he held the door for me.

A gentleman. Very few of those in my world. As soon as I stepped into the huge foyer, my attention turned to the obvious wealth reeking from the room.

A huge chandelier with many crystal lights hung from the cathedral high ceiling. The foyer had to be larger than my whole apartment. A curved staircase led to the second story.

"This way, please."

I followed him down the hallway into a room which obviously served as an office and library. To my shock, I found myself doing it again. Staring with admiration at his tight muscular butt as he strolled ahead of me. I stopped myself from going too far down that road and brought my thoughts back to the interview at hand.

He held the door and let me pass.

I felt his eyes boring into my back.

"Please have a seat," he said, walking over to take his seat behind the big desk.

"Thank you, Mr. Meyers."

"Please call me Luke."

I sat down and tried to keep my dress from riding up too high on my thighs. When I looked up, Luke was staring at my exposed thighs. So, it wasn't just me. We had some serious chemistry going on.

Then I remembered the landlord. I really, desperately needed this job. Luke Meyers was my potential employer.

With that, I beamed what I hoped was a professional smile at him and began my prepared spiel. I intended to shower him with all my charm. I would land this job. It was exactly what I needed.

# LUKE

*T*his was Molly's potential nanny!

*Fuck me!* I had seen many women who could be described as sex on legs, but never would I have attributed this description to a five-feet nothing nanny. Until now. Everything about her just screamed sex. That red hair, her juicy mouth, the way her green eyes narrowed in on my dick, and that smoking body! Even her ponytail just made me want to grasp it and pull her head back as I rammed into her.

I actually had to hurry behind my desk to hide my growing hard on. I couldn't keep my eyes off her smooth creamy thighs. Her choice of dress didn't help matters. If it had been a couple of inches higher, I'd have seen her panties.

If she wore any.

I adjusted my cock subtly. It didn't help how her breasts were pushing against the thin material of her dress and I could make out not only the shape of her heavy breasts, but I could see her nipples. They were hard. I forced my gaze upwards, away from her curvy little body, up to her face. She bit down on her plump bottom lip, and I felt it like a punch in the solar plexus. I wanted to suck on that juicy lip… so hard.

She let out a small moan.

*Jesus!* This was not the way to start out with her. Especially, if she turned out to be a good candidate. Although, I highly doubted it. For one, she wore a dress that fell short of being indecent. To be fair, on another woman, it wouldn't have been a big deal. I guess it wasn't her fault, she had the kind of body which would induce wet dreams. Small and compact. I could easily lift her up and fuck her standing, without even breaking into a sweat.

My cock throbbed painfully at the image of fucking her against the wall. Angry with myself, I pushed away the image and concentrated on the interview. "So, Miss Cooper," I began.

"Please, call me Ella," she said. Her voice sounded soft and unhurried. A soothing voice.

I liked all of her and her voice. "Okay, Ella. I didn't tell you much about my daughter in the email. Her name is Molly and she's five years old."

She smiled and leaned forward enthusiastically. "Yes, I know she is five that is exactly why I wanted this job. My sister has a five-year-old daughter and she's so much fun. I love them at that age."

A sudden sadness washed over me. My Molly was anything but fun. I leaned back in my chair. "Well, Molly is a little different from other five-year-old girls. Since she lost her mom, she hasn't been the same."

Ella's gorgeous green eyes widened and filled with sympathy. "Oh, I'm so sorry for your loss."

I almost laughed at this. My ex-wife Penelope was alive and kicking. In fact, the last time I'd seen her, she had been on all fours getting fucked from behind on our bed by a strange man. After that, we have only spoken through the lawyers. "Oh, my ex-wife is not dead. She ran off with another man," I said, my tone cold.

Women were all the same. Disloyal. I looked at Ella dispassionately. She probably had a boyfriend somewhere and I was sure I could seduce her. We hadn't even been introduced and I caught her gaze on my cock. She had looked at it as if she couldn't wait to put her mouth on it.

I almost groan aloud at the thought. I hadn't had a woman in months. After Penelope left, I'd been like a wild man, sleeping with as many women as I could. Just sex. But sleeping with anonymous women lost its allure very, very quickly.

"I'm sorry," Ella said.

I waved a dismissive hand. "It's been a while now. The problem is Molly has not gotten over her mom leaving. First things first," I said, barely glancing at the paper in front of me. "Do you have any health issues I ought to be concerned about?"

I'd had so many nannies in the year and a half since Penelope left that I had the interview questions down pat. I'd gone the formal way and hired nannies from an agency. They had been good on paper, but none managed to get Molly out of her shell.

Desperate to see my daughter come out of the world she had locked herself in, I decided to advertise on the internet, hoping for a different caliber of nanny. I never expected this, as my eyes were drawn once again to Ella's nipples showing through her dress. I imagined capturing her swollen nipple in my mouth and sucking on it hard.

"None, I'm as healthy as a horse," Ella said.

I dragged my mind away from her nipples and went through my check list of questions. She gave all the appropriate answers. The trouble came when we moved to her experience with children. It didn't take long for me to decipher that she had zero experience. All the experiences she had listed which had caught my eye and impressed me were just glorified baby-sitting for friends and family.

If I were being straight, I was glad she wasn't right.

True, Ella had a sunny disposition, something Molly solely needed, but she was too distracting. I'd want to fuck her all the time. Hell, I couldn't even work with her in the house. It would be cold showers and hell on earth, sleeping a few doors away from her. "I'm sorry," I said, putting regret into my voice. "But I really need someone with more experience. Someone... um, older."

*Someone less delicious.*

## LUKE

*H*er face fell and she bit her bottom lip again. My cock jumped and I felt happy I hadn't hired her. There was no way I could wake up every morning to her in my kitchen.

"Okay, I understand... but sometimes children don't need experience. They need someone who truly cares for them. If your child is missing her mother, she doesn't need a nanny with a lot of experience, she needs someone she can confide in, trust... even come to love with time."

I stared at her. I'd never even thought of that. But it suddenly occurred to me... she was right. This was what I had done wrong. I kept on getting the most professional nannies. Women who seemed more like nurses rather than warm, caring people a child could fall in love with.

Ella saw my indecision and went for the kill. "Look," she said reasonably. "Why don't you let me meet Molly and see how we get along? She might hate me..."

I stared at her. What if she didn't? That would be terrible for me.

"You owe it to Molly," she added persuasively.

A big, a *very* big part of me didn't want her to meet Molly in case Molly liked her. Then I would have to hire Ella, but another part of me, knew I had to give her a chance. What if she was perfect for Molly and could bring Molly out of her shell. I would walk through fire for Molly. So keeping my dick in my pants and taking cold showers would be a small price to pay.

I stood. "Fine. Let's go meet Molly."

She stood and smiled at me. "Thank you for giving me this chance."

I nodded and led her to the first floor where the playroom was. Molly was playing quietly on the floor, arranging her dolls against the wall from the shortest to the tallest.

"Pumpkin," I said as we entered the play room. "I have someone I want you to meet. This is Miss Cooper. Ella, this is my daughter Molly."

Molly looked up without changing her facial expression.

It tugged at my heartstrings that as her father, I couldn't make her smile or laugh. I took full responsibility for this. I had brought my childhood into my own home and became my father all over again.

In the early years of our marriage, I worked like the devil to build up my architectural firm. Meyers Designers and Architects was one of the largest architectural firms in South

Carolina. The cost had been high. My wife and I grew apart and I didn't know my own daughter.

Molly had been almost a stranger.

I had been the distant dad who came home late at night when she had already gone to sleep and left early in the morning while she would be parked in front of the TV, watching cartoons on mute. When I think of the kind of man, I was... I cringe. I'd been so caught up with becoming the biggest and best, I lost sight of everything. I could have lived with regrets, wishing I had done things differently but I wasn't that kind of person. I made mistakes, analyzed them, and did better the next time.

Reversing my mistakes with Molly was proving to be a difficult task. She had only known her mom and when she left, Molly stopped trusting everyone. Lost, as if her soul had been locked away somewhere without a key. But I was determined to get that key. I needed to bring joy back to my sweet daughter, no matter what it took.

Several times a week, I worked from home, and when I didn't, I made sure to be back home by five in the evening. Not that it made a difference with Molly. She greeted me like the stranger I was, and nodded politely when I asked her a question.

"Hi Molly," Ella said in her soft soothing voice. "Do your dolls have names?"

Molly said nothing, didn't even look up. Well, here it was. I don't know what I expected, but I felt disappointment. How would I ever get Molly to be a normal little girl again?

Apparently, Ella wasn't giving up. She went and crouched beside Molly. "Is her name Winabanana?" Ella asked, picking up a doll.

I tore my gaze from her curvy ass and tried to concentrate on what she was saying.

A giggle floated out of my daughter!

I froze and stared unbelievingly at Molly. I wanted to tell her to laugh again. It had been so long since I heard her giggle. I took a step forward like a man in a trance.

Molly gazed at Ella with interest. "Her name is Penny," she said softly.

My heart shattered into a million pieces... her mom's shortened name.

"She's beautiful," Ella said.

"I know," Molly said.

"I hope we'll be friends."

Molly didn't reply. She went back to her silent, pitiful, lonely play.

My heart pounded as we left the playroom. I wanted to go back in there and hear my daughter's giggles one more time. It had to be the sweetest sound I'd heard in a long time. "You've done something no one has been able to do, not even Molly's therapist," I said to Ella when we returned to the library.

"What's that?" Ella asked as she sat down.

"You made her giggle. That's all I want. A happy child. The job is yours if you want it."

Ella was all wrong on paper, but she had trounced all those professionally trained nannies by making my daughter laugh.

A gorgeous smile came over her features. "Really?"

I nodded and smiled at her childlike enthusiasm. "Really."

"Yes, please. When do you want me to start?"

"You do know that this is a live-in job, right? I need you here all the time for the times when I have to work late. I have a cook, and a cleaning service that sends maids to come in a few times a week, but I have no one to watch Molly."

"I know and none of it is a problem," Ella said.

"Good. You can move in immediately. I'll show you to your quarters."

Pleased with how everything had gone, I led Ella back to the first floor and showed her the room next to the playroom and Molly's room.

"It's nice," she said as she took in the double bed and the matching furniture.

"There's an en-suite bathroom as well," I said to her and gestured to a door on the left.

"Thanks," Ella said and then sat on the bed. Her breasts bounced along and her dress rode up her thighs.

My body reacted immediately. My cock formed a tent in front of my trousers. So, I immediately turned and left the room. "Find me downstairs when you're done," I threw over my shoulder.

I was sweating by the time I reached the library. How could I resist Ella while living in the same house? I wanted to grab her curvy butt and slam my cock into her sweet pussy.

The throb in my cock had become painful. I desperately needed relief, but I knew I wouldn't get it. Ella was now officially Molly's nanny and out of bounds. More importantly, she had done something no one else had been able to do. She'd gotten a reaction from Molly.

I wouldn't jeopardize Molly's recovery because of how badly I wanted to fuck her nanny.

# ELLA

"*I* got it! I got the job," I screamed into the phone.

Ruby laughed. "Hey, slow down and tell me everything."

I gave her a rundown of everything that had transpired from the time I arrived at the house. I didn't leave out how gorgeous Luke was either. I told her about the giggle.

"You got the job because you made the girl giggle?"

"Yeah, I used the same trick I always use to make my sister's little girl laugh. I called her doll by a nonsense name. And it worked."

"That was lucky. Now about the boss?"

"Oh, my God, Rubes. You cannot believe what a Greek god this man is. I mean I was fantasizing about his cock from the first moment I met him. I mean, when have you *ever* known me to do something like that?"

"Never!" she cried empathically.

"Exactly!" I cried back.

"Don't mess this up though," she warned.

"I won't, but the funny thing is, I think he kinda gave me a hungry look too."

"Work affairs don't work," Ruby said flatly. "Why would you want to mess up such a cushy, well-paying job?"

"If you saw him, you'd understand."

"Are you actually planning on having an affair with him?" she asked incredulously.

"I'm not," I admitted with a sigh. "I guess, I'm just being a bit silly. I need the job more than I need the sex."

"Hey, I'm about to leave work. Want me to drop you off at your new place of work?"

"Yes, please," I said gratefully. If I paid my rent tonight, there wouldn't be much left in my account and an Uber trip might drain away the last remaining bit and even put me into the red. Until I got my first paycheck, I needed to live like a pauper. And even after that, I would have to squirrel away as much I could for the next rainy day.

"Be there soon," Ruby said, and disconnected the call.

I glanced at the pile of clothes on the bed and got to work packing. I felt lucky that I didn't have to stress over furniture and stuff. I had rented the house furnished and owned almost nothing in the apartment, apart from my clothes. Actually, the only things I valued were my clothes, my precious notebooks, and my Singer sewing machine.

Ruby came while I was struggling to shut the suitcase. "It would help if you folded the clothes neatly," she said and proceeded to dump all my clothes back on the bed.

"Do you know how long that took me?" I protested.

"Relax, Aunt Ruby is here." She folded my clothes one by one and arranged them neatly in the suitcase.

Every so often, she stopped to admire one of my creations. "I don't get why you refuse to design clothes for people? Everyone is always complimenting the dresses you design for me."

I didn't want to talk about my lofty dreams. It was one thing to design and sew dresses for myself and Ruby for free but to charge for my designs would be impossible. I felt relieved when Ruby didn't wait for a response.

"So tell me more about this Greek god. Is he someone you can have a little more than a physical relationship?"

I frowned. "No. He's totally out of my league. Anyway, after Stan—"

She stopped folding clothes and whirled around to face me. "Every man is not Stan. He was nasty and you're right to be careful, but you can't judge every man by his standard, Ella. It's not right."

I shrugged. I didn't expect Ruby or anyone to understand. I'd been with Stan for over a year and for the last five months, he had abused me in one form or another. The burns on my thighs had been the last straw.

After therapy, I'd come to a conclusion... the biggest mistake I'd made was allowing myself to be vulnerable. He had manipulated me into a situation where I felt responsible for all his pain and hurt and he had a lot.

When he hit me, then sobbed and said he was sorry, it hurt him more than it hurt me—I made excuses for him. Always in places where no one would see the bruises. At the time, I didn't see how calculated his cruelty was. I still believed the horrible stories he told me of how his father had abused him. Mentally and physically.

It took a long time on the psychiatrist couch to understand how he had his way of manipulating people. Making them excuse his inexcusable behavior. It made me understand the one time I met his father, he struck me as one of the nicest human beings I'd ever met.

The story with Stan didn't even end with the restraining order. There were anonymous phone calls. All I would hear was him, breathing down the line. Sometimes, I'd felt sure I saw him following me from afar. Then one day, he stopped. I found out through a mutual friend he had been arrested for starting a fight and beating a man outside a bar. No doubt, he'd picked out a wimp, but he'd chosen the wrong guy. Turned out, the wimp's father was a rich criminal lawyer who made sure Stan got a prison sentence.

Once he was gone, I'd been able to analyze my relationship with him and I came to a conclusion. The way to never to get manipulated like that again, was to simply not open my heart to anyone like him again. Sure, I loved sex like any other healthy female did, and I wouldn't deny myself that pleasure.

But my heart was mine and mine alone.

I quickly changed the topic, knowing Ruby would never understand what it had been like to live with a psychopath.

Ruby had been seeing her boyfriend for as long as I could remember. He proposed every six months and each time, Ruby said she wasn't ready. I never understood this and she never gave me a straight answer about it either.

"You're a genius," I declared, when we closed the suitcase with room to spare.

"Yes, I know," she agreed, nodding with satisfaction. She looked around us. "Are we all set to go?"

I could see she was excited about meeting Luke. So was I. My sex twitched at the thought of seeing him again. Maybe the second-time around wouldn't be so intense. Perhaps I'd let nervousness and my imagination run away with me and he was just like any other man.

He wasn't.

"Fuck!" Ruby exclaimed when Luke stepped out of the front door. "Is he real?"

"Told you," I said with a little nervous laugh. My stomach was already in knots. No, it hadn't been better than the first time. It was worse.

"I wouldn't mind a taste of that," she said.

"You have a boyfriend," I reminded her.

"If I didn't," she said with a chuckle, as she released the latch to the trunk of her convertible.

I hopped out of the car just as Luke came down the steps. He smiled and my legs weakened. He was that delectable.

"I'll take that," he said, reaching inside the trunk for my suitcase.

"This is my friend, Ruby," I said and stifled a laugh at the way she kept gawking at him.

"Hi there, I'm Luke," he said and flashed her a smile. The man had gorgeous teeth. His parents must have spent a fortune on them.

"Nice to meet you," Ruby said, and licked her lips cheekily.

*"Stop it,"* I mouthed from behind him.

She winked at me.

I knew he could see her doing this. Quickly, I grabbed the box with my sewing machine in it. "All right then. I'll see you soon. Thanks for the ride," I called out to Ruby brightly before she could embarrass the both of us further.

She put the car into gear and with a cheery wave... she was off.

"You should have told me you needed a ride," Luke murmured as we walked up the steps. "I could have sent my driver to collect you."

"Thanks, but it was great to catch up with Ruby," I said. I followed him up the stairs and to my room.

He put the suitcase on the dresser top at the far side of the room.

I set down my sewing machine box and faced him.

"If you need anything, let me now." He gave me a nod.

I need plenty, I thought as I stared at his lips. My blood pounded in my ears when I realized his gaze was also stuck on my mouth. Unconsciously, my lips parted.

He cleared his throat and tore his eyes away. "Dinner is usually at six. We eat on the deck when it's warm like this. You can't miss it. I mean, it's just off the dining room."

"Okay, thanks. I'll unpack and take a shower," I said.

He blinked.

Ugh... too much info, I scolded myself.

Then he looked me over, one more time.

I couldn't seem to help it as I pushed my chest out a little.

He seemed to have a hard time leaving.

It was mutual. I wanted him to stay a little longer. I wanted to feel his admiring glance on my body. His hungry gaze made me feel hot and sexy.

He shook his head slightly and walked away.

The door shut and with that, I made myself unpack my clothes and went to take a shower. I needed it.

## ELLA

*A* cooling breeze blew, as I stepped out onto the deck. Luke and Molly sat side by side like strangers.

My heart-strings pulled. I still couldn't wrap around my head the fact that Molly's mom had left her. Who in their right mind would leave such a sweet girl? Her mother must have been a fool. I looked at the child. She had her father's brown hair and his wonderful blue eyes. I wanted to wrap her in my arms.

Luke pushed his chair back and stood when he saw me. "There you are, we were about to send a search party, weren't we, Molly?"

Molly did not respond. She merely glanced at me with an expressionless face.

Her staring made me wonder what she was thinking. "I got lost," I said, desperate to coax a smile out of Molly. "I found myself in a maze."

"There's no maze in the house," Molly said.

"The hallway then," I said as I sat down in the chair Luke had pulled out for me. "This house is perfect for playing hide and seek. Would you like to do that tomorrow, Molly?"

"I don't know how to play hide and seek," she said.

My heart squeezed. How could a child of five not know how to play hide and seek? I smiled at her. "It's not hard at all. I'll show you."

She nodded.

Molly had already stolen my heart. And one way or another, I would bring joy into her life. Also, she and her father were going to be dad and daughter again.

Seconds after I sat down, a uniformed chef brought steaming plates of food. My eyes almost popped out at the sight. I felt like I was in a five-star hotel. He proceeded to serve us daintily curved baked potatoes, with salmon, and a variety of buttered vegetables.

"Yum, yum, this is delicious. Thank you," I said as I tucked into my food. I'd always had a healthy appetite and hence, all the extra curves. Stan used to say I was fat, but fuck him. I refuse to stop eating for any man.

"You're welcome, Miss Cooper," the chef replied with a polite smile.

"A person could get used to such luxurious treatment," I said, returning the smile.

His eyes twinkled with pleasure as he left us to eat in peace.

Molly's meal was different. Chicken nuggets, veggies, and some sauce. She seemed to enjoy her food too, and ate without a fuss. I wished she would talk though. I decided to let her be. Pushing her too hard too soon would be counter-productive. She would come out of her shell when she was ready.

Luke and I made light conversation at the table. I couldn't concentrate and found myself watching the movement of his mouth as he ate. His mouth was made for kissing and something told me he would be good at it.

After dinner, Luke excused himself and went to the library.

Molly and I went to her playroom. I got her into the bath, then afterwards, sat with her and read her a storybook. Less than an hour later, her eyes were drooping. So, I took her to the library to say goodnight to Luke.

She kissed his cheek without showing any emotion then hand in hand, we left for her bedroom.

"Do you want me to carry you up the stairs?" I asked her.

Molly tucked her thumb into her mouth and nodded.

I scooped her warm body up and she buried her face into my neck. I held her little body tight and felt my chest tighten with emotion. I really didn't get how a person could leave such a sweet child. As I climbed the stairs, I heard footsteps behind us.

"Do you want me to carry her?" Luke asked.

"No, I'm fine. She's not heavy."

Luke leaned on the doorway and watched as I tucked Molly into the bed.

I kissed her forehead and whispered goodnight.

She smiled sleepily.

Luke moved closer and did the same.

We both reached for the doorknob at the same time. Our hands touched. Electric current sizzled through me and went straight to my pussy. I really wanted this man. I ached for a touch. A lick. Anything.

"Would you like a drink downstairs?" Luke offered. "We ought to get to know each other a little bit."

"Yes, that would be nice." I noticed he kept his distance. Clearly, he was one of those men who kept their emotions and behavior under control. The kind of man who thought everything over carefully before acting. You did not get to be as rich as he obviously was by acting impulsively.

We went down the stairs together and into a cozy living room, with comfortable couches and a fireplace.

"What would you like to drink?" he asked, over his shoulder.

"A glass of wine would be fine," I said, while perching at the edge of the couch. I couldn't even relax. My body was just too affected by Luke to enjoy the marvelous surroundings or the prospect of a relaxing drink.

## LUKE

*J* handed Ella her glass of wine while being careful that our hands wouldn't touch. Then I sat down opposite her. A mistake. It felt like torture while staring at her creamy thighs and fighting the urge to run my hands up them.

Up to heaven…

"What were you doing before you decided to apply for a nanny job?" I asked before my thoughts ran away with me. She had the perfect hourglass figure. The kind men masturbated to.

"Well," she said, then paused to take a dainty sip of her wine before continuing, "I sold real estate."

I imagined Ella showing male clients a house… while they admired her gorgeous ass. Jealousy speared through me, and I shook the negative feeling away. How stupid could I be? Jealous, when she wasn't even mine, it was disconcerting. I'd never reacted in such a possessive way with any woman. Especially not with one I hadn't even slept with.

When I found my ex-wife, Penelope, with another man, it hadn't been jealousy that I felt. All I felt was red hot anger at the disrespect she had shown by bringing a man to our home. Our daughter was sleeping in the same house. The sheer audacity of it had shaken me. She had cared so little about me that she had brought a man to our home.

I brought my mind back to the present. "Did you like it?"

She shrugged. "It was a job and it got the bills paid."

I suspected taking the nanny job was a way of getting her bills paid, but I had no problems with that. I respected people who worked hard and shouldered their responsibilities. I thought of Penelope. She didn't work and relied on the alimony checks I sent for her upkeep.

"What do you do?" Ella asked.

"I'm an architect," I said.

Then she asked the next question and I answered it. And so it continued. Talking to Ella seemed to be so easy. She laughed easily and I found myself looking for more ways to make her laugh. She was good company and she made me realize how much I had missed adult company at home. Time flew by and before I realized, it was nearly midnight.

She stood up unsteadily. "Oops... I'm not used to drinking so much wine."

"Fortunately, your bed's not too far."

She giggled. "Yes, it's just up the stairs, second room on the right."

I felt my cock stir at the thought of her in her bed. "Third room," I corrected.

She giggled again. "Is the second room yours?"

My eyes widened. "Yes." For a second, I stared at her. I felt the kind of hunger I hadn't experienced for a very, very long time. Then I realized where I was. Who she was. And I swallowed hard. "Come. Let me take you upstairs."

I kept some distance between us, as I escorted her up the stairs to her room.

Outside her bedroom door, she turned to me and stepped closer. Her chest lightly touched against my chest.

I stopped breathing.

"I just want to say thank you for giving me a job," she said, her voice slurring slightly. "I promise to take care of Molly as if she was my own."

"I know you will," I said softly.

"I'll get that little girl out of her shell if it's the last thing I do."

"Thank you," I murmured.

At this, she impulsively threw her hands around my neck.

I understood it wasn't meant to be sexual, but of their own accord, my hands went around her small, perfect waist. She hugged me tighter. Her nipples were hard bullets against my chest. I needed to break the hug before I lost my mind.

I pulled back.

Ella raised her gaze to mine. As soon as I stared into her green eyes, blazing with passion, I was lost. She brought her mouth to mine and our lips touched. She opened her mouth and invited my tongue in. I tasted her sweet flavor and forgot everything. All the promises not to touch her—everything.

Maybe I could have stopped… before my hands cupped her curvy bottom. Then the ache in my cock overrode my common sense.

I wanted everything she had to offer. She smelled of flowers and sunshine. I wanted to taste every inch of her skin. I wanted to claim every part of her. All those months of being without a woman roared to life.

I lifted her and she wrapped her legs around my waist. I growled like a wild animal when her dripping wet pussy rubbed against my rock-hard cock.

"Mmmm," Ella moaned.

My phone vibrated in my pocket and pulled me out of my trance.

An icy cold filled my stomach. With a jolt, I realized what I'd been doing. My hands were on the nanny's ass and I was grinding into her pussy. Like a sick pervert. I went cold all over. Shame came over me.

She sensed a change and opened her eyes.

I carefully lowered her to the floor. I couldn't meet her gaze. "I'm so sorry."

She started to speak.

I raised a hand. "I promise it won't happen again." Then I turned abruptly and returned to the living room.

I couldn't believe I'd allowed my carnal urges to take over. I'd taken advantage of a tipsy woman. Sweat gathered on my forehead. I'd have to look for another nanny. No way would Ella agree to continue working for me after this.

I fisted my hands and threw a punch in the air. How could I have messed up so badly? Losing control of my own body. That wasn't me. Never in my whole life had I *ever* lost control.

*Fuck!*

# LUKE

*A*s soon as I woke up, I remembered the firm flesh of her ass cheeks when I'd cupped them. Immediately, my already hard cock became painfully rigid. Not even the shame of what I had done could stop me from remembering.

The taste of her mouth had been exquisite. Like water to a man who'd been wandering in the desert for days. Without even seeing them, I knew without a doubt that she had big nipples. Nipples, I would have given my last cent to swirl around in my mouth and bite softly. I groaned with need.

I needed a shower really badly before going downstairs. In the bathroom, I tried to empty my thoughts of the visions of Ella, naked and on all fours sucking my cock. The image refused to go away. I wrapped my hand around my cock and closed my eyes as the water cascaded down my body from above.

*Soap.*

I poured a dollop of shower gel into the palm of my hand and gripped my cock again. I imagined Ella's plump lips wrapped around my cock, my hand at the back of her head, keeping her in place. I rocked my hips as my hand worked my cock, stroking faster and faster.

I imagined Ella's tongue teasing the tip of my cock and licking off the pre-cum. Her dazzling green eyes, looking up at me as she took all of my big cock into her mouth. Her whimpers as I pumped into her mouth.

Her voice, begging me to take her. To drive my big cock into her sweet tight pussy. Fuck. I pumped into my hand harder. I could feel a climax building up. Relief only a few seconds away.

Visions of Ella crying out as I drove my cock into her over and over again filled my head. I muffed the roar rising in my belly as cum burst from my dick, mingling with the water.

When it was over, humiliation washed over me. The last time I had jerked off over a woman had been when I was a kid. I had just now jerked off to fantasies of the nanny. It might be a good thing she was leaving. I'd allowed myself to get consumed with the thought of fucking her.

I finished showering and toweled off. The sooner I dealt with Ella the better. After dressing, I left my bedroom, feeling angry and disappointed with myself at the thought of losing her before she had even begun working for us. Molly would lose out on having a nanny who understood her for the first time and all because of my selfish behavior.

I'd made a huge mistake and I would be paying for it. I found Ella and Molly in the dining room, having breakfast and chatting. Or rather, Ella was doing the all talking and Molly was licking the jam off her toast.

Ella looked up when I walked in. Her face immediately flushed and her lips parted.

That was all it took for my cock to roar to life. Panic came over me. *What am I going to do?* I wanted this woman with an uncontrollable, yet primal need. I had become a fucking caveman. "Good morning," I growled, angry with myself.

Ella smiled sweetly. Then her gaze dropped to the bulge in front of my pants before rising up to my face again. She knew how much I wanted her and she liked it.

I'd been sure she would be handing in her resignation, but it suddenly dawned on me she had no intention of leaving. Relief made my knees weak. I walked over to the coffee machine and flicked on the switch.

"Morning," Ella said. "Molly and I are just about to finish our breakfast. We're planning to go swimming later."

Images of Ella in a wicked bikini-that left nothing to the imagination-filled my head. I imagined her curvy ass cheeks pushing out at the sides of a thong. My hands palming her ass and slightly spanking it, so it would shake and bounce.

"Can I get you something to eat?" Ella offered.

"Thanks, but no need. Chef will bring in my usual." I turned to Molly.

She wore her usual *leave-me-alone* expression. The one that made me want to wrap her in my arms and protect her from the world. "Would you like to swim, Molly?"

She turned to me with her sad eyes and nodded solemnly.

"Okay, we're done here," Ella announced and got to her feet.

Molly stood up too.

I kissed her cheek before they left the dining room. When they were gone, I let out the breath I hadn't realized I'd been holding. After my breakfast was brought, I wolfed it down, and retreated to the library to work. I needed something to get my mind off Ella's hot body.

But no—I had lost control of my thoughts. I stared at my laptop unseeing. I forced myself to recall my ex-wife's betrayal. The image of the man fucking her hard was fading. In her place, I saw Ella.

And the man pumping into her was me.

# ELLA

*M*olly's sweet laugh danced around me. It was obvious she loved swimming. It seemed to be the only place where she truly became a child. At first, she'd been her usual reserved self, but when she realized there were no rules and we could just have fun, she had relaxed. She had already learned how to swim like a champion at five years old and it made me wonder what kind of education and training she'd had.

She swam after the colored ball we were playing with and when she got it, she turned and threw it to me.

I saw it coming straight for me. I could have ducked, but I didn't. Instead, I let it hit me smack on the head, and gasped out with a mock sound of surprise.

At first, Molly looked frightened, but when she saw me burst out laughing, she started laughing too.

A deep chuckle sounded. I turned to look and saw Luke standing by the pool watching us. My insides trembled. I'd never wanted a man as much as I wanted Luke Meyers.

I wanted, no—I needed to feel him inside me. I didn't even care if he was my boss. As long as I kept my emotions out of it, I should be okay. Sex without feelings. Women all over the world did it all the time. Why not me?

Boss and employee with benefits.

"Hi ladies, I'm the one who's been sent to spoil the fun. The chef said that Molly's snack is ready."

"That's fine. We've swum enough, haven't we Molly?"

Molly swam to the edge of the pool where Luke lifted her up and wrapped her in a towel. She padded into the house without looking back.

My breathing came out in gasps. Would Luke follow his daughter, or would he stand there until I came out. I slicked water out of my hair as I waded through the shallow end towards the edge.

Luke watched me with hooded eyes.

I couldn't tell what he was thinking as I grabbed the ladder and started to pull myself out. Water ran down my body. I knew I looked good in the leopard print bikini I wore. I'd had Luke in mind when I put it on earlier today. Somewhere in the back of my mind, I'd hoped he would come out to the pool at some point.

Luke stepped forward and offered his hand, which I quickly took. He pulled me effortlessly upwards and onto stable ground, but my knees wobbled and don't ask me how, but I tripped on my own legs. I definitely didn't do it on purpose. I wanted to look sexy and glamorous, not like some clumsy creature, flailing like a fool at the edge of the pool.

But the effect of me tripping was a nice surprise. Strong hands immediately went around me. When I steadied myself, I was wrapped inside Luke's warm embrace and my wet breasts were squeezed against his hard chest. Electricity zapped between us. I suppressed a shiver as Luke's ocean blue eyes bore into me.

My whole body heated under his gaze.

His stare dropped to my mouth. I parted my lips. A clear invitation. He took it. In seconds, our tongues were dancing together and our hands were exploring each other's bodies. He palmed my ass. One of my hands went to his thick hair and the other did what I had lain at night fantasizing about.

It dropped to his cock. I froze as I felt him... huge. I mean, massive. Like bigger than anything I'd even seen or touched. God, I wanted to feel that monster inside me. I felt myself being pushed. We were moving. Seconds later, we had entered the changing room.

All... without breaking our breathless kiss.

Luke's hands frantically roamed over my back before moving to my front. With a growl, he snapped my bikini top open and it fell off me. My breasts spilled out. His hands cupped the heavy flesh as if weighing them. He grazed his fingers wonderingly over my nipples and I moaned into his mouth. His hands did things to my nipples that sent electric bolts, straight to my pussy.

He broke the kiss and moved his mouth to my jaw and then my neck. With my eyes closed, I arched my back, lost in the sensation of being in the arms of a man. A man who knew his way around a woman's body, judging by the sensations he was evoking in me.

*Suck my tits*, I wanted to beg.

I had to bite my lower lip to stop myself from voicing my thoughts. I wasn't going to jeopardize what was happening with my mouth. The last time Luke had broken our kiss because of an interruption. This time, I gave him no reason to stop. I needed this and if it meant taming my mouth, I would do it.

He squeezed my tits together, then sucked one nipple hard while rolling the other between his fingers. I shuddered. It had been so long. Actually, no man had even done it like this. No man had ever made me feel the way I felt right now. As if my body had caught fire… a fire threatening to overwhelm me.

# ELLA

*A*s if my body belonged to Luke. He could do anything to me and I wouldn't stop him.

I cupped his cock and tried to undo his zipper. Luke's hand came down and in a flash, his zipper was open and his cock sprung free. Then his mouth found mine again, and we kissed each other greedily.

I reached for his cock then with shock, I gasped into Luke's mouth. His cock was just like I'd guessed... massive. Even bigger than I'd thought and I wondered for an instant if he would fit inside me. Then he deepened the kiss and I started to imagine how it would feel to be stretched and filled by him. My pussy clenched and gushed at the thought of Luke pushing his large, throbbing cock inside me.

I wrapped my hand around his silky shaft and stroked it. It jerked against my hand as if it had a life of its own.

I wanted his cock desperately. Pounding me senseless. It didn't matter that we weren't far from the kitchen and there were people there. All I wanted him to do was relieve this unbearable, aching need in my core.

Luke's hand snaked between us and outlined the edge of my bikini bottom. I whimpered with animal need. I needed his fingers in my pussy. As if sensing what I wanted, he dragged his fingers over the soaked material and caressed me. He slipped a finger through the edge of my bikini bottoms and I saw stars.

I widened my feet further as his finger rolled over my clit and it took every ounce of control not to scream. His expert fingers worked my clit, rolling it and teasing it to near unbearable pleasure. Guttural groans surrounded us and it took awhile for me to realize they were coming from my mouth.

My hand worked his cock furiously. It was so huge that my hand couldn't close over it completely. I should have been afraid of its size. Instead, it excited me. I wanted to taste it. See if my mouth could take all of it in. Have it in my pussy, inch by delicious inch.

Luke grunted as I palmed the head of his big cock. I was desperate to see it.

Before I could make a move, Luke broke the kiss and dropped to his knees, his face directly in front of my pussy.

He blew hot air into my panties and I let out a small cry. I wanted him and I was not afraid to say it. "Please," I pleaded thickly.

"Please what?"

"Please, eat me out." My voice trembled with desire.

He pushed my bikini bottom to the side and his tongue snuck in.

My knees became like water as his tongue probed my folds. Holding on tightly to his shoulders, I parted my legs even further and pushed my hips upwards to give him better access. My whole body trembled as he gave a long agonizing sweep from one end of my folds to the other.

He licked, nipped, and tongued me with the abandonment of a man who loved eating pussy. I ground my hips against him. His tongue found my clit and teased it mercilessly until my eyes rolled into my head. I bit my lip so hard... I tasted blood.

He couldn't stop now, could he?

While teasing my clit, he inserted a finger, then another. I lost it. I gripped his head as he pumped his fingers in and out. I tried to fight the orgasm building up inside me. I didn't want to come. Not so soon. But it had been too long. My breath came out in gasps as the orgasm worked its way from my stomach, lifting me and then exploding.

Juices flooded his mouth. My body shook and clenched and he continued lapping it up. Until it was all over and I sagged over him. Only then, did he stop and drop his head. Like a boy who'd been caught stealing.

I wanted to reassure him that it was okay. I had wanted it. Been desperate for it. "Luke?"

He swiped at his mouth with the back of his hand and looked up at me. His expression, unreadable. He got to his feet with his hands clenched by his sides.

I took a step back.

"I'm sorry," he said quietly while sounding controlled, but it remained clear that he was furious with himself. "I can't understand why I keep losing control around you. You're my child's nanny. She likes you. You might be the one person who can bring her out of her shell. I won't be so selfish again. I won't be so weak."

Before I could react, he strode out, leaving me standing in the changing room, half-naked. My hands trembled as I clipped my bikini top back on. No one had ever spoken to me like that. No one.

I took a shower in the changing room and as the water cascaded down my body, it washed away the confusion and if I was honest, anger. I could understand Luke, but I hated the feeling of being cast into the role of Jezebel, leading him astray. We stayed out of each other's way the rest of the day.

Dinner was a stilted affair, and afterwards, I took Molly to bed and retreated to my room. I plopped on the bed and turned on my cell phone.

"Where have you been, I've been trying to call you!" Ruby said by way of greeting.

I let out a great big sigh. "Working and more."

"I want the *more* part," she said gleefully.

I laughed. I told her all of it. She gasped when I described the size of Luke's cock. "Anyway, I'm tired of him blowing hot and cold."

"Didn't you tell me that his wife left him for another man?"

"There's no accounting for taste," I said. "If I ever meet that woman, I would have one question I'd want an answer to.

Why?" Luke had strung my body like an instrument, knowing where to apply pressure and where not to. Good, unselfish lovers were hard to find. How could she let him go? If Luke were mine, nothing would make me give him up.

I startled myself with this thought. It would be foolish and dangerous to think like that. Luke was not mine and I didn't want him to be mine. And by the sound of it, he didn't want to be mine either. This kind of thinking would only bring heartbreak.

"Are you there?" Ruby asked,

Her voice jolted me back to the conversation. "Yes, I'm here."

"So someone who had been betrayed by their wife will be careful about any future relationships," Ruby went on, sounding wiser than her experiences.

"After Stan, I don't want a relationship. I just want to have fun," I said.

"He doesn't know that you don't want a relationship."

I sat up straighter as what Ruby was saying started to make sense. "You mean he's frightened?"

"Exactly. He's frightened of being hurt again," Ruby said.

"Well in that case, I'll have to let him know that the only thing I want is his hot body."

Ruby giggled. "God, how can you be so direct?"

"Easy, I open my mouth and the words just pour out."

## LUKE

*I*'d been staring at my laptop in the library for hours without making progress. I'd requested a sandwich to be brought to the library for my dinner. Anything… to avoid seeing Ella.

It seemed as if every time I saw Ella, something in me went off and I became an uncontrollable Neanderthal that couldn't contain his horniness.

Darkness had set in and I flicked the lights on. I should have been thinking about the elevation for an art house project my company was working on. Instead, all I could think of was Ella. All the blood in my body immediately rushed down to my dick. Ever since she came to live in this house, it seemed as if I had a permanent hard on which was becoming painful and unwelcome.

I ached to have her hand stroke my cock again. I couldn't forget the softness of her body and how responsive she was to my touch. I wrestled with myself moving from one decision to another. She was my employee and if we started a relationship, it would ruin everything.

Women were trouble. This I knew for a fact. But then another voice reminded me... I wasn't looking for marriage. Just sex. And everything Ella did seemed to suggest she was looking for the same. Just sex. What if we just had sex? Surely, a few nights of unbridled passion would be enough to get Ella out of my system. In my experience, after the first time, sex always became less and less exciting until it completely fizzled out.

Maybe that was the answer. Just fuck a few times and let it naturally die out. Then she would be able to concentrate on her work and I could get down to mine.

Yes, this might be the solution. One night and we could move on with our lives. The other option would be to resign myself to having a permanent hard on. At this rate, at some point I would probably have to be hospitalized.

One night of passion with Ella sounded a whole lot better.

A slight knock came on the door before it swung open. Molly walked in.

I found myself smiling. She did that to me. She made me happy. I wish I could do the same for her. "Is it bedtime?"

She looked at me with her big eyes and nodded.

"Okay, come here for a hug and a kiss."

Molly came to my side.

I hugged and kissed her. Her small hands went around my neck and I almost wept. She had never done that before. I forced myself not to show my excitement. I pretended that my daughter hugging me back was the norm.

Molly left the library. So, I looked at the door expecting to see Ella. When it became clear that she wasn't going to come, it did something strange to my heart. I realized I'd been looking forward to seeing her. It had already become a ritual in my mind. I'd only caught a couple of glances of her during the day as I had been determined to keep my distance, but now I hungered to see her again.

I forced myself to work for another hour with the hope that Ella would come to say goodnight. No such luck. Finally, at nine, I switched off my computer and left the library. All the lights downstairs were off as I climbed the stairs. I walked as if in a daze. Slowly, my feet dragging.

My heart pounded as I found myself standing outside Ella's bedroom door. I should go to my room, I told myself, but I couldn't move my feet. I wanted to see her so fucking badly. To feel her soft body against my own. To hear her sweet moans. To hear the words she tried to keep in by biting her lower lip.

I shoved my hands into my pockets and then took them out again. I squared my shoulders, took a step forward, and knocked on the door. I held my breath as I waited for a response.

I had just taken a step back when the door opened and Ella stood there.

For a second, I couldn't speak. She looked so beautiful and relaxed with her red hair loose, flowing down her back. I tried. I really tried to keep my eyes on her face and not on her towel clad body. The soft curves of her shoulders begged to be touched. Her neck begged to be kissed. My gaze dropped to her chest and I almost came.

"Yes?" Ella asked in a serious tone.

My mind went blank. Why was I knocking on her door at night? "Um… do you need help drying yourself?" I stared into her gorgeous eyes.

They widened and the silence between us dragged on as she contemplated me. Then she nodded and dropped her hand from the doorknob. "Sure."

My cock swelled in response.

I followed her in and shut the door behind us.

Ella stopped in the middle of the room and turned around. Her chest rose up and down, making her gorgeous tits bounce just the slightest bit.

Every single thing about her drove me crazy.

*Control, Luke, have some fucking control.*

# LUKE

*I* went and stood in front of her, then ran my fingers lightly over the swell of her breasts, over the top of the towel. I gripped the hem of the towel while looking into her eyes. This was my way of giving her the last opportunity to say no to what would be happening next.

She licked her lower lip.

I tugged the towel and it fell to a heap at her feet. "God, you are so beautiful," I whispered in awe, almost unable to comprehend how a human form could be so pleasing to the eye.

"There are condoms in the drawer," she said thickly, gesturing to the bedside table.

My instincts told me to quickly quench the fire inside me, except I wanted to fuck Ella slowly. Make it last forever. I was dying to eat her shaved pussy. I wanted to take her to heaven. I took her hand and led her to the edge of the bed. There, I sat down and ran my hands over the hard peaks of her tits.

She groaned, reacting for the first time.

I buried my nose into her belly button and inhaled her sweet scent. When I'd had my fill, I traced a line downwards with my tongue. Then I couldn't wait a second longer. I dropped to my knees and went straight to her nectar.

She opened her legs. The sweet aroma of her arousal wafted up into my nostrils and my last dredges of control evaporated. With a growl, I parted her pussy folds with my fingers and licked her swollen clit. I lapped up her juices, groaning as I did so.

"Oh God, Luke," Ella cried out. "Eat my pussy…. please."

I did her bidding. Delicious. I teased her clit mercilessly and fucked her with my tongue.

"Fuck, yes. This pussy is yours," she cried, almost delirious with pleasure.

My cock throbbed painfully at her words. Yes, I wanted her pussy to be mine… at least for the night.

"Luke, please," Ella begged.

I paused long enough to ask. "Please what?"

"Your cock," Ella moaned. "I need your cock inside me. Fuck me with your big cock."

"Yeah?" I got to my feet. I pulled her into my arms, wrapped my hand around her waist, and kissed her. Let her taste her own flavor on my tongue.

She moaned at the sweetness.

My hands cupped her as I pulled her up against my cock. I wanted her to feel just how hard I was for her. "See how much I want you?" I growled into her ear.

"Then have me," she whispered back.

I lifted her and threw her on the bed. Our eyes, blazing with passion met. I shed all my clothes without breaking the stare. This was a woman who knew what she wanted—and she wanted me.

I shed my boxer briefs and my cock sprung free. Then I got the condom packet and slit it open with my teeth. I rolled it on carefully. I had split them open in a rush before. The hazards of having a very big cock. When I was done, I put my knees on the bed.

Ella grabbed her ankles and pulled them all the way, until they were touching her shoulders.

*Wow!* I stared astonished at the beauty of Ella. Her pussy glistened with juices.

"See how fucking wet I am for you?" she whispered.

As I watched, more nectar dripped out of her. I couldn't help myself, I sucked that open throbbing clit into my mouth. All of it.

She whimpered and came right there. Her body convulsing and clenching like crazy.

I kept on sucking until it was all over. Then I placed my cock over her swollen, pulsating entrance.

"Yes," she gasped.

Instead of pushing my cock in, I dragged my tip up and down her slit. Her slick juices and my saliva coated the head of my cock.

"Luke, please." Her voice was tinged with desperation.

I wanted to oblige but I had to be careful. She was so small and I was so big. Besides, I wanted everything from her. I wanted her to reach the kind of ecstasy she had never experienced.

"Your cock feels so good," she murmured.

We both moaned as I rubbed my cock over her clit. Ella rocked her hips, trying to coax my cock into her pussy. Her big beautiful tits jiggled with the movement. I made out like I would push it in. The very tip of my cock disappeared into her hot folds.

"Oh," she gasped.

I fought the temptation to thrust it in.

I imagined my cock nestled in between her big curvy tits. I put it down on my things to do before the night was over. My cock felt like it would explode. I pushed it in just a little bit deeper. Her pussy felt so hot, like I'd thrust myself inside a hot water bottle.

I pulled my cock out and made circles on her clit.

Ella's fingers fisted the sheet and her head rolled side to side. She raised her hips to force more friction on her pussy. "Come on," she begged.

"You want my cock, sweet Ella?" I taunted.

"Yes. Please. Now."

A dark pressure came over me. If I gave in to Ella, I wouldn't be able to control myself. I needed time to control myself. To stop myself from coming. I pulled away and slid down the bed. I worked one finger into her pussy and teased her clit with my tongue.

Ella screamed. I licked her furiously knowing she was close to coming again.

"I'm going to come," she yelled.

"Then come in my mouth," I urged, and lapped up all the juices rolling out from her. Her body shook and her pussy walls clenched against my fingers.

"Oh God, oh my fucking God!" she shouted.

I added a third finger and she unraveled, shouting expletives as she came.

# ELLA

$\mathcal{T}$he next thing I felt was the bulbous head of his cock pushing into my pussy.

He took my legs from my shoulders and placed them on his shoulders. The overwhelming feeling as his cock went in inch by inch, made me want to scream. To cry. The feeling of it seemed to be too much. "God," I gasped, shocked at the sensation.

Luke froze, his face creased with concern. "Are you okay? Am I too big?"

"Yes. No." I didn't know what I was saying. It felt like I was being split open, but it was also the greatest feeling in the world to know I could take his massive cock inside my pussy. "Don't stop. Keep going. Go all the way in."

He pushed in some more. "Like this?"

"Yeah, like that. Fill me up." How had I made it for so long without this? I'd never had a cock as big as Luke's, and nothing compared to having a man stretch and fill you up so completely. I didn't know what I had been missing. I felt feverish with desire. I wanted more. Somewhere in the back of my mind, I knew he'd just ruined me for all other men.

My body felt like it might just break in two.

Then Luke plunged into me until he was balls deep, as I screamed and clawed at the sheets. It felt like he had gone all the way into my belly.

He stayed still for a few moments to allow my pussy to stretch to his width.

It felt absolutely delicious. I looked into his eyes. "You feel amazing inside me." It was like I'd been walking around with a hole in me and all the while, this was what it took to fill it. He fit perfectly inside me.

I craved more friction. I rocked my hips and Luke pulled out and then slammed his cock back in. I might just be the first woman to die from too much cock-pleasure. Sex with Luke was unlike anything I had ever experienced. Deeply intense. A spiritual connection, not just physical.

"I've thought of fucking you so many times," Luke admitted as he pumped his cock into me over and over again.

"Like that," I managed to say as his cock hit a particularly sensitive spot, deep inside me. I felt every ridge in its length. Every delicious vein, as his thrusts took me closer and closer to another orgasm. Like a tornado, the fire in my belly grew.

"Luke, Luke," I cried repeatedly. I needed to hold onto something. I grasped the air desperately as if sanity remained just out of my reach. I whimpered and moaned. I was so close. At the edge. One more thrust and I felt myself spiraling, flying, and then exploding.

"Fuck, fuck, fuck." I'd never climaxed with such force. Such feeling. He continued fucking me and another climax tore through me. Oh, my God, I was having multiple orgasms. I shuddered with intense bliss. Tears ran down my face.

As that climax ebbed, I heard a roar escape Luke's lips. His cock felt as if it had swelled even larger inside me. Just from this sensation, another climax came to sweep over me. We came together... our names on each other's lips.

He rolled over to the side and we remained like this as we tried to catch our breaths.

Moments later, he got up and went to the bathroom.

Attuned to all his movements, I heard the toilet flush, before he returned to the bedroom.

My heart pounded hard. Was he going to leave? I wasn't close to being satisfied. I needed more of him. I planned to make up for those months I had stayed without a man.

To my delight, he made his way back to the bed, lifted the covers, and slipped in.

I turned to face him and could barely make out the outline of his face.

He reached out and caressed my cheek. His hands dropped to my breasts. "I love your body," Luke said, trailing a finger around my nipple.

Every man I'd been with loved my nipples. "I'm kinda running into fat," I confessed and placed my palms against his chest. I could feel the strength of his chest under my hand.

"Nope. No danger of that," he murmured and lowered his body until his face was directly in front of my breasts. He sucked a nipple into his mouth.

I closed my eyes to revel in the sensation.

He worshipped my breasts, licking and sucking my nipples hungrily, while muttering how gorgeous they were. He seemed particularly fascinated by my nipples. He couldn't stop sucking and biting them. My fingers raked through his thick hair. Soon, my pussy was clenching again, while I was wriggling under him as heat burned between my legs.

Luke rolled me onto my back. "I want to fuck your tits."

"Yes, please," I said to him and pressing my breasts together, I lifted my head.

Luke straddled me and pushed his hard cock between my breasts. He pumped effortlessly in the valley of my breasts and straight into my open mouth. I greedily took in his cock's big head as it emerged from the top of my cleavage. I peered up at Luke. He looked down at me greedily and his mouth almost open. He looked as if he was in heaven.

It did feel like heaven.

He pulled out his cock and rubbed it against my nipples. It was clear he had a thing for this part of me. I moaned and arched my chest. Then he slipped it back between my breasts. He did this several times, each time returning to the hard knobs of my nipples.

"I'd love to see you in nipple clamps," he growled.

"Get them then," I replied. I'd never had them, but I was willing to try anything with him.

"I will," he promised.

Luke moved further up my body and replaced my hands with his. His thumbs rubbed and pinched my nipples while his cock thrust in and out. Every time the head emerged, I licked it furiously then watched it disappear and come up again. This had to be the most erotic dance I had ever done.

I lost my mind as we rose higher and higher into the heights of orgasm.

Then Luke began to tense. I could see he was at the edge. He threw his head back and hot cum shot all over my chest. He let go of my breasts, gripped his cock, and used it like a paint brush to spread his cum everywhere as if marking me.

The thought excited me.

"You're mine," he growled, his gaze glued onto mine.

A shudder went through me. I had fantasized about this and yet, I truly never imagined it would happen… to belong to Luke and him to me, even if only for a few hours.

He lay on his side, facing me and his hand immediately sought my pussy, dripping with juices. His teeth glistened in the darkness when he smiled. "I love how ready your pussy always is for me."

I raised one leg, inviting his fingers in.

He caressed my clit unhurriedly, as if he wanted to master every bit of it. His cum had dried on my breasts. "How about a shower?" he asked.

"Tired of me already?"

"Not a chance," he said. He withdrew his hand and helped me up.

We padded into the shower and as I slid the glass door shut, Luke turned on the faucet.

And yes, I admired his muscled, taut butt.

He grabbed the shampoo and poured a generous amount into his hand. Then he turned me around to face away from him. His large hands went to my head and he worked the shampoo gently into my hair.

I let out a sigh as his hands massaged my scalp. I'd never had my hair washed by a man. So many new experiences crammed into one night. A night I never wanted to end.

When he was done, he guided me under the shower spray and raked my hair with his strong fingers as he rinsed it.

I expected him to turn me around. Instead, he grabbed the shower gel, poured some into a sponge, and proceeded to wash my back. He rubbed circles over my ass. "Beautiful," he murmured, as he deliberately worked the sponge between my ass cheeks to my mound.

I leaned forward, as if bending to pick something up and I felt Luke go on his knees. He ditched the sponge and used his hand to wash my folds. Warm water ran down my back and between my legs, rinsing away the soap.

"Push your ass out," he instructed.

I obeyed and another sensation came over me as his hands parted my ass cheeks and his tongue replaced his hands. I moaned softly as it probed my folds, sucked and licked. I parted my legs further and groaned as he nipped my clit. Then he withdrew.

I let out murmurs of protests.

"We need to wash your front now," Luke said, a chuckle in his voice.

I straightened and turned around to face him. "If you must," I stated primly.

"I must."

"You're so bossy," I grumbled.

He frowned. "Only because I *am* your boss."

His words reminded me of the precariousness of what we were doing. But I knew myself well enough. I wasn't the clingy or needy type. My life experiences had taught me the futility of clinging to a man. When the time came to let go, I would walk away without looking back. I felt sure I could walk away from him. All I had to do was make sure this never became anything more than just sex.

Luke used the sponge to wash my neck and then my breasts. He gave a lot of attention to them.

"There's more of me, you know," I reminded him.

"I'll admit I'm fascinated by your tits. I've never seen such big nipples. The way they swell up is utterly mesmerizing. I saw them through your dress even on the day you came for your interview. And even then, I wanted to suck them."

"They're all yours," I said.

He sucked the swollen buds until they were hardened to his satisfaction. Then he cleaned the rest of me.

I took the sponge from him. "Now, it is my turn to wash you." I then took more than two minutes to wash his erect cock, jutting out from his body.

"There's more of me, you know," Luke teased me back.

I giggled. "It takes time to clean something this massive, you know?" But in my mind, I wanted to see how big it could get. I couldn't believe I'd taken in the whole of it. No wonder I'd felt so completely filled.

Luke merely grinned.

I stroked it with both hands. My pussy pulsing at the memory of having that magnificent piece of man flesh inside me.

"If you keep doing that, I'm going to have to fuck your sweet pussy again," Luke warned lazily.

"Maybe that's what I want," I flirted back.

Luke slipped his hand around my waist and pulled me close, crushing my breasts against his chest. He brought his mouth to mine as I parted my lips to welcome his tongue in.

He cupped my face with his hands as he kissed me before dropping them to palm my ass. I caressed his shoulders, loving the hard muscles underneath his satiny skin. His tongue probed my mouth, teasing places that had been neglected for too long.

He broke the kiss and nibbled on my neck. "I want to do things to you all night. Indescribably erotic things. You're going to let me?" he growled the words.

His growling, deep voice turned my legs to jelly. I couldn't get enough of him. "Yes," I replied, my voice trembling, hoarse, begging.

His gaze dropped further down to my nipples, which were taut, swollen to twice their size, and waiting for his attention. Luke did not disappoint. He rolled them between his thumbs and index fingers, making me gasp and arch.

"What do you want me to do to you my, sweet Ella?" he asked.

My heart leapt at his choice of words. I liked being *his* sweet Ella even though it could never be more than sex between us. But no one said we couldn't enjoy ourselves while we were at it. "I feel greedy… I want you to fuck me again with that incredible cock of yours."

He inhaled sharply. "You can make a man come with your words alone." His finger snaked between us and into my pussy. "You are… so beautiful… so responsive… so damned tight."

His words were spoken softly while interlaced with kisses, seducing me. Making more juices gush out of me.

"Turn around," he ordered.

I did as he asked. God, how I wanted to take his cock in from behind. I planted my palms on the wet tiles and leaned forward.

His hands caressed my ass cheeks before parting my thighs further.

I panted in anticipation, all my nerves on edge as I waited to feel filled up again. I felt his cool lips on my back as he planted several kisses along my spine. His hands circled me to play with my nipples. I wiggled my ass impatiently.

He chuckled. "My sweet Ella loves cock."

"I love *your* cock." I'd become shameless because of him. It just felt so new and exhilarating to meet a man who had a filthy mouth. I suddenly realized that I loved vocal sex. I really liked being able to let him know how I loved every-thing he did to me.

Luke's hand returned to my ass and the other to his cock because the next thing I felt was the head of it probing my entrance. He gripped my waist and shoved his cock in. For a second, I couldn't breathe as he went all the way up inside me. Good God, he was so powerful!

Then he moved into me, slow and steadily.

Then suddenly, I realized he wasn't even balls deep yet. I pushed my ass back to take more of him. My pussy made slurping noises from all the juices gushing out. I couldn't believe how ready my body remained for him. Not just ready, but already desperate for more.

His cock expanded my walls, filling me in a way I had come to crave, in the last couple of hours. His grip moved to my hips, keeping me in place as he thrust hard into me. My body slammed forward. And it felt almost too good.

"Is this how you like being fucked, sweet Ella?" Luke growled.

"Yes… yes, I like it… like that," I moaned the words out. My legs felt like they were giving way. Losing their strength.

As if sensing I was nearing my climax, Luke increased the pace of his thrusts to hard and fast. The world outside stopped existing. There was nothing but his body ramming into mine. With his hard cock so deep inside me, I thought I would go insane. He fucked me until I felt myself begin to coast. I wanted to come, but I didn't want this amazing feeling to end either.

"I'm going to come," I choked out.

"Then come!" Luke commanded.

As if I had been waiting for his permission, my body shuddered and shook. Then using one strong hand, Luke held me up, keeping me from falling.

## ELLA

*J* woke up to the summer sun streaming in through the sides of the curtains. I blinked against the light. I shifted then my pussy protested and my thighs protested. I grinned at the memory of the previous night. I turned to the side. Luke was gone. Of course, it could never be, but it would have been a nice way to start the day with something hot and hard inside me.

I gripped the hem of the covers and remembered. All night fucking. And I still wanted more, despite my sore body. The man was a beast. A beast, I'd gladly keep permanently. I frowned at the thought. This was a summer thing. By the time summer was over, I'd have a new job and Molly wouldn't need a nanny, as she would be starting school.

Something akin to bereavement came over me at the thought. I quickly shook it off. This wasn't the time to feel sad about leaving. I told myself to stop being silly. I had the whole summer to enjoy that hot bod. The man had skills too. All those other times I'd had sex, now faded in comparison. It had been just foreplay compared to what I had experienced last night.

I hadn't slept for more than four hours but I had never felt more alive. My alarm shrieked, shattering the silence. I turned it off and dragged myself from the bed. The shower held more memories of our night together. Luke's strong hands around me, holding me up as my orgasm rocked me.

I touched my folds. They were so swollen between my legs, I wondered how I could even walk.

I felt good though. Really good. I sang softly as I showered and dressed. Joy bounced off me as I left my room and tiptoed into Molly's room. She had thrown her covers off and was snoring gently, her hair like a halo on the pillow. I stepped next to her bed and gently arranged the covers around her.

Molly seemed to like sleeping in a bit, which was a good thing as it gave me time to prepare for the day. My sister's girls were up at the crack of dawn and ready to annoy the hell out of the whole household.

I tiptoed out and made my way to the dining room. My stomach clenched at the sight of Luke, solemnly reading a paper. Oh, but he was so beautiful, first thing in the morning.

"Morning," I said almost shyly.

He looked up and smiled politely. "Good morning Ella. I trust you slept well."

My own smile wavered. What happened to Sweet Ella? Had I imagined the whole night? I'd expected some teasing and joking. Not this stranger who acted like we hadn't spent the whole night together fucking our brains out.

"Have a seat. Paul will bring you breakfast," Luke said and continued reading his paper.

I was too proud to call him out on it. If he wanted to play stupid games, then he could very well play them alone. I sat down and told myself I had enjoyed a good night of sex. Now I needed to focus on my work. I wasn't going to beg Luke to give me what he clearly wasn't ready to give.

I sat there stewing until Paul came in with a plate of pancakes and sausages. My mouth immediately watered and I forgot how angry I was. "Thanks Paul," I said happily and pounced on my breakfast. I felt Luke's gaze on me, but I ignored him.

"What are your plans for today?" Luke asked.

I had been stuffing my last bite of food into my mouth. So, I took my time chewing and swallowing before I answered his question, "We want to do some painting this morning. Which reminds me, I need to go and look for paint." I pushed the chair back. I could do the formal, cold tone too.

Still, Luke's coldness stung. I flounced out of the dining room, pretending not to care, but the truth was... I did. I hated things without explanations. I went up the stairs and back to the playroom. On the shelves, all the toys and board games were neatly arranged.

Nothing looked out of place. In the few days I had been here, one thing that struck me was how little time Luke and Molly actually spent together. I might not be an expert on kids, but I did know one needed to spend time with them.

I remember how neglected my sister and I felt while our mom was at work all day and evening. As a single mom, she sometimes worked two jobs to make ends meet. I pushed away memories from my past. Luke had no excuse. He was home a lot, but he never actually spent time with Molly. It almost seemed like he was afraid of her.

I didn't understand him. Last night and then this morning made it worse. He seemed to act like two different people. I sighed as I recalled his tenderness. The perfect lover, more concerned about my pleasure than his. Then this morning, he'd been a complete jerk. But then again, what was I expecting? We had daytime roles to play. I was the nanny and he was daddy. He couldn't be obvious about fucking the nanny.

"Miss Cooper?" a small voice said.

I turned and smiled at the sight of Molly standing in the doorway, her long black hair mussed up and her eyes still heavy with sleep.

"Ella," I reminded her. "Call me, Ella."

"Okay. Good morning, Ella."

"Good morning to you. Come here sweetheart." I dropped to my knees and opened my arms.

For just one second, she hesitated, then she came straight into my arms and rested her head on my chest.

"Did you sleep well?"

She nodded.

"Good. Let's go get some breakfast for you, and afterwards we can come here and paint. Did I tell you that I'm good at drawing?"

She raised her head and stared at me. "Can you draw a cat?"

I nodded.

"Can you draw me?"

I grinned. "Bet, I can. Drawing you is easy because you're so pretty."

She smiled.

"Now, shouldn't we go brush all these small teeth of yours?"

She giggled prettily.

I took her by the hand and hung around while she got ready. She was a neat little thing. She even folded her nightgown. Afterwards, we went downstairs for breakfast.

It was already hot outside when we went to sit on the outside tables.

"It's Daddy!" Molly said pointing at the pool.

I swallowed to clear my rapidly closing throat. Sure enough, cutting across the water in strong sure strokes was Daddy. "Mmm… yes," I said. "I'll go get your breakfast." I noticed how my breath was coming out in gasps. My brain filled with his hot kisses and his delicious body while my thighs tingled at the memory.

In the kitchen, I deliberately waited around as Paul prepared Molly's breakfast with the hope that by the time I returned, Luke would have left.

No such luck. He was coming out of the pool as I stepped out. I faltered in my steps as I took in his body in his swimming trunks.

His hair clung to his scalp and drops of water trickled down along his very muscled chest. I longed to lick that chest. I didn't care about being mad at him for not showing even a tiny bit of caring towards me. If he kissed me, I'd respond, and resume my anger afterwards.

He kissed Molly's forehead sweetly and teased her about being a sleepy head. "Hey you," he said to me.

I gave a stiff nod in reply and kept my eyes off his body, afraid I would embarrass myself by doing something stupid. Like running my fingers over those rock-hard abs and maybe lean in for a kiss. I reminded myself about being angry with him. Yes, we had jobs to do, but a little wink or secret smile wouldn't have been amiss.

"Are you angry at me?"

I glanced at Molly to see if she was listening.

She wasn't. She was wolfing down her breakfast.

I looked at him and met his steady gaze. My pulse quickened in response. "Why would I be angry that this morning you pretended that nothing happened last night?"

He frowned. "Can we talk later?"

I nodded nonchalantly. "Sure."

"Right. I'll see you in my study after you put Molly to bed."

# LUKE

*I* paced the width of the library and practiced what I wanted to say to Ella. There was no good way to say it, except to say it. I could not offer her what she wanted. I wasn't relationship or boyfriend material. I owed her an explanation.

I remembered the hurt look on her pretty face. I had caused it and I never wanted to hurt her. She was sweet and beautiful. She deserved a man who could give her his heart. That man would not be me.

I was done with women. The only female who had my heart was my Molly.

No matter how sexy she was—and Ella was easily the sexiest woman I'd ever laid eyes on—I didn't want to go there. Penelope had been enough. I didn't need another lesson in betrayal.

Soft footsteps sounded on the hallway before Ella knocked softly on the door.

I pulled the door open and stood aside to let her pass. Her sweet scent teased my nostrils as she glided past. I admired her gorgeous legs. Ella dressed almost exclusively in short dresses and I loved her in short dresses. The shorter the better.

I yanked my eyes away. It did feel shocking how proprietary my thoughts were towards her. She did not belong to me. I reminded myself of this fact as I shut the door.

She turned to face me and crossed her arms under her chest, pushing her tits up. She jutted out her chin and waited for me to speak. She looked so sexy with her flame-red hair flowing to her shoulders and her green eyes blazing with an emotion I could not identify.

"You wanted to talk, I'm here," she said.

I couldn't stop staring at her lips. What I wanted to do was kiss that pouting mouth senseless, not talk. But that would be a stupid thing to do. I needed to set the record straight. "I want to kiss you and suck on your lips," I blurted out.

Her eyes widened. "Then, why don't you?"

I closed the distance between us and pulled her into my arms. I groaned with the pleasure of molding her soft body into mine. Logic said this was wrong. Reason said it was idiotic, complicated, stupid. Our bodies though, told a different story. They fit together like two pieces of a puzzle.

Her mouth, sweet and yielding, parted for me. I tilted my head and assaulted her mouth with mine. I sucked on her lower lip and her tongue. Like a drowning man, I grabbed her ass and pulled her hard against me. "Can you feel how hard my cock is for you?" I growled.

This woman was driving me insane. How could it be that I had intended to explain to her why we couldn't be together and then she ended up in my arms?

Ella broke the kiss, but did not move away.

The hardness of my cock pressed into her stomach.

"I don't play games, Luke. I don't like them and I'm not good at them." She kept her hands wrapped around my neck.

Her nipples pressed against my chest. My hands were on her soft curvy hips. A caress away from her sweet pussy. Did I really want to end it?

"Luke?" she said.

I cleared my throat. Through the thick fog of desire, my brain tried to list for me all the reasons why Ella and I could not be together.

She was my employee.

I had nothing to offer her.

Women were disloyal. Once she tired of me, she would find another willing replacement, leaving me to pick up the pieces of my heart. This reminder broke through my desire. "Look Ella, I like you very much, but I can't do relationships. I'm not ready and I doubt I ever will be."

She burst out laughing as she dropped her hands from my neck.

I wasn't ready to let go of her. I kept my hands firmly on her hips and glued to my erection. Her reaction puzzled me and if I were honest, unnerved me. "What's so funny?"

"I shouldn't laugh," she said. "But where did you get this idea that I want a happily ever after with you?"

"You don't?"

"No, I don't. Like you, I'm not ready and I doubt I ever will be," she said, her tone sure.

"Does that mean…"

She held my gaze. "We're adults, you and I. We enjoy pleasuring each other, so why not continue? No feelings involved. A physical, undemanding relationship."

I couldn't believe what I was hearing! Could I be this lucky that Ella wanted the same thing I did? Uncomplicated sex.

"We could be friends too," she said. "Nothing wrong with that."

I frowned. "You sound pretty experienced in this." The thought of Ella with another man made me want to break something.

She laughed. "Let's just say, I've had a relationship that has put me off of ever having another one."

For the first time in my life, I wanted to pry into a woman's private life and ask a lot of questions, but I didn't. She had laid down the rules and I should be happy. Very happy and it was exactly what I wanted too. I didn't question the odd feeling of unease in my gut. "In that case, we need to celebrate. What would you like to do? A glass of wine and—"

"Dance!" Ella shouted. "I'd love to dance."

I grinned at her infectious energy. "Dancing it is."

We left the library hand in hand, and I felt like I was walking on air. Ella had agreed to be my lover. My undemanding lover. This was what they called a win, win situation. Everyone's happy. She, me, my cock…

In the living room, I left her to select the music and went to the fridge bar to fish out a bottle of champagne, which I carried back to the living room together with two flutes. I slowed my steps as Ella came into view.

Her eyes were closed as she swayed to the music.

I locked the double doors, placed the champagne and glasses on the table, then went to her. "May I have this dance?" I asked.

Her eyes popped open and she laughingly came into my arms.

How could it be that she felt so perfect in my arms when I had barely known her for a week? When we were together, sparks flew. The song probably wasn't for dancing as closely as we were, but I didn't care. The music could have been screaming hard metal and I would still keep Ella in my arms. I lifted her hair from her neck and kissed her soft skin.

Her hands caressed my shoulders. She turned her face, seeking my mouth. "Kiss me, you sexy man!"

This time, our kiss was unhurried. A leisurely joining of mouths and tongues. Ella raked her fingers through my hair. I caressed her ass and snaked my way under her dress to feel her naked skin. My hands roamed the curves of her hips as our kiss deepened. So soft. So sweet. Her thong barely covered her ass. Unable to resist, I cupped her soft ass cheeks and gloried at her near nakedness. My hands roamed over her ass and back.

In one movement, I pushed her dress up and over her head. "The less clothes you have the better," I said to her as I took her back into my arms.

Her hand went to my crotch and fumbled with my zipper.

At the promise of her hand wrapping around my cock, it twitched and throbbed. I opened the zipper for her and pulled out my cock.

"I want to taste your cock," Ella said and without waiting for my response, she dropped to her knees.

I hissed when her hand wrapped the base of my cock and her tongue tentatively flicked over the head. I closed my eyes as all sorts of wicked sensations came over me. Holding my balls in one hand, she licked the length of my cock. I rocked my hips to the beat of her strokes.

I made a strangled noise when she took my cock fully into her mouth. "Yes. Suck my cock."

Except she took in only the head when I knew she could deep throat. I rocked my hips to make her take more of my cock into her mouth and throat, but she deliberately pulled back. I groaned in frustration.

She licked the tip, making sweet noises as if my precum tasted delicious. "I love your beautiful big cock," she said.

"Then suck it properly," I growled.

"Be patient, cowboy," she said and continued to give me slow agonizing licks.

Her sweet tongue made me want to grab her head and fuck her mouth.

Her hand caressed my inner thigh as her mouth worked my cock and her other hand worked my balls. She finally took me in, a little at a time. Expertly, she swirled her tongue around my sensitive head.

Then when I was almost screaming with frustration she sucked me in slowly, swallowing more and more of it. It was wonderful to watch my cock disappear into her beautiful face. Then she began to suck me so hard her cheeks hollowed out as she bobbed her head. I groaned with pleasure as she increased her speed. I rocked my hips faster and faster. I came hard, my hot seed spurting into her mouth and throat. I watched the muscles of her throat as she swallowed it all.

I gently pried my cock from her mouth and pulled her to her feet.

"Why did you do that so quickly?" she asked in an exaggerated pout.

I laughed. I had never met a woman who loved cock so unashamedly like Ella did. "Because we're supposed to be dancing and drinking wine." I tucked my cock back into my trousers and pulled up the zipper.

"Should I dress?" she asked uncertainly.

"No, you look beautiful. In fact…" I released the clasp of her bra and out tumbled her beautiful breasts, her nipples already erect. I resisted the urge to take them into my mouth.

My hands rested on the swell of her ass cheeks and hers around my neck. I'd found something wickedly erotic while dancing with a near naked woman while I remained fully dressed.

"You've changed me forever," Ella said. "From now on, I'll be expecting to strip off down to my panties for a dance."

I laughed. "It'll take a lot of sacrifice, but I think I can manage that."

Now, since I was temporarily sated, we moved quietly. I could hear her heart and a realization hit me. Ella was peaceful. She made me relax just by being in her presence. The song we were dancing to came to an end.

"A glass of champagne?" I offered.

She threw her head back and looked at me with those beautiful eyes. "What are we celebrating?

"Our arrangement," I replied as I filled our flutes while keeping my gaze on her. She looked unbelievably hot in a black thong. I handed her a glass.

"To us," she whispered.

"To us," I echoed.

She took a sip while staring at me.

I took a sip of mine and placed the glass back on the table. "I can't fucking keep away from you," I said to her as I closed the distance between us and cupped her heavy tits.

"That's okay. I don't want you to keep away," she murmured.

I flicked her big nipples as she closed her eyes and moaned softly. I leaned forward and licked her cleavage, running my tongue down as far as it could go.

My cock throbbed painfully. Knowing Ella, I knew her pussy was already dripping and I was dying to lick it up. I took her glass, placed it on the table, and moved her to the side of the couch. Then I turned her around and made her bend down from the waist. Obediently, she placed her hands on the arm rest of the chair and wriggled her hips for me.

I loved Ella's ass. So round, fleshy and curvy. "I love your body, sweet Ella," I said and kneaded her ass cheeks.

When she wasn't expecting it, I slapped her ass.

She jumped and grunted.

I watched my handprint turn red on her gorgeous ass.

She turned her head, looked me in the eye, and said, "That all you got, cowboy?"

I spanked her until my hand was stinging, her ass was red all over, and her juices were pouring down her legs.

"Fuck me, cowboy," Ella said and swayed her reddened ass enticingly.

I opened my zipper and fished out my rock-hard cock. I sheathed it swiftly, then placing my hands on Ella's inner thighs, I spread them apart.

"Fill me up with your big cock. Fuck my tight pussy," Ella pleaded throatily.

A primal feeling came over me. I gripped my cock and plunged it into her saturated warmth. Her pussy engulfed my cock and squeezed it. Balls deep, I gripped her hips and began thrusting in and out.

Ella arched her back pulling my cock in deeper. "Fuck, yeah," she moaned. Her hand dipped between her legs. She was touching herself.

*Hot as hell.* "Tell me what you're doing?" I asked.

"Touching my clit. Teasing it," she moaned. "Pretending it's your big hand."

"Fuck, Ella," I said. "I want to see that later. I want to see you playing with yourself."

"I'm going to come," Ella yelled suddenly.

My own climax was rapidly building up. "Come hard for me, sweet Ella," I growled, pumping harder.

She screamed my name as her orgasm ripped through her. Just knowing I was responsible for the pleasure Ella was experiencing was enough to make my own load spurt from my cock.

ELLA

*I* felt like I'd been in a fuck fest the last couple of days. Luke and I fucked whenever and wherever we could. Two starving people with insatiable appetites for sex had been brought together. Luke never ever had enough of me and I of him. I couldn't even begin to imagine how much more we would have fucked if not for Molly.

Sometimes, I thought we'd make a great couple and then I would remind myself of the danger of such thoughts. I'd taken to waking up a little earlier to take a shower before Molly woke up and we would start our day together. Luke and I slept together, but he always went to his bed usually just before dawn.

It did seem to be the best idea, I thought as I threw the covers away. It would have been nice to wake up to his hot male body but I understood his need to leave. We had to maintain some sort of distance between us. We couldn't afford to get too close.

As I headed to the shower, I planned the day for Molly and me. On Fridays, Luke usually went to his offices, so we'd be alone all day. We could go to the park, I mused. Paul, the chef, had told me about a park close to the house.

Molly would enjoy leaving the house and seeing other children. I quickly showered and returned to my bedroom. I was about to drop the towel and apply lotion on my skin when a slight knock came on the door

The door swung open and Luke walked in.

My eyes widened at the sexy vision he made. He looked so hot in an expensive looking grey suit. His eyes roamed over me as if seeing my nakedness for the first time. I loved how he openly loved my body.

"Thought I'd say goodbye before I left," he said. He shut the door behind him, locked it, and stepped into the room. "But I realize I can even do more than that. I can help you with that lotion." His voice had thickened. A sign of his arousal.

"Okay," I said, aroused at the sight of his tented formal slacks. I licked my lips in anticipation.

His eyes on me, he shrugged off his jacket and tossed it carefully on the dresser. He loosened his tie and pulled it up over his head. He came to me and took the lotion from my hands.

He squatted down, poured a dollop of lotion into the palm of his hand, and then spread it to his other hand. "I like to start with the legs… and have I ever told you, you are exceptionally beautiful."

"Many times," I said thickly.

He rubbed the lotion on my right leg in gentle circular movements. Slowly, he rose higher and higher, each time adding more lotion to his hands.

By the time he reached my thighs, my pussy was dripping. I'm sure Luke could smell my arousal and feel the stickiness of my thighs but he acted as if his only interest was in applying lotion to my skin. My pussy felt as if it was on fire. His hands were so close and yet, so far.

I shifted my weight from one foot to another, eager to feel his hands on my pussy quenching the fire building up. "My skin is rather dry further up," I finally said, unable to wait.

Luke chuckled. "I like your impatience, but you'll have to wait, my sweet Ella. I intend to take my time enjoying your sexy body."

I knew how to solve that problem. I loosened the knot of the towel and let it fall to the ground. Luke looked up and saw my pussy inches away from his nose. He inhaled sharply as my scent invaded his nostrils.

There was no more talk of impatience now. He lifted a finger and probed my folds, the lotion completely forgotten. "I've never seen a pussy that drips so much. Look at it." He slipped a finger into me.

I couldn't hold back a moan. I'd craved his touch so much that when he finally touched me, I felt like I would unravel. Come apart. "Luke," I whispered.

A second finger went in. "So beautiful," Luke murmured as he pumped his fingers in and out of my pussy making me moan and writhe.

My pussy clenched hard on the digits. "Don't stop," I said, grinding myself against his hand.

"You look so hot with your tits bouncing like that," Luke said.

I should have been embarrassed at the indecent figure I cut, standing there naked while he finger fucked me first thing in the morning, but I wasn't. He made me feel that way and I wanted him to know it. Luke's other hand played with my clit, flicking it and rubbing circles over it.

It didn't take long before my body began to tremble and I seemed to lose all my senses except for what was happening in my pussy. I threw my head back and let out a strangled scream as I climaxed.

"Not too loud," Luke warned before he covered my clit with his mouth and sucked it. With his fingers deep inside my sex, and his tongue on my clit and slit, a second orgasm came on the heels of the first, and it took a long time before I stopped shaking.

Knowing that his cock was burning, I fell back on the bed, lifted my legs into the air, and spread them into a V, exposing my open pussy to his greedy eyes. "Aren't you going to be late?" I asked sweetly.

"Fuck Ella, how is a man supposed to resist that?" He unbuttoned his pants as he spoke and pulled them down along with his boxer briefs.

"He's not," I said. I expected Luke to fuck me as soon as he got between my legs. After all, I was wet and ready for him. Instead, he slid up higher and lowered his head to suck on my sensitive nipples.

I squirmed. The sensations in my breasts became almost unbearable as Luke thumbed one and sucked on the other and then interchanged them.

"So sweet, I could do this all day, except I'm scared of embarrassing myself," Luke said.

"How?"

"By ejaculating even before I reach the final destination," he said.

I giggled.

He raised my legs and pushed them back to my shoulders. He held his cock in one hand and guided it to the entrance of my hungry entrance. We had stopped using condoms two days ago. I was on the pill and it just seemed wrong to have even the thinnest skin of rubber between us.

"Oh, yes!" I gasped out as his cock stretched and filled my pussy. His balls were against my ass as he pumped in and out in deep strokes that penetrated deep into my body. "Fuck me… yeah," I hissed. "I love your big cock, cowboy."

"I'm going to fuck you till you can't walk," Luke growled.

"Is that a promise?" I managed to say.

"You better believe it."

It had been enough warning for me. I reached behind and gripped the headboard of the bed. And sure enough I needed something to hold on to. It felt as if I was about to fly out the window. Luke fucked me faster and faster. The bed rocked. Our breaths came out hard and fast.

We came simultaneously. Luke groaned his way through his orgasm and mine rolled into my pussy and spread to the rest of my body.

After a moment, Luke supported himself with his hands and stared at me, a solemn expression on his face. He kissed my forehead. "And now, I really do need to go."

For some reason I couldn't explain, I wanted him to stay longer. I told myself it was because I liked his company... nothing more. Plus, I needed to speak to him about spending more time with Molly. "Are you coming home early today? I thought it would be nice if you spent some time with Molly. You don't spend enough time with her."

He stiffened. His face, which had been open and laughing earlier became devoid of all expression. He rolled off me and sat up. "I spend a lot of time with Molly. Today is the one day I go to the office and I might come home late."

"Tomorrow then?" I insisted.

He rose from the bed, pulled up his pants, and headed to the bathroom.

I got up and managed to tie the towel around me.

Luke reentered the bedroom and made sure a lot of space remained between us.

"You didn't answer me?" I said.

"Look, I pay you generously to mind Molly. If I wanted lectures, I'd have invited my ex-wife to come for a visit. All I need from you is to be the nanny. That's all."

I took a step back, stung by his words. I didn't understand his reaction. His controlled anger. "All I'm saying is that you need to spend more time with Molly," I said, my voice rising.

"I didn't ask you for parenting advice." He took his jacket from the dresser and slipped it on. He glanced me over dispassionately.

His stare shrunk me. Made me feel small. I shivered, as if I felt cold just from the ice in his eyes.

He turned away and left.

# LUKE

*I* waited impatiently for Jeremy, one of the promising junior architects to wrap up the client presentation, and as soon as it was over, I made some small talk with the clients, then escaped the conference room.

"Hold all calls," I barked at the temporary secretary who'd been covering for Janice, for a few weeks.

"Yes, sir," she mumbled.

I closed the door shut, dropped myself down on my chair behind the desk, and swiveled around to face the floor to ceiling window. I stared out at the view, seeing nothing. I'd been in a lousy mood all day. I couldn't get rid of the image of Ella's face from my head all day long. The absolute hurt in her big green eyes.

I told myself it had been a good thing for me to lay down the boundaries. Her job was to be a nanny to Molly and mine was to earn a living for my family. I had done the right thing. My reasoning told me so. Yet, I kept seeing images of her eyes.

Like a video, I saw our spat from this morning. My contempt as I let her know in no uncertain terms that she was not to ever give me parenting advice. Shame came over me. Ella hadn't deserved the tone I had used. I'd spoken to her like an employee.

Hell, I didn't even speak to my employees like that. The real truth was I had treated her like she'd been nothing because she had touched an old wound that never healed. I knew I wasn't a good daddy to Molly, and I hated it when she had pointed it out. As the day progressed, I felt worse and worse. I needed to apologize to her.

I wondered how Ella and Molly's trip to the park had fared.

Had Molly enjoyed herself or had she been intimidated by the sight of many children? A pang of longing came over me. I would have liked to have gone to the park with them.

I ran my hand through my hair. I never wanted to be like my dad and here I was. Doing the same shit. Never at home. If I didn't build a bridge now with Molly, she and I would always be distant.

Problem was I didn't know how to be with Molly. I didn't know how to pull her out of her shell. I was afraid of the awkward silences. Afraid she would start to get bored of our time together. Worse, she would come to dread having to spend time with me. Maybe, Ella's suggestion to spend time together was a really good one. Ella could be the temporary bridge between us… until I built one of my own.

I felt glad when evening rolled around and I could go home. I walked out of the building with confidence in my step now, since I had a plan. I would apologize to Ella and then we would have a nice dinner washed down with a glass of good wine. Maybe I would run her a bath with lots of bubbles and give her a long massage. I visualized my muscles relaxing from spending an evening in good company.

The drive back home took the usual twenty minutes and I found myself hurrying out of the car, eager to see my girls. I frowned at the thought. Ella wasn't my girl.

I got into the house and went through to the living room. I really did want to know how the visit to the park had gone. I found no one there. My next stop was the playroom. The door open, and there they were.

"Next, you draw the eyes, just like this," Ella was saying.

They were on the floor, their heads bowed close together. Their concentration was so complete they hadn't even heard me open the door. Molly was the first to sense my presence. She looked up and when she saw me, her face lit up.

My heart swelled at my daughter's unguarded reaction when she saw me. Seconds later, her smile faded.

"Hi sweetheart," I greeted brightly, as I stepped into the room.

Ella looked up. There was no expression on her face. "Hi," she said, scrambling to her feet. "I'll leave you two to it. I'm sure Molly would love to show you the things she drew this afternoon." She gave me a curt nod as she passed.

She wore a short white dress and the image of me lifting it and sucking on her sweet pussy flashed into my mind. The door shut behind her and a heaviness settled in my chest. Clearly, I had wounded Ella, but I had a plan. An apology. Dinner. Wine. A bath. And a long, long massage. After which she would be putty in my hands.

"May I see your drawings?" I asked Molly.

She nodded.

I joined her on the floor and for the next ten minutes, we looked at the pictures she had drawn. I asked her to explain each.

She gave me one-word answers, a big improvement from the unresponsive Molly I was used to.

"You are so talented," I said, and planted a kiss on her cheek.

Soon, it was time for her to have her bath. Dinner was nothing like I had imagined it. Ella ate without speaking and if I asked her a question, she gave me the simplest, shortest explanation possible. I deserved it after the way I had treated her this morning.

I got an opportunity to apologize after Molly went to bed. I was in the living room flipping over a file of one of the projects my guys were working on when Ella walked past towards the kitchen. She returned with a glass of water.

"Would you please sit down, I'd like to speak to you," I said, closing my file.

"Okay," she said casually, and perched on the chair.

"I want to apologize about this morning," I began. "I shouldn't have spoken that way to you. You deserve respect—"

"I don't understand why you got so mad," Ella said, her cool face crumbling. "I meant what I said. Parents do need to spend time with their children. It makes them happy and I know you want Molly to grow up happy."

I felt like a complete idiot. "I'm sorry. It's a sore spot for me. I know I don't spend enough time with Molly, but I'm afraid if I do that, I'll bore her and she'll start to resent having to spend time with me."

She stared at me with surprise. Then she chewed on her bottom lip as she thought about what I said.

It made blood surge to my cock.

"I don't think you could ever bore Molly," she stated softly.

"She's not the same with me as she is with you."

"Start with little things," Ella suggested. "Maybe you can take her out for an ice cream. She loves McDonalds. The Chef told me you think McDonalds food is not really food, but take her there for a burger. As a treat. Another day, you can take her to the movies."

"I was thinking maybe you should come with us," I said.

"Of course, I'll come along." she nodded.

Relief surged through me with her answer.

We sat there awkwardly like two people who didn't intimately know each other's bodies. We both stood up at the same time.

"Forgive me for being such a brute this morning."

She smiled softly. "You're completely forgiven."

Something inside me shifted. God, what an angel she was.

"I'm off to take a shower now," she murmured. "Maybe I can join you for a drink later."

"Actually, I was thinking I should run you a nice bubble bath, then give you a long, hot oil massage."

She cocked her head to the side and a twinkle came into her eyes. "Sounds like a very, very, very good idea, but I really can't wait that long. How about a tour of the master suite first and a stop off on the master's bed?"

I grinned at her. "A much better plan."

We nearly ran out of the living room and up the stairs to my bedroom.

I opened the master bedroom with relish. I couldn't wait to see Ella's reaction. I had paid extra attention to the master bedroom when I was designing the house. I had imagined it like a sanctuary.

That dream had quickly died back then though. I spent a lot of time at work, which had been my first mistake. When I did make time to be with Penelope, she hadn't wanted to be home. She'd wanted to be out having a good time.

Ella stepped in and I followed her.

"Oh, my goodness, is this for real?" she asked, her voice filled with awe.

Pride swelled in my chest. I had been pleased with the space I had created and it felt good to have my work acknowledged. Natural light flooded the room from the floor to ceiling windows. The huge four poster bed sat in the middle of the room and in one corner, a fireplace stood

The show stopper though as far as I was concerned would be the bathroom. I guided Ella through the door leading to the bathroom.

"Just wow!" she exclaimed when she went in.

The bathroom was almost entirely made of glass. The custom whirlpool bathtub sat in a corner and overlooked the grounds of the house. You could see out but no one on the outside could see in.

"My God! That tub!" Ella gasped. She kicked off her shoes and climbed into the tub, fully dressed. She leaned back and shut her eyes. "I'm imagining those silky bubbles popping all over my body."

"You, young lady, just talked yourself out of a relaxing bath on your own."

Her eyes snapped open. "What do you mean?"

I offered her a hand. "Let's get those clothes off and I'll show you exactly what I mean."

# ELLA

*I*t seemed like a shame that Luke and I couldn't be anything more than lovers. Tears filled my eyes at the gentleness with which he held my legs and massaged them as we sat opposite each other in the whirlpool.

"Tell me about your family," I said to Luke. I wanted to know everything about him. It made sense to be fascinated by a man who played my body like an instrument.

He continued massaging my feet under the water but his gaze shifted to a spot behind my head. "I was the only child of an authoritarian father and sweet mother."

"What, no siblings?" I asked.

He shook his head. "I wish there had been."

"Shame. Where are they now?"

"Both my parents were killed the year I graduated from college," he said quietly.

"Oh, I'm so sorry." My heart went out to him. I knew how it felt like to lose your parents. Luckily for me, I had my sister Angela, even if we weren't as close as I'd have liked.

"How about you?"

"One sibling. An older sister. She has three kids. She met her husband in high school and married soon after," I replied this with a wistful sigh.

Luke chuckled. "Does that sigh mean that you'd have liked to have married your high school sweetheart?"

"Yes, if I'd had one. As it was, I was a plump unattractive girl and I had my first boyfriend when I was twenty-two."

"I don't believe that," Luke said.

I laughed. The past didn't bother me anymore. I had moved on and become secure in my own skin. "True story."

Talking with Luke was easy. If he asked a question I didn't want to answer, he didn't take it personally. He simply moved on to other topics. There were a zillion things I didn't want to talk about.

Like the fact that I had an ex who had abused me. It shamed me how I had allowed a man to beat me. That I had kept quiet for too long. I didn't like what that said about me. Like I'd been some kind of a doormat. This wasn't at all how I wanted Luke to envision me.

I wanted him to see me as a smart, confident, passionate woman. Not a woman who could be slapped around and she would still try to believe the man was somehow a creature to be pitied and rehabilitated. I might have been that person once, but not anymore.

"You look deep in thought," he commented.

I smiled at him. "I was thinking that this is exactly where I want to be at this very moment. There is no other thing I would rather be doing than being naked with you in this gorgeous glass tub."

He stared at me solemnly. In a serious way.

The expression he wore made my heart beat nearly out of my chest.

"Me too, sweet Ella," he said softly. "Me too."

Afterwards, we dried each other and then slipped into his bed. We then made slow, sweet love. It turned out to be such a magical night. We seemed to be in perfect sync all evening and now... this amazing, amazing sex. The kind of sex that had been almost like making love... if I was honest about it.

I put the thought away as I drifted off to sleep. Love didn't come into this arrangement.

Best of all, when I woke up in the early hours of dawn, Luke was sleeping right there next to me. I propped my head on my hand and watched him sleeping. His lips were curled into a smile and the creases on his forehead ironed out. It became so tempting to kiss him but I didn't want to wake him up.

"Had enough of staring? Can I open my eyes now?"

I jumped nearly out of my skin. I grabbed a pillow and beat him with it. "You should have said something!"

He grinned and pinned me down with his body. "Why spoil your fun? And now it's time for me to have *my* fun."

I widened my eyes and pretended to be frightened. "What do you have in mind, sir, and will it hurt?"

"Only in the most delightful way."

"In that case, I'm all yours," I said.

He lowered his mouth to mine. His lips were warm and demanding. He covered my body with his and I wrapped my legs around his waist. He groaned into my mouth as our bodies ignited on contact. I ran my heels over his back and tight muscular ass.

Bracing his hands on either side of me, he moved his mouth down the column of my neck and then nibbled my ear.

I purred from the sensations trailing along with the movement of his lips.

His cock grew and he shifted his body so it sat between my legs, teasing my pussy. Luke's tongue found my taut nipples and first flicked them, then took them one at a time into his mouth.

I groaned as my body ached with need. I gripped his shoulders. "The fire in my pussy needs to be put out with your big hose."

Luke looked up and grinned. "You have an unusual way with words, Ella."

"Does it bother you?" I waited with suspended breath to hear his answer.

"Everything you say and do makes me hot as hell. I wouldn't have you any other way," he said and moved up by body.

Instead of taking me as I thought he would, he flipped me around to lie on my stomach. He nudged my thighs apart and raised my ass a little higher. Moments later, he plunged his cock into me. "Tell me how much you like my cock," Luke purred into my ear as he pushed his cock deep inside my body.

"I *love* your cock. I wish… I could have your cock inside me… all day long," I said, barely able to get the words out. Every single time he pushed into me felt like the first time. As though his cock was stretching me to the limit, but I knew how to stretch him to the limit. "Sometimes, I think I should make a mold of your cock and have it strapped into me as I go about my day. I'd be buying groceries and your cock will be inside me. I'll be getting into the car and your cock will be inside me. I'll be talking to complete strangers and your monster cock will still be inside me, fucking me."

"Christ, you really know how to twist a man," Luke growled. His breathing matched mine. Raspy. He fucked me harder and harder.

I raised my hips meeting every plunge with my own thrusts.

"I won't last long, sweet Ella," Luke warned. "I can't."

"Me neither." My orgasm had already coiled itself into knots in my belly and was working its way downwards.

Before too long, my body felt as if it had liquefied. Shudders rushed through me. Over and over again, the sensations carried me like waves. I lost myself in them. My sense of time and place left me. I was only aware of my body and Luke's relentlessly thrusting into me.

My pussy was flooded with hot cum.

"That was amazing," I gasped, as he withdrew his cock from my body.

He rolled off me to lay by my side with his hand resting on my ass. He caressed it slowly as our breaths returned to normal. "What are your plans for today?" he said.

I rolled onto my side and faced him. "Molly enjoyed the park. We might go back there this afternoon."

A frown came over his gorgeous face. "I would join you, but I have a lot to do today. There's a project that has stalled because of some delayed permissions."

I didn't mind that he wasn't coming to the park with us. It was enough that he wanted to. The seed had already been sowed. Maybe the next time he would, but I'd learn that with Luke, it just progressed better if you took it slowly.

"What project is it?" I asked.

He proceeded to explain to me the current projects they were working on.

"Sounds fascinating," I said to him. "Seeing an idea grow from the mind to paper and then to real life."

"It is," Luke said, his hand reaching out to play with my nipples.

"Did you always know you wanted to be an architect?"

"Not really. I went with my father once to a construction site. His friend was the architect. I was fascinated as I listened to their conversation and realized that he was the one who had conceptualized the whole thing. After that, I was hooked. I couldn't get enough of construction sites." His voice tinged with passion.

Admiration flowed through me. I couldn't imagine how it felt like to earn a living doing what you loved.

"What about you? Did you always want to be in real estate?" Luke asked. He stopped playing with my nipples and looked at my face.

Usually, I answered such questions flippantly but now I found myself telling him the truth, "No, I did it to earn a living and it sort of grew on me."

"What did you really want to do?" he pressed.

"I wanted to be a fashion designer," I admitted.

He nodded. "I've noticed that you're really good at drawing. I saw the pictures you drew for Molly. Why didn't you pursue it?"

"Fashion Design degrees require money," I answered simply.

He nodded but didn't pursue the topic further. His hand went to my nipple and he played with it again.

My body tingled in response. I played my own game. I would stay as still as possible.

"What are you thinking?" Luke said. "You've made a funny face."

"I'm trying not to react to your touch," I explained with a laugh.

"I like a challenge." Luke grinned and took a nipple in his mouth as his hand dipped to my pussy and he ran his fingers over my folds.

Before long, I was twitching.

"You need to try harder," Luke whispered.

"I'm trying," I moaned.

Luke chuckled.

"Okay, I give up. Touch my pussy," I ordered, throwing my legs open wider. I needed his hands on me, challenge be damned.

His fingers parted my folds and he worked one finger into my pussy.

I writhed. "Oh yes. Like that."

A soft insistent noise penetrated into my brain. Luke heard it too and withdrew his fingers. It came again—a soft knock on the door. I froze. It could only be Molly. I stared at Luke questioningly.

He smiled at me in reassurance, got up and padded to the door. He opened it. "Hey sweetheart, are you awake already?"

She mumbled something I couldn't quite make out.

"Give me a moment to get dressed and I'll be along shortly," he said.

I could hear the smile in his voice. I knew then, things were going to be all right for him and her.

# ELLA

We strolled through the park hand in hand. Molly hopped as we walked and looking at her, you'd think that she was like any other kid. She still didn't speak or laugh much. Still, we had made progress. She wasn't as solemn as she used to be.

And she smiled more often.

It's odd how the human brain reacts to trauma. The doctors had told Luke that there was nothing physically wrong with Molly. She had withdrawn into her own world to escape the trauma of losing her mother whom she was very close to.

No one knew what went on in her lovely, little head. I couldn't imagine the frustration and sadness her dad had gone through while trying to help her.

Molly slowed down. Her attention focused on an older girl playing on the grass with a puppy. A ghost of a smile covered her face.

I guided her to a bench near where the girl was. Her mother sat on the opposite bench and smiled at us.

Molly sat at the very edge, completely entranced by the dog.

"You can go and touch the puppy," the woman said to Molly.

I shot her a grateful smile. "Go on, Molly."

The girl who looked to be about ten years old looked up and smiled at Molly. "She won't hurt you."

Slowly, Molly got up and joined the girl on the grass. The white puppy jumped on her lap. Molly let out a loud laugh and I found myself laughing along. I wished Luke had been here with us to see it.

An idea came to me.

I fished out my cell phone, went to camera, and proceeded to record Molly as she played with the puppy. After a minute of recording, I hit share and sent it to Luke.

Seconds later, my phone beeped.

*Unbelievable.*

I sent him a smiling emoji in return. Seconds later, another message came in.

*I have an idea. Let's get Molly a puppy.*

A smile split my face into two. Molly would love that. *Yes please,* I texted back.

I sat back and continued watching Molly, her new friend and the puppy.

It seemed like the puppy sensed that Molly needed a lot of love. She kept licking her face and hands. Molly loved it.

My phone beeped and I grinned. It felt nice to be texting with Luke. I felt like he was here with us. I frowned when I read the message.

*You're still beautiful.*

The number was unfamiliar. Wrong number, I decided. As I made to slip my phone back into my pocket, it beeped again.

*We belong together. We always did. I hope you know that now.*

The hairs at the back of my neck stood up. My gaze bounced around the park. No one was watching me. I read the message again. As I was reading the messages, a new one came in.

*You were a wildcat in bed. I miss that.*

My heart pounded hard against my chest. Fear came over me. It sounded like Stan. Except he was locked up in prison. With trembling fingers, I texted Ruby to ask her about Stan.

Her reply came shortly afterwards. *Let me ask Elijah.*

I sat stiffly on the bench, my mind arguing on whether or not it could be Stan. It was the word "wildcat". Any man could say that to any woman. The only problem was Stan used to say it to me and he used to say it in that context. In exactly the way the text was formed.

I desperately hoped and prayed it was a case of mistaken identity. A horn blared and I jumped in fright. I felt eyes on me.

The mother of the girl was staring at me like I'd lost my marbles.

I tried to smile reassuringly.

IONA ROSE

It seemed to have the opposite effect. She got up abruptly. "Cathy, it's time to go," she said to her daughter.

Molly got up too and watched the puppy until it disappeared from view.

Guilt gnawed at me. My jumpiness had chased them away and it was probably nothing. "Let's go to the swings," I said and took her hand.

We stayed in the park for the next hour but I couldn't still the restlessness in me. I kept glancing at the phone waiting for a message from Ruby while frightened to find another message from whoever was texting me.

With distance and time, my fear of Stan had dissipated. I wasn't the same person he had pushed around. But he wasn't a man you wanted near you. He was a violent man and he got a mad glint in his eyes when he got violent. I'd had a lucky escape.

I felt glad when it was time to go home. During the short walk back home, I kept glancing behind us. I only relaxed when we got home and the door was locked behind us.

Molly and I had lunch and then I took her to her room for a nap.

The chef left shortly after for a shopping spree and he had taken Molly with him. I was alone in the house when I heard the sound of a car. I raced to the front window and almost cried with relief when I saw Luke.

I was being paranoid... I scolded myself.

With Luke in the vicinity, the ice-cold fear that had surrounded my heart melted. I let out a chuckle. What silliness. It couldn't be Stan. Of course, he couldn't have texted me. He was away and locked up. I knew he wasn't due out of prison for another two years.

Besides, what would he want with me?

Revenge, a voice inside me said and I shuddered. He never forgave me for leaving him and he always said, acid was too good for bitches who didn't know their place. Then I got a restraining order and that pissed him off so bad.

I shook my head free of those thoughts.

I kept thinking the worst and it was only serving to increase my anxiety. "I'm not a victim, I'm a strong, powerful woman who can take care of herself," I muttered to myself. Besides, he couldn't come anywhere near me. They were the conditions of his restraining order. I repeated these words like a mantra to myself, again and again, until the knots of anxiety in my stomach untangled.

By the time Luke bounded into the house, I was actually almost back to myself. I greeted him with a lingering kiss on the mouth. It was a new experience for me eagerly waiting for a man in the evening.

I'll never forget the dread that had always filled my stomach whenever Stan's hours for returning home neared. When he stepped into the house, I'd search his face for signs of which mood he was in. If his top lip was slightly curled, that could mean by the end of the evening, I'd be sporting an ugly purple bruise somewhere.

Dammit, I was thinking about Stan again. He would ruin my evening and the rest of my life if I let him. I needed to erase all those terrible memories and concentrate on the present—my very eye-pleasing present.

"Hey, sweet Ella," Luke murmured and pulled me back into his arms.

My hands skimmed over his strong arms and glided over his smooth broad chest.

"Is Molly napping?" he asked.

"No, she wanted to go shopping with Paul. They just left," I said and then added in a suggestive tone, "I'm afraid, we're all alone in the house."

His hands dropped to my butt and squeezed.

Tingles of pleasure rose from my pussy. He angled his face and brought his mouth to mine. We kissed each other hungrily. His cock pushed against my pelvis. I slipped a hand between us, and cupped his cock over his pants. I stroked his hard, thick length through his pants.

Luke groaned. "There's something I've been wanting to do. Let's go to my office." He grabbed my hand and led the way to the library.

Pulling me in, he shut and locked the door behind us and pushed me against the wall. He massaged my breasts through my top, running his thumbs over my protruding nipples.

I groaned and pushed my chest out. I needed his touch desperately. Our mouths found each other again, and we locked lips.

Every inch of my skin awakened and tingled with longing. I wanted him badly. My fingers threaded through his hair and we kissed as though our lives depended on it. The only noise in the room was the sound of our moans and groans.

Luke's hands dropped to my waist and then my hips before he raised my dress and cupped my pussy.

"Please," I begged, unaware of what I was begging for.

"All in good time, sweet Ella," Luke said. "I love your very sexy panties but right now, I need them gone." He hooked his fingers on the waistband and pulled them down.

I stepped away from them and like two magnets drawn to each other, we closed the gap between us again. I tugged at the zipper of his trousers, a sense of urgency pushing me. I sighed when my hand wrapped around his throbbing cock. "Fuck me, Luke!"

He gripped my right thigh and raised it. I wrapped it around his waist. Without warning, he took his cock from my hand and pushed it against my folds. I whimpered when his hard-throbbing cock slipped into my pussy.

"Raise your leg," Luke commanded.

I did as he asked and his body braced me against the wall, holding me up as his cock pushed into my pussy.

"You're too damn sexy for your own good," Luke said.

I clung to him as he fucked me, going deeper each time. "Yes!" I moaned over and over again.

We fucked fast and hard while our orgasms were just as intense. When it was over and we'd quenched that desperate need for each other, Luke gently lowered me back to the ground.

Our gazes met and we laughed.

"I've never done that before," he said.

Warmth spread from my chest to the rest of my body. I felt glad we had experienced something that had been a first for him. I glanced down at his cock and giggled. It jutted out from his body as if it hadn't just emptied hot cum into my pussy.

"Now go to the desk and bend over it."

The tone of his voice made my thighs tremble and an ache rose from my core. Instead of lowering my dress, I pulled it over my head. Then, dressed only in my lacy bra, I sashayed suggestively to the desk. I placed my hands on the edge and bent over it.

I looked over my shoulder just as Luke let out a whistle.

He took two steps and his hands palmed my ass. "Fuck Ella, you can turn a man into an animal," he said.

"I never get enough of your cock," I said to Luke as his hand caressed my dripping pussy.

He rubbed my clit with his thumb. "I need to taste this." He dropped to his knees and parted my thighs.

I screamed when his tongue swiped over my slit. "More."

He did it again and again, until I was a whimpering mess. He pushed his face into my ass and took my whole labia into his mouth. I collapsed on the desk as he ate my pussy with a shocking greed.

"Your pussy tastes so good," Luke said as he dove in again, swiping, licking nibbling and tongue fucking me.

"Yes, yes, oh yes, Luke. Please," I begged and moaned over the slurping noises.

"What else do you need, baby?" he asked, pushing a finger and then another one in.

"That, yes that," I groaned, desperate for release.

He pumped into me furiously while I panted and writhed. Just as I was about to orgasm, he withdrew his fingers and in a beat, replaced them with his cock. He gripped my hips and thrust into my pussy hard. I pushed my ass back to take all of him.

I felt like I was floating, with Luke's hands gripping my hips, his cock filling and fulfilling me. My pussy tightened and clenched uncontrollably around his cock.

Luke growled in response. "You love it when I fuck you hard, right sweet Ella?" He increased the speed of his thrusts.

"Yes. H-harder," I gasped the words out.

"Like this?" he said, holding me in place and ramming into me.

Tears of pleasure flowed down my cheeks. For the first time in my life, I had met a man whose enjoyment of sex matched my own. Luke made me feel all woman when we fucked. He made me feel like the sexiest woman alive.

"Oh, y-yesss," I said as his cock plundered me repeatedly.

"Come for me sweetheart," Luke said.

*Sweetheart.* He had called me sweetheart. I didn't care whether it was just in the throes of passion. It felt damn good. My legs suddenly lost all strength as a delicious release came for me.

# LUKE

*I* had made several calls and finally we had a puppy. A potential puppy. Ella and I had agreed to go get it in the afternoon, after Molly had woken up from her nap. In preparation, I had also bought a kennel and had one portion of the garden partitioned off. That would be the new puppy's playground.

Excitement coursed through me as I imagined Molly's reaction.

I had watched that video from the park countless times. I had never seen Molly so animated and entranced with anything. And it was because of a puppy.

I should have thought of a puppy earlier.

I forced myself to concentrate on work for the next two hours.

At three, a soft knock came on the door then Molly and Ella walked in.

*My girls*. I arrested the thought as soon as it formed. I couldn't afford to think of Ella as my girl.

We had an arrangement. I needed to keep this in mind and not get too attached to her. Molly had grown very close to Ella in a short time. The instant bond they had made seemed to have grown stronger every day. They were holding hands as they walked in.

Ella looked so pretty and hot in a dress that stayed a few inches away from her knees. I couldn't control the pounding of my heart.

"Hello Daddy," Molly said. She seemed different.

I turned off my laptop and walked around my desk. "Ready? Did Ella tell you that we have a surprise for you?"

My little girl looked at me with big blue eyes and nodded. Her eyes shone with a rare excitement, which lifted my heart.

"We're ready," Ella said, a gorgeous smile on her face.

It hit me then how nice it felt to be with a woman who had a natural love for life. I compared Ella to Penelope who had sulked almost three quarters of our married life. Ella met every day as if it was a gift while Penelope had behaved as if life was something to be endured and suffered until she received a party invitation. Then she became animated.

I had my car keys with me and was ready to leave.

Molly walked between us and held both our hands.

It felt like we were a real family.

"Can we have the sunroof open please?" Ella asked.

"Yes ma'am," I said. "Your wish is my command." I did as she asked. "Anything else, my ladies?"

Molly giggled from the back.

I tried to play it cool but I couldn't keep the huge grin from my face.

It looked like a gorgeous day for a drive. The sun spilled into the car casting a golden glow on the girls. The wind blew in and messed up Ella's hair which made Ella put all of it into a mad bun on the top of her head. Then she turned around to make comical faces at Molly, which made Molly fall over laughing.

Every so often, I stared at them through the rear-view mirror as my transformed daughter and I felt light, as if I didn't have a care in the world.

I searched my mind to identify and name the emotion I was feeling. I found it. *Happy.* I felt… happy. I hadn't felt this way in a long time. My marriage to Penelope had been a miserable mistake. I could admit that now. But it wasn't a mistake I regretted because it had given me Molly.

I'd been humiliated and angry when she left me for another man, but as time went by, I relished the peace in our lives. Had Molly not been affected so badly by her mother's leaving, I would have celebrated her leaving us because for the first time in years, I had peace in my life.

Our destination was a farm on the outskirts of the city. It took forty-five minutes to get there.

Ella sang silly songs and made us both laugh with her antics.

The man who married Ella would be a lucky man indeed.

A stab of jealousy pierced through me, surprising me with its intensity. I shook my head as if clearing it of the fog of possessive fury. A part of me, the caveman part, wanted to keep Ella for myself, but the rational side of me recognized how unfair that would be-I couldn't offer her what she needed-what she deserved.

Ella had the heart of an angel, and was such a good person. She deserved a man who could love and cherish her completely. Marry her and be willing to start again. I was not that man.

Once, I had been that man. I wish we had met then. Instead, I had met Penelope, a woman as selfish as they came. We wanted different things in life. When she found out I wasn't the party guy she needed, she had left.

Which would have been fine, if not for what it had done to Molly. I couldn't give Molly another mother who might walk out on her again. I'd vowed to myself that I'd never place her in such a vulnerable situation again.

"We're here!" Ella announced breaking into my reverie.

I drove the car down the graveled road to the farmhouse and killed the engine.

The door of the farmhouse swung open and a man in a straw hat stepped out. "How y'all doing?" he shouted coming to the car. "You must be the folks my Maggie told me about, coming for the puppy."

## LUKE

*I* glanced at Ella and smiled. She smiled back. Then I got out of the car and opened the back door for Molly.

"My, what a pretty girl. I bet you're excited about your new puppy!" the man exclaimed.

Molly shifted a questioning, wide-eyed, disbelieving glance at me.

The look nearly broke my heart. I nodded. "Yes, we're getting a puppy for you."

"I'm getting a puppy?" Molly echoed in disbelief.

"That's right."

Tears filled her eyes. "I'm getting a puppy?"

I crouched next to her. "Yes, my darling. You're getting a puppy."

Suddenly, her mouth opened wide and crying soundlessly, she threw her arms around my neck.

"Don't cry, Molly. Please don't cry," I whispered, distraught to see her crying like this.

Ella crouched next to me. "It's okay, Luke. She's just happy. These are happy tears."

I scooped my daughter up in my arms and carried her towards the farmhouse.

The family of ten was all in the large kitchen, having their four o'clock snacks. Eight children with identical blond hair looked up from their meal.

A pang of envy came over me as I observed their simple, yet full life. You could tell they all loved each other. They had the kind of family that most people dreamed of but never got to experience.

I glanced over at Ella and I knew marriage to her would be like that. She laughed a lot and loved easily.

"Is this the very special little girl that has come for her puppy then," the mother asked with a smile.

"It is," I said.

One of the bigger girls stood and called to Molly to go outside.

Molly cast a worried glance at me.

I nodded at her reassuringly then I put Molly on the ground and we followed at a more leisurely pace behind the girls.

The dogs were housed in comfortable kennels at the back of the house.

"We're giving away only one, but you can choose which one you want," the girl said with a warm smile.

It warmed my heart to see strangers being kind to Molly. It made me question what kind of person Penelope really was to take off without a backward glance. She had treated Molly like a burden that she'd been happy to drop. In the early days, I had lain awake most nights wondering if she ever thought of Molly at all. And if so, did she feel guilty and wonder how our little girl was fairing?

Molly didn't even have to think about this. "That one. I want him." She pointed.

The puppy was a two-pound black and white Boston terrier.

The blonde girl crouched on her knees and picked him up from the enclosure. She handed the puppy to Molly.

Molly immediately hugged it close to her chest while fresh tears poured down her face.

The puppy looked up at Molly with big trusting eyes.

For a few seconds, no one spoke as the puppy and new owner bonded.

"Thank you, Daddy. Thank you," Molly sobbed.

"What are you going to call him?" the girl asked.

"Bean," Molly announced. "I'm going to call him Bean."

Ten minutes later, we were in the car, on the way back home. Every time I looked at the mirror, Molly was staring at her new pet lovingly.

Bean was returning the love too and was staring back at Molly with big trusting eyes as if she had owned him all his life.

The ringing of a phone broke through the purr of the car engine.

I watched Ella talking on her phone. Her forehead creased. Whatever the other person was saying had Ella worried. Spending a lot of time with her meant I could read changes in her very quickly.

She made one *ah* noise, then listened quietly. When the call was done, she looked away, but not before, I caught the worry in her eyes.

"Is everything okay?" I asked.

She smiled but I could see it was strained. "Yeah, I'm fine. Just a friend pouring out her troubles."

Back home, Molly carried Bean to the backyard.

Ella and I stood outside the picket fenced in area.

Bean seemed to be busy getting used to his new play area. He ran back and forth the square space and explored his kennel.

Molly laughed and plopped down on the grass to watch him.

He wagged his tail and ran around her.

Ella and I exchanged a look and smiled.

Just seeing Molly this happy gave me hope that she would soon come out of her self-imposed shell.

"You have made one little girl very happy. You're an awesome dad and Molly is very lucky," Ella murmured.

Her words touched me. All I'd wanted was to be a good dad to Molly. I wanted to make up for all the pain she had gone through in her short life. Pain, Penelope and I had unthinkingly caused. "Thank you, but it was your idea."

Ella nodded. "True. But you made it happen."

"See you girls later," I said. I had a few calls to make

Molly didn't take her eyes off Bean. "See you later, Daddy."

"Catch you later," Ella said.

I turned back to look at Ella before I entered the house. Her expression looked troubled, and though her gaze remained on Molly, I could tell her mind was elsewhere. I headed to the library, feeling anxious over the change in Ella. No matter what she said, I knew something was wrong.

I asked myself hard questions. Like why it bothered me so much. It was Ella's business not mine. Then I quickly answered my own question in a way, so I wouldn't have to think too hard about that question. I needed Ella to be happy to enable her to do her job well.

I got the chance to question Ella again after dinner, when Molly went to bed. As we sat companionably in the living room, I waited for the perfect moment to broach the subject. Ella was leafing through a magazine while I was reading an architectural book.

"You don't seem like yourself this evening?" I said. "If there's something I can do to help, please tell me." I surprised myself by meaning every word. I would do anything to remove the worried look I'd seen on her face in the car and in the backyard.

Her eyebrows rose in surprise. "I don't know what you're talking about," she said, sounding genuinely surprised.

I shrugged. I'd probably read her wrong. Maybe it was like she said. Something had happened to her friend she'd already forgotten about. Relief flowed through me. I felt relieved that everything with Ella was okay. "Well, if everything is fine..." I let the words trail away, distracted by the expression on her face.

"I can prove it to you," Ella said with a wicked grin. She placed her magazine on the table and got up. She came over to me and straddled me, raising her dress before sitting down.

I hissed when I felt her bare pussy. She had no panties on. All night long, she had been sitting around with no panties. My breath hitched. Her sweet feminine scent teased my nostrils and senses. I fought down the instinct to take charge and sat back with my hands on the side, waiting to see what she had in mind.

Ella placed her hands on my shoulders and inched forward until she was sitting on my hardened cock. She gyrated her hips, rubbing her bare, open mound against my cock.

"I can feel every inch of your big cock," she said.

My cock jerked against her and she let out a soft moan. She ground down on me. I had locked the door earlier, so I raised my hips and pulled down my pants along with my boxer briefs. I settled back down with my cock hard and ready between us.

Ella wrapped her hands around it lovingly and stroked it.

I lay back and closed my eyes.

"I want to bounce on your cock," Ella whispered.

My cock jerked against her hands in response. "Whatever you want, minx. I'm all yours." I watched her with hooded eyes.

She raised her hips, positioned my cock at her entrance, and slid down on me. She hissed as she impaled herself on me.

"Fuck," I growled as her tight pussy enveloped my cock completely.

She wore one of those wraparound dresses and I pulled apart the two front pieces to expose her breasts. Her nipples were hard against the lace. I freed them and her breasts popped out close to my face. I pressed her breasts together and sucked both nipples into my mouth. They were still swollen from last night when I had sucked them for ages.

She began whimpering.

With her nipples inside my mouth, she started to ride my cock. At first, I let her slide slowly up and down my cock, but I could only control myself for a short time. Before I knew it, I was fucking her like an animal. Hard. Just the way she liked it.

My eyes were glued on her tits as they bounced up and down. She had her head thrown back with her eyes half closed. Soft moans escaped her mouth as I bounced her on my cock.

I knew her orgasm was close. I pulled her hips close, so my groin would press her clit every time I pumped upwards. I increased the pace and rubbed her clit harder.

Before long, she was screaming my name. Her pussy clenched impossibly tight around my cock. "I'm coming!

Don't stop," she gasped. Her legs shook and her body convulsed.

All the while, I kept pumping into her as my own climax built up. Hot cum shot out of me and I growled with the relief of it.

When it was over, she lay her head against my chest and I caressed her with circles on her back. I tugged her dress over her neck and head as she sat on my lap completely naked.

Her tits pressed against my chest and my hands rested on her curvy ass.

"Let's go to bed," I whispered into her ear, as I pushed two fingers into her pussy. It was full of my thick cum.

She shuddered.

I pulled my fingers out and brought them to her lips.

Eagerly, she sucked my fingers into her mouth. Her eyes never left mine while she licked them clean.

My cock recovered and began to swell, pushing hard against her pussy. I stood up, threw her over one shoulder, and carried her naked body upstairs to my bedroom.

The night was only beginning and I wasn't ready to sleep yet. I threw her down on the bed and she opened her legs wide. Judging from the juices still running out of her pussy, I guessed that Ella wasn't ready to sleep either.

## ELLA

*L*uke made me forget my worries that night but in the morning, when I woke up, they were there, waiting to consume me.

Stan had been let out of prison on parole. I had let Ruby convince me that he couldn't possibly be the one contacting me. His restraining order was still in place. He could never come anywhere near me, or he would be going straight back to prison. The way she put it, even if he had sent those messages there was no way he was dumb enough to actually try and make physical contact.

Besides, she said, her boyfriend had heard from one of his friends that Stan absolutely hated prison. He'd made an enemy of a bully and he'd gotten beaten up real bad a few times. So, there was no way he wanted to go back to prison. She managed to convince me somewhat, but a little of the anxiety remained.

Only I knew about the murderous, reckless glint I'd seen when he had attacked me that last night. If I hadn't kicked him in the balls and ran out of the apartment who knows what would have happened.

Ruby had been utterly and totally convinced about it being a wrong number and if I didn't respond to that sick person, he would eventually give up. When I thought about it now, there was really nothing to connect Stan with those messages. Wildcat was a generic term. Lots of men refer to women as cats in bed. Wildcat, kitten, pussy...

I decided there and then not to give in to my fear.

It was past time to put Stan in the past where he belonged. I had no reason to believe those messages had been from him other than my own paranoia. I had to stop letting him into my head and spoiling my life.

For the first time in a long time, the future looked colorful. I had no concrete plans, but I knew my life was about to take a different course. Something was growing in me. A longing to do more. To reach all my potential. To go after my dreams.

I knew a lot of it had to do with Luke. He had worked hard for the life he had created for himself and his daughter. A number of times I had caught him in the library immersed in his work, he had a rapt expression of a man who enjoyed his work.

I wanted the same for myself. It wasn't too late to chase my dreams and live a life I could be proud of. I had never once woken up before him. Luke was always the first in the household to get up. This was what it took to make a successful career.

By my side, Luke slept soundly, his right hand cupping my breast as if claiming ownership.

I wouldn't mind belonging to Luke. With a sigh, I reminded myself we weren't about that. We didn't own each other. We were two people who enjoyed sex with each other with no emotions attached. But just for a few seconds, I gave in to temptation and allowed myself to fantasize what it would be like to be Luke's woman.

He was the kind of man who would shower attention on his woman all the time. With Luke, you would never feel neglected. He always, *always* thought of my pleasure before his. I stared at him as he slept. His gorgeous, dark hair lay in unkempt waves, giving him an *I-just-fucked-hard* look.

My sex clenched as memories from the night came over me. My hand snaked down between my legs and I slowly began to rub my clit. Soft moans escaped my lips.

"Not fair," Luke grumbled.

"What's not fair?" I gasped.

"You playing with your pussy without letting me watch." He opened his eyes. "I want to watch." He got up from the bed. "I won't be long. Don't do anything."

I admired his naked form as he went into the bathroom.

Moments later, he strode back into the room, his cock rock hard and jutting out from his body.

I drooled as I watched him grab a chair and bring it near the bed.

He sat down, wrapped his hand around his cock, and softly stroked it. "Spread your legs wider, little Ella," he urged.

I opened them as wide as they would go and slid down the bed so he would have a really good view. "Can you see my pink pussy?" I asked, heat pulsing between my thighs. I felt like a sex vixen as I brazenly showed off my most private parts to Luke.

"Oh, yes," he replied, his eyes blazing. "Pink and wet. Go on, play with yourself for me."

"You sure you won't come and play with me instead?"

"This time I want to watch."

"If you're sure..." His words spurred me to make him break his intention of simply watching. My hand drifted down my body to my pussy. I parted my folds, and as my fingers came into contact with my clit, I groaned and let my body arch.

"You're dripping," Luke muttered, his gaze glued between my legs.

"For you. I'm always dripping when you're around," I purred and rolled my clit between my fingers. Then I finger fucked myself slowly.

Lust shook Luke's body as he stroked his huge cock. Beads of white liquid formed at his tip. "I need a taste of your sweet pussy, Ella," he growled, and in one swift movement, he was kneeling by the bed and tugging me downwards.

I laughed softly, victoriously. I did feel glad he couldn't keep away.

He moved my hand away and replaced it with his tongue.

At the first touch of his tongue, I whimpered. "Oh yes," I moaned as his tongue lapped up my juices.

"You taste so good... like honey," Luke muttered.

"My pussy's hungry for your wonderful cock," I said as I writhed to get as much of his tongue inside me as I could.

He climbed onto the bed, flipped me onto my side roughly, and raised my right leg up. "Is your hungry little pussy ready to get fucked?"

I almost came from his dirty talk and the anticipation of getting fucked while in this position. It was one of my favorites. It always felt as if his cock went so deep, all the way up into my belly. "Yes please," I cried.

It felt like I had died and gone to heaven when he shoved his cock into me. "Please... please." Every time he did it at this angle, I felt surprised anew to feel this filled up. I needed nothing else in my life, except the feel of his cock thrusting in and out. Each time Luke thrust in, his cock touched a hot spot while rendering me helpless and desperate to come.

I raised my hips higher and Luke pumped into me harder. The fire in me flared. I started to feel lightheaded. "I'm going to come."

"That's it, baby. Come for me. Come all over my cock," Luke urged.

I fisted the bedsheets as scalding pleasure exploded in me. I screamed and called his name repeatedly. Luke slammed into me harder, intensifying my orgasm. My body had never experienced such pleasure as it had in the weeks since Luke and I had started having sex.

Seemingly, from far away I heard his growl, and I knew his orgasm was imminent. I squeezed my pussy, gripping the length of his shaft.

"Fuck Ella. I'm about to shoot my load inside you."

"Fill me with your cum," I urged, loving the intense pleasure drawn on his face.

Hot, thick spurts of cum filled my pussy and still, Luke kept pumping. I felt another wave of yet another climax coming on. I threw my head back and reveled in the intensity of another multiple orgasm.

"That was so damn hot," Luke said a few seconds later, his cock still buried in my pussy. He offered me a hand. "Let's go shower together. I got a big day ahead of me, but I think I have one more fuck inside me for you."

# LUKE

"Would you girls like to come to my office in town, later in the afternoon?" I asked Ella and Molly as we were having breakfast.

Where had that come from? I'd always kept my home and work life private. Perhaps it had begun with Penelope because she had never been interested in my work life and had made that clear from the beginning.

Whenever I spoke about work, a bored look would come over her features. It hadn't taken long to realize Penelope liked money but never cared about how it got made. All she had cared about was spending the money as quickly as possible… on herself.

I tensed as I realized the vulnerable position I had placed myself. I suddenly realized I wanted Ella to say yes. It would hurt if she said no. Now it was too late to withdraw the offer. I started castigating myself. *I shouldn't have asked. I should have continued to keep my work separate from what Ella and I had.* The sheath I had wrapped around my heart was beginning to melt off and this wasn't a good thing for me.

"We would love that, wouldn't we Molly?" Ella said and looked at Molly, who nodded enthusiastically.

When she turned her gaze back at me, I searched her face for any signs of her faking it. Her expression looked as open as it always was while her eyes were sparkling. Relief flooded into me even as warning bells rang in my head. Why was it so important to me for Ella to say she would love to see my office? I pushed away the taunting voice and launched into mundane words, "I'll send the driver to pick you both up." I looked at Ella.

"Great," she said with a big grin. She turned to Molly. "Tell Daddy what naughty Bean did this morning."

Molly immediately launched into her story about Bean chewing up one of her shoes.

I listened, but part of me couldn't believe this was really my life. Was this really me, sitting here with Ella and my daughter playing happy family? Or was I dreaming?

After breakfast, I kissed Molly and lingered near Ella.

She winked at me. "Not today, but one of these days we're going to have to christen your desk at work."

My eyes widened as all kinds of wild images ran through my head. I drove myself to work, all the while whistling as I drove.

"Morning Robert," I greeted the security guard standing by the entrance, as I walked through the glass doors of the building.

He stared at me in surprise before replying in a stuttering voice. As if my friendliness had shocked him.

I searched my memory as I slipped into the elevator and realized how sometimes I would be in such a foul mood that I never said hello to anyone.

Shame flooded me. I'd never given it a second thought before. Such behavior reminded me of my father when I was growing up. He'd been in a perpetual bad mood and his usual response to questions had been barks.

I vowed to be friendlier to my employees. One of the strengths of Meyers Designers and Architects was our employees. We'd gotten top notch designers and architects as the company expanded. We also paid the best in the industry and our benefits couldn't be compared to any other company in South Carolina.

Still, a little friendliness went a long way. It cheered people up. I knew this because when Ella aimed her gorgeous smile at me in the mornings, it lightened my heart and made my whole day.

I stepped out of the elevator on the tenth floor where the company offices were. My company occupied the eighth, ninth and tenth floors of the building. I got the same reaction Robert had given me from everyone I greeted as I went through the wide carpeted corridors to my office at the end of the hallway.

My mornings were usually taken up by a series of meetings with our architects and designers and this morning would be no different. The only difference was the sense of anticipation I felt in my stomach. I had a quick sandwich lunch at my desk. Then I had a client meeting in the conference room at two P.M.

Before I knew it, two thirty came around and I was back in my office, waiting for Ella and Molly. Lightness filled my chest and I found myself smiling for no reason. Perhaps it was because it would be the first time Molly had ever been to my office.

This notion rang as false even to myself. At five years old, it wouldn't really make much of an impact for Molly to see where her dad worked. It was mostly for Ella. Warning bells sounded again. I told myself, I rarely got a chance to show anyone what I had created.

By the time my secretary buzzed me to let me know they had arrived, I'd actually started to grow impatient. "Show them in," I said, getting up. I grinned widely as the door swung open and Molly walked in followed by Ella.

Molly looked around my office wide eyed.

I shifted my gaze to Ella and immediately my body heated up.

What was it about her? She was sexy without even trying. She wore the kind of short dresses she favored and I loved. This one showed off her figure without appearing overly sexy. My hands itched to slide her skirt up, and cup her ass.

"I love your office," Ella said, looking around. "Isn't it nice, Molly?"

My daughter held my gaze and nodded.

"Thank you," I came around the desk and stepped closer to them. "This is my favorite spot," I told Molly and led her to the ceiling to floor glass window. It had a gorgeous view of the city.

She placed her palms on the glass and peered down.

I looked back at Ella and we exchanged a warm smile.

Moments later, my secretary brought in some coffee for myself and Ella, and a glass of apple juice for Molly.

We chatted as we drank our coffee.

Molly drank her juice while standing by the window and taking in the view of the city below.

"I have somewhere else I want to show you," I said to Molly when we had all finished our drinks. "It's on the eighth floor. Let's go."

Molly slid her small hand into mine as we walked, and I pretended this was a normal occurrence, but inside my chest, my heart felt like it might burst into a million splinters of joy. We were making progress. My daughter was beginning to trust me.

On the eighth floor, I greeted the receptionist and led my girls down the hallway to a huge room at the end. I pushed the door open and we were met by a burst of color and children's voices.

Molly padded in.

Ella turned to me. "What is this place?"

"A play area for kids. It's for our employees who have no child care at home and they have to work. This way, their children are taken care of, and they get to be productive at work."

I felt proud of the play area we had created. In a survey, our company had been ranked up there with one of the best places to work. I firmly believed that to get the best out of your employees, you also needed to provide the best for them.

Child care, benefits and enough rest time, so when they were at work, they focused and gave the company their best. They also got to bring their dogs to work if they had well-behaved pets. It was a symbiotic relationship.

"Wow!" Ella exclaimed, clearly impressed.

I introduced them to the two ladies who took care of the kids. Today, there were four kids, all under ten years old.

Molly seemed drawn to the playhouse in a corner and she entered, joining the little girl playing there.

"Looks like we've lost our Molly," Ella noted with a laugh.

I laughed too. When we were ready to leave, we asked Molly if she wanted to stay longer and she nodded happily.

"I'll let you know when she's ready to go," one of the ladies said.

We left soon after and returned to my office. I explained to Ella my policies with regards to my employees.

"You appear so aloof and yet, you're a teddy bear inside," Ella commented with a grin.

I frowned. "I'm not aloof. And neither am I a teddy bear."

"You're thawing," she said. "I like the new you."

I hadn't ever thought of myself as aloof. If anything, I associated that word with my dad. I didn't like the comparison. My dad's aloofness had ensured that I had grown up without being close to him. I needed to try harder. I never wanted Molly to grow up and describe her dad as 'aloof.' "I told my secretary not to disturb me until I was done with my *meeting.*"

"Meeting?" Ella asked.

I shut my office door and locked it. "Yes. Didn't you get the email?"

"I like the sound of that," she said, her tone throaty, a sign telling me she was turned on. Her heels barely made any noise on the carpet as she padded to the glass window.

I remained by the door while admiring her hourglass figure as she stood with her back to me. She placed her palms on the glass like Molly had done. I swallowed heavily and my whole body stiffened with need.

Ella looked over her shoulder. "The view is just beautiful."

"Not as beautiful as you are," I said and meant it. Ella's beauty shone from the inside.

"Thank you," she said and continued looking out. "So, what is the agenda of our meeting?"

"Well," I replied and closed the distance between us. "The first agenda is to find out if you're wearing any panties beneath that dress."

"If I am?" She giggled softly.

I loved the sound of her laughter. "If you are, I'll be very upset."

"Will there be consequences?" she whispered.

143

I wrapped my hands around her waist and rubbed my erection against her ass. "Very *severe* consequences." I leaned into her ear and inhaled a whiff of her scent. So musky and sexy.

"Agenda number two?" Ella asked.

"Mmm, we'll move to the matter arising from the first agenda." My hands moved up her body to cup her tits.

A quiet moan escaped her mouth. She arched her back as I grazed my hands back and forth across her hardened nipples. "Your tits feel so good." I leaned forward to taste the skin on her neck. My cock pushed against Ella's ass and I humped her softly, loving the feel of her curves.

"We have to begin the meeting," Ella said. "We're short on time."

"Agenda one," I said, trying to keep my voice serious. My hands wandered to her hips as I caressed her soft skin gently, rising higher and higher. "You're so fucking beautiful. Lean forward."

Ella did as I had said and presented me with her beautiful behind.

I lifted her dress up to her waist, exposing her thong clad ass. "Someone is in trouble." I lifted the thin strip of black thong.

"They don't qualify as a pair of panties," Ella defended as her breath rasped.

"That's true," I agreed, as I snapped her thong several times. From her reaction, I knew it had the desired effect. I dropped to my knees and pulled the thong down. I needed it out of the way. I wanted full access to Ella's sweet pussy.

I was hungry for it the way a thirsty man needed water on a hot day. Her thong looked completely soaked and I grinned as I threw it on my desk. I gripped Ella's inner thighs and my tongue slid up and down the length of her pussy.

"Oh yes, please Luke," Ella pleaded. "Eat my pussy."

I nibbled, sucked, and drank all the juices leaking from her insatiable pussy as I breathed in the sweet scent of her arousal. Her juices just kept gushing out, no matter how fast I lapped it up. She needed more than my tongue. She needed my cock.

I stood up, unsnapped the button of my pants, and brought my zipper down. I pulled out my painfully rock-hard cock. I gave it a few strokes and then spread Ella's thighs even further apart. I gripped my cock and rubbed it over her pussy and ass. "Can you feel how hard you make me?" I growled.

"I am so ready for you," Ella moaned. "Please." She arched her back, her pussy gleaming against the afternoon sun rays.

I didn't need a second invitation. I arranged my cock at the entrance of her pussy and plunged it in. Ella gave a muffled cry as my cock ripped through her walls. I stayed still, allowing her pussy to stretch enough to accommodate my size.

A moan escaped Ella's lips and I knew she was ready. I slowly pulled my cock out all the way leaving only the head.

"Fuck me hard, Luke," Ella said.

I loved it when Ella told me what she wanted. I loved her unashamed nature that made having sex with her so different and a whole new experience.

Ella uttered some incoherent words as I plunged in again and again. Her breathing became ragged and so did mine. Ella's moans deepened and I knew she was close to coming.

"Oh, yes... fuck," she cried.

"I want you to come hard," I said, afraid I wouldn't be able to hold on until I had satisfied her first.

In the next moment, her body convulsed as she whimpered like she did when she came.

My cock seemed to get the memo and it exploded into her pussy, shooting cum into her. I held her tight as our orgasms rocked us both. When it was over, I grabbed some napkins off the table and pulled my cock out. I wiped and tucked it back into my pants.

Then I cleaned Ella up, knowing she would be ultrasensitive at this point. I pulled down her dress and arranged it around her hips.

"What about my thong?" she asked, turning around to face me. Her hair looked messed up while falling in gorgeous red curls around her face.

I arranged it back as well as I could. "I like the idea of you going back bare. Make sure you stay that way until I get back." I picked her thong off the floor. "This belongs to me now. I'll keep it in my drawer and sniff it whenever I miss you too much."

"Ooo... I like the sound of that," Ella purred.

On a whim, I turned to her. "How about dinner tomorrow night?"

She raised an eyebrow at me.

I knew what she was thinking. We weren't about that. I knew it too, but this was different. I felt a need to thank her for everything she'd done for my daughter. She had gone beyond what had been expected of her and I felt grateful.

Is that the whole truth? A voice in my head asked. Of course, it was the truth. No one knew how to keep their feelings in check like I did. After Penelope, I'd locked away my feelings and thrown away the key. I was a man and wasn't averse to the company of a beautiful woman. And Ella certainly was beautiful. "I want to thank you for taking care of Molly so well," I finally spoke.

"You don't have to and besides, who would watch over her?"

I liked that just-fucked look in her eyes. The look that no other man would feast his eyes on. I caught myself. *What is the matter with me?* Ella did not belong to me and even if she did, I wasn't the clingy possessive type of man.

I wasn't a Neanderthal. I was an educated, sophisticated man.

"You could ask your friend Ruby," I suggested. "I also meant to tell you that you can have a friend over anytime. I know it can get lonely with just myself and Molly for company."

Ella smiled suddenly, her whole face lighting up.

It felt like a ray of sunshine was shining directly into my heart.

"I'd love to go for dinner with you. I'll ask Ruby."

# ELLA

"I think it looks better up," Ruby said, holding my hair at the top of my head. She turned to Molly. "What do you think Molly? Up or down."

"Hmmmm," Molly said thoughtfully.

Molly and Ruby had taken to each other almost instantly, but it wasn't hard to like Ruby. She knew how to be silly and fun. A child's dream babysitter. Her green hair helped too. She had recently dyed her hair with streaks of green.

Molly's eyes had widened when she first saw her. "She has green hair. Is she a witch?" she had gasped when Ruby jumped out of her car.

"No, she just likes colors. Last week her hair was pink."

"I like colors too. Can *I* have green hair too?"

"Um… let's see what your father thinks about that first, okay?"

Molly smiled and hadn't stopped smiling since.

"Molly thinks up, and that's what we'll do," Ruby announced seriously.

"You can't read Molly's mind," I pointed out.

"Am I right, Molly?" Ruby asked.

Molly nodded a huge grin on her face.

I stared at my reflection as Ruby heaped hair at the top of my head and pinned it into place. The end result was a sexy ruffled look that made me look quite hot.

"I love it! Thanks. What do you think Molly?"

"It's nice," she said approvingly, as she picked Bean off the floor and cuddled him in her arms.

I got up and smoothed down the turquoise off shoulder dress I had decided to wear. One of the few designs I owned that was long and flowing. Feeling suddenly nervous, I grabbed my clutch bag from the bed, and turned to face my audience of two. "I'm ready," I told them.

Ruby turned to Molly. "Shall we take pictures of Ella and your dad?" When Molly nodded, Ruby turned to me. "You heard Molly, phone please?"

I let out an exaggerated sigh, clicked open my clutch bag, I handed her my phone. We left the bedroom and headed downstairs to the living room.

Luke stood at the French doors, his back to us when we entered. He turned around when he heard us.

My heart stopped.

He wore a black dinner jacket over a white casual shirt, made to fit over his very masculine physique. As my gaze hungrily raced down his body, he'd already stripped me with his eyes.

"You look beautiful," he said, his voice thick and husky.

His voice told me what he would do to me if we were alone. My panties became damp as I imagine him closing the distance between us and taking me into his arms.

Ruby coughed, breaking the sexual tension in the room.

I laughed to cover up for my embarrassment. For a minute there, it had just been Luke and me, lost in our own bubble.

He came to me and offered his arm. "I wish we were alone," Luke whispered into my ear. "I'd have you right here and now."

His husky voice trembled through me, heating my blood, leaving me incapable of rational thought.

"Pictures, please," Ruby said.

"Pictures?" Luke asked, looking at me.

I laughed. "Yes. Let's pose."

"All right," Luke agreed. He arranged himself behind me and slipped his hands around my waist.

"I like that pose," Ruby said and proceeded to take pictures. Then she gave my phone to Molly and showed her how to capture images. We took several more pictures with Molly standing between us then a few of her and her dad.

Then we were out of the door and we were alone again. The night air felt warm as we walked to the car. I felt a strange burst of excitement. We were officially on a date. *Like a real date.*

Luke opened the passenger door for me.

I thanked him and slid in.

He closed the door and walked around to the driver's side.

His aftershave filled my nostrils. I turned to him. His face was lit by the light coming from the dashboard. I felt my heart contract. *Whoa! What the hell was this sensation?* I turned away quickly. "Where are we going?" I asked him, trying to keep my voice normal. Casual. As if I wasn't all out crazy about him…I was just a woman going on a date with a man.

Luke navigated the car onto the road. "I thought we'd check out this new Japanese restaurant. I think you'll like it."

I smiled. "I'm sure I will."

Luke went on to tell me about the owner of the restaurant, a Japanese chef who had won top awards in restaurant competitions in Japan. He'd since opened an exclusive restaurant in the States and people were loving it.

It felt so nice to be out with him.

After parking the car, quick as a flash Luke was around to my side. He opened the door and helped me out.

I shot him a grateful smile. It would be easy to fall in love with Luke. Once you got to know him beyond his cold exterior, you found a gem underneath.

Another warning bell rang in my head.

We could never be anything more than lovers. Luke had made that very clear. Still, I couldn't help but wonder how it would feel to be in a real relationship with him.

In the low-lit restaurant, Luke gave his name to the hostess, a Japanese lady with a gentle manner and welcoming smile.

"Please come with me," she said after checking the reservation. She led us to a private cubicle with a low table on a highly polished wooden platform.

Luke slipped off his shoes and I followed suit before we went in. We sat on cushions around the low table.

"Someone will be with you in a moment," the hostess said with a nod. Then she withdrew, sliding the screens shut.

We were once again, alone in our own little world. "Wow! This is the real thing, isn't it?" I said looking at the gorgeous black and pink paintings of lotus flowers on the screens.

"Yes, very authentic," Luke agreed.

"Thanks for bringing me here. I've never been to a place like this," I said, meeting his eyes. In the soft glow of the lantern over us, he seemed beyond beautiful. A god almost.

"You're welcome," he said. "I hope you like the food."

"Don't worry. I'll like it. I'm not fussy about food. I usually eat whatever's on the table," I told him with a laugh. Then I leaned closer to him. "I'm only fussy about the cock I swallow."

Luke's eyes widened.

Before he could answer, a faint knock came on the door, and a waiter opened the screens to take our order.

Luke recommended the hot sake for our drink and I was more than happy to try it. Luke's idea was to order a variety of meals, so we could sample a lot of their dishes.

It sounded fun but terribly expensive. "Isn't this going to cost the earth?"

"This is the reason why I work hard. Relax. Enjoy it. What's life without enjoyment?"

He was right. He did work hard and he deserved this. We fell into an easy conversation. Luke made me feel like his equal, asking my opinion about important things and making me feel as if he genuinely valued my thoughts.

As we were sipping our warm sake, Luke leaned on the table and stared at me. "Tell me something about you I don't know."

I cocked my head and searched my memories. Laughter bubbled up my throat as a memory came to me. "I can pole dance, or at least I could."

His jaw dropped. "Really?"

"Yes, Ruby and I took pole dancing classes when we were younger. Before we became boring," I told him, a wistful note in my voice.

The screen doors were opened again by a woman and two waiters appeared bearing our food. They arranged the various dishes around the table.

A laugh escaped my mouth at the sheer quantity of food for just two people.

"Dig in," Luke said when the waiters left.

I didn't wait for a second invitation. I tasted every single dish, making a face at one.

Luke laughed. Darn it, I loved his laugh. It relaxed his face and made him look younger and carefree.

"That is octopus. It tastes horrible by itself, but you have to dip it in this sauce here."

"No, I think I'll pass, thank you."

"It's delicious," he insisted. "Here try it." He picked up a piece of the meat that had made me want to gag between his chopsticks, dipped it into the brownish sauce, and held it out for me.

I leaned forward and opened my mouth. The sweet and sour flavors mixed with the meat and burst in my mouth. "You were right. It's delicious," I agreed.

"Here's another one," Luke said and fed me again.

It felt weird but fun and scary how much I enjoyed Luke's company. It would have been far easier if his company had been dull. But no, he had to be charming and attentive. He would always go out of his way to ensure I was kept entertained and tantalized. No man had ever paid such attention to me.

"You were telling me about pole dancing," Luke reminded me.

I laughed. "You're not going to let me forget that, are you?" I told him about the lessons and how terrible we were in the beginning.

"Did you ever practice on a boyfriend?" Luke asked, the laughter gone from his voice.

I didn't know what to make of his question. "Once, but it didn't go down well. Stan accused me of behaving like a slut." Why the hell had I said that? I hated talking about Stan to anyone.

"He was a fool," Luke said. "Some men can't tell their good fortune when it's right in front of their eyes. How long were you together?"

Stan and I were together for too long. "One year one month and five days. It was good at first, for maybe six months. Once he persuaded me to give up my apartment and move in with him, it then went downhill all the way."

He nodded at this answer, a strange expression on his face.

Curiosity about him came over me. I knew that he'd been married then his wife had left him and Molly. "Do you date at all?" Surely, a handsome man with such a voracious appetite for sex like Luke had, couldn't stay alone for long.

He shook his head. "No. My life has been about work and Molly. This is the first time I've been out on a date since my wife left."

My face heated up and my heart took off on a wild gallop.

He held my gaze. "You're the first woman I've been interested in in a long time."

I tried to smile and stopped when my lips felt like they were held together by glue. I didn't want to look any deeper at the meaning in his words. We'd already had that conversation, and we had both agreed what we had was just fun and games.

I steered the conversation to safer topics. Like his family. From what I gathered, Luke had grown up in quite a privileged household, but with a father who was too busy for his kids.

"You're different with Molly," I told him when he expressed a hope to never be like his father. "I don't think it's a deliberate choice on the side of the man. But work has a way of consuming you. Before you know it, your child's all grown up."

Luke ordered another little ceramic bottle filled with hot sake. We sat talking and drinking it. By the time we finished it, I was sure we must be the last customers in the restaurant.

"I'll bet they're happy to see the last of us," I laughingly said to Luke as we walked to the car.

Luke opened the car door for me but before I slipped in, he hooked a finger under my chin and kissed me deeply.

When he broke the kiss, I felt quite dizzy with happiness. I slipped into the car seat feeling almost high with joy.

Luke started the car and we were on our way home.

I couldn't wait to get home. The heady combination of the wine and Luke's company had made me desperate to feel him inside me again. Or at least, to taste him. "There is only one thing I've truly missed tonight."

He glanced at me. "What?"

"Cock," I said and casually placed my hand between Luke's legs.

He inhaled sharply, and his cock jumped, but he did not look at me.

I stroked his cock, enjoying the feel of it as it grew and swelled to crazy proportions. Growing braver, I edged closer, unzipped his pants, and pulled it out of his boxer briefs. I loosened my seat belt and lowered my head to his pulsing cock. I loved the musky masculine scent of him. I blew hot air over the tip and was rewarded with a stream of expletives, muttered under his breath.

"Should I stop?" I asked innocently.

"Don't you dare," Luke growled. He shifted in his seat but his concentration remained on his driving.

I grinned, knowing how hard he tried to ignore what I was doing. I wasted no time in taking his whole cock in. It jerked in my mouth as I bobbed up and down. I let go of his shaft and dipped my hand further down to cup his balls. They were big and tight. I massaged them softly as my mouth sucked on his cock.

I slowly built up the speed with which I was sucking his cock. Each time I raised my head, Luke raised his hips, thrusting his cock into my mouth. I sensed a change in his driving before the car came to a stop.

"Let's finish this inside," Luke growled.

I gave the tip of his cock one last lick and withdrew my mouth. "Couldn't concentrate, huh?" I teased.

"No. I thought I could, but I can't," he admitted, and started the car again.

My panties were soaking wet and my pussy was on fire. I couldn't wait to get into the house and have Luke put out my fire.

# LUKE

*M*y anticipation of exactly what I intended to do to Ella disappeared at the sight of a blazing red BMW parked outside my house. It couldn't be, I told myself.

She couldn't just turn up like this, could she?

Even Penelope in all her denseness knew better than to show up after two years without warning me first. Except I knew that car well, after all I'm the one who'd bought it for her. Obviously, she hadn't found a sucker to replace it. While she was married to me, she wanted a new vehicle every year.

Rage rose in me that she would actually come to my house without warning me. I could feel my insides clench as if in the grip of a cold hand. I broke into a cold sweat at the thought of what she might have told Molly. Penelope was a terrible liar. She told some of her friends I used to beat her up. I was shocked when one of them cornered me at a party and started to scold me for being such a prick to her.

I jumped out of the car. If she had tried to ruin the progress Ella and I had made with Molly now... progress that even therapists had been unable to make. All Molly had needed was stability and people who loved her. She had found that with me and Ella.

And now Penelope was back to spoil it all. My fury was such I even forgot Ella was in the car. All I could think of was getting rid of the poison in my house before it infected everything good in my life. I could barely contain my rage as I strode to the house. The door flung open before I even touched it.

Ruby stood there, her brow creased, her face tight with tension. Penelope had that effect on people.

"Hi," I said and tried to smile. I touched her shoulder. "Everything will be fine. Where is she?"

"In the living room. She told me who she was and then went to the playroom to see Molly," Ruby said in a low tone. "I couldn't stop her."

I stiffened. "What did she tell Molly?"

Ruby shook her head. "I don't know. She closed the door on me."

"Where is she now?" I asked urgently.

"In the living room."

"And Molly?"

"In bed," Ruby replied.

Ella came running behind me.

I turned to her. "Sorry. I have to deal with this. Give me a few moments, okay?"

"Of course," she said, looking at me worriedly.

In the living room, I found Penelope leafing through one of my architectural magazines. Something she had never done when we had been married. She heard my footsteps and looked up. She had changed a bit. It was only two years but her face had lost its youthful look. Her eyes looked tired. As if life had disappointed her.

It should have pleased me to see she hadn't been happy since she left us, but it didn't. If life had been good to her, she would have left us well alone. That would have been the ideal situation.

"Luke!" she cried and stood up, her face arranged in a pageant-winning smile. The same smile that had won her the Miss Connecticut title.

I had come to learn that Penelope could summon any emotion she needed at will. She could cry on cue, laugh convincingly, and show emotions she wasn't feeling.

So I was extremely skeptical of her over-enthusiastic reception. "Penelope," I said formally.

She ran towards me and looped her hands around my neck.

Her strong perfume made me feel sick. I grabbed her hands and pulled them away from my neck.

She pretended she didn't notice the snub, took a step back and grinned at me. "It's so good to be back. You've done well for Molly, Luke. You got her a nanny who seems like she knows her job."

It jarred me to hear her praise me on the job I'd done with Molly. "Ruby is not her nanny. She is her babysitter for the night. Molly's nanny is Ella. It's her who managed to bring back a smile to Molly's face."

"Oh, that's wonderful. So… were you out… on a date?" Penelope asked.

I tried to control the tight knot of anger in my stomach. How dare she? She had broken our daughter's heart and for that, I would never forgive her. "What are you doing here?" I asked her bluntly, tired of playing catch up when I had no interest whatsoever in knowing anything about her life or telling her anything about my life.

"I came to spend some time with my daughter and husband," she said and sat back down.

I frowned. I didn't like where this was going. "*Ex*-husband."

She waved a dismissive hand.

I wanted to shake her. Hard. To remind her she had left her daughter for another man without a backward glance. "Do you know what happened to Molly after you left?" My voice was deceivingly casual.

She looked at me with interest. "What?"

"She stopped talking, Penelope. For nearly a year. Then she went into her own little shell. You fucked up our daughter when you left without a word of goodbye. When you chose a man over her."

A sob broke out from her. She covered her face with her hands and stood there as still as a statue.

I tried to dismiss it as acting, but it looked too real. I waited for her to regain her composure.

"I was a fool Luke. A damned fool and I hate myself for it," Penelope said, dropping her hands, her eyes filling up with tears. "That's why I'm here. To make amends."

*I was a fool. A damned fool.* Where had I heard this before? *Oh, my God. It was a line from one of those daytime soaps.* I shook my head. For a moment there, I had almost believed her. Still, I shouldn't have been surprised that she was back. No one had told beautiful, spoilt Penelope that life did not work like that. You didn't do something like she had done and then retrace your steps when you decided you'd made the wrong choice.

"That's not possible," I told her, my voice calm. "You don't get to walk back into our lives now. Not after what you did."

She tilted her chin. "Molly is my daughter."

"Wasn't she your daughter when you took off for a better life, somewhere else? You never called once to check on her well-being." My breath came out fast.

Her cheeks colored. "I admitted that I made a mistake. A huge one. But I'm back to make amends. Everybody makes mistakes. I'm not perfect. I want to get to know my daughter and I want her to know me. Every girl needs her mother."

That last sentence penetrated my brain. Penelope was Molly's mother and I couldn't do anything to change that. The anger that had fueled me ebbed away. I thought of my Molly and the shell she had wrapped herself in. Even though we'd made progress in the last few weeks, maybe she still needed to have her biological mother around her. Maybe that was a sacred bond too. One that I had no right to cut off. That should be Molly's decision.

I would do anything for Molly, even having Penelope back in our lives.

"Please, Luke. You were never a cruel man. All I want is to spend time with my own daughter. The child I carried inside my body for nine months. I still have stretch marks to show for it. Remember, it was me who breastfed her. Not you. So, I made a… mistake. Are you going to punish me forever for it?"

The image of Penelope on all fours getting banged from the back by her *mistake* came into my head. A lot of women, if caught in that situation would have been ashamed and terrified. Not Penelope. She had looked at me as if she had felt pleased that she had been caught.

I looked at her now and felt pity for her. No anger and no pain remained inside me. I was truly over her betrayal. In fact, for the first time in my life, I felt truly happy, but it was clear she was an unhappy, broken woman. "What happened to what's-his name?" I asked.

"He doesn't matter," Penelope said, her lips drawing into a thin line.

"He left you, didn't he?" I asked.

She shrugged. "I was going to break it off with him, anyway. I'd already realized that I had made a mistake. He was not you. I don't even know why I went with him. I was just lonely. You were never here for me. Maybe I just wanted to show you that other men wanted me even if you didn't."

She was easy to read. Her pride had been wounded and because of that, she had come back. But maybe that experience had taught her to put her daughter first. The only part I didn't like was the way she was trying to imply she still had feelings for me. "If I agree to this Penelope, you're going to have to follow my rules."

Her face lit up. "Yes, of course! You're Molly's dad and I'll do exactly what you say."

"You can only see her in this house to start with. If I see that you are a positive influence you can start to take her out of the house for little trips to the park or for a meal," I told her.

She agreed eagerly. "Yes, I agree. That sounds absolutely fair. I always knew you were fair and—"

I held up my hand. "I have more rules for you. I don't want to upset Molly anymore, so you're not to tell her that you left her for a man."

A horrified look came over her features. "What do you take me for? I wouldn't do that. I'll tell her that I left for work."

I let out a humorless bark of a laugh. *Work indeed.* "If I see one hint that your presence is affecting her negatively, that will be the last time you see her."

"Yes, I understand." Penelope nodded eagerly.

"Where are you staying?" I asked her.

"In town. I've taken a room at the Sheraton hotel."

Of course, she was. Penelope loved to spend money. She was staying in the most expensive hotel in town at my expense. But no matter. If she could bring even a little happiness to Molly, it would be worth it.

I'd gladly pay double what I already was if she could make my daughter happier.

She made a praying gesture with her hands and adopted a sickly-sweet voice as she spoke, "I can see you've probably had a long day and you're tired, but before I go... is it okay if I see Molly one more time. If she's already asleep, I won't even disturb her. I just want to see her face again. She's so big and beautiful."

Once I had believed Penelope was this sweet. Not anymore, I knew this sickly-sweet facade was what she used when she wanted something she knew you didn't want to give her. I almost refused, but then thought better of it. What harm would it do when I'd already agreed to allow her to see Molly? "Sure," I said curtly.

"Thank you," she murmured and was careful not to look too victorious.

We climbed up the stairs to the playroom.

Molly was actually awake and she and Ella were on the floor playing with dolls. They looked up when we entered.

Ella scrambled to her feet and excused herself.

I longed to pull her into my arms for a quick hug, but I didn't want any questions from Penelope.

Penelope joined Molly on the floor and sat smiling at her.

Molly stared back at her mother, but didn't make any moves towards her.

Penelope leaned forward and kissed Molly's cheek.

Still, Molly did not react. She had retreated back into her shell. I started to frown. Had I made a mistake in letting Penelope speak to her? Was all the progress Ella and I had made going to be lost?

"It's late so I'm going now," Penelope said softly. "But I'll be back tomorrow and the next day and the next. I'm not going anywhere, Molly. I promise, I'm going to be here for you from now on."

She was good… I had to give her that. She spoke softly to Molly and with just a few sentences, she had conveyed to Molly what her intentions were.

She stood up. "Goodnight, Molly. I'll see you tomorrow."

Molly peered up and gave Penelope a tiny smile.

"I'll walk you to the door," I told Penelope and led her out of the room.

A myriad of emotions came over me. I felt glad Molly seemed happy to see her mom, but I was worried sick as well. What would happen if Penelope left again? How would Molly survive a second loss? I closed the door firmly behind us.

"I can't tell you how happy I am to see her," Penelope said.

I stared at her grim faced until she stopped smiling. "What happens when you decide to leave again, Penelope? Molly can't handle having her heart broken again."

Penelope dropped her head. "I deserve that, and I'm sorry. People change, Luke. I was immature and selfish and all I could think about was myself and my own happiness. I'm not going to hurt her again. I promise."

I was desperate to believe her, but I really didn't have much choice. "If you break your word, I promise you'll never see Molly again."

"You'll never have to worry about me breaking my word. Just give me another chance and you'll see how much I've changed."

After seeing her off, I went to the kitchen. I desperately needed a strong cup of coffee. I found a cup, put it under the machine, and waited.

Not too long ago, I wouldn't have given Penelope the time of day. I would have immediately escorted her out of the house and as for seeing Molly, that wouldn't have happened, but over the last few weeks, I had changed. The anger and bitterness I had held close to my heart had melted away.

Ella was the reason. She had softened my heart and taught me that there were good women in the world. Every woman wasn't like Penelope. I sipped my espresso and felt my insides relax. I had made the right decision.

It was important for Molly to know her mother again. Then I went upstairs.

Ella looked at me worriedly. "Is everything okay?"

I smiled at her. "Everything is A-okay. Now, where were we?"

She smiled back. "I think I had to stop giving you a blowjob because you couldn't concentrate on driving."

"Well, I'm not driving now," I said, my fingers moving to my belt.

## ELLA

*It's none of my business.*

I'd been chanting this same phrase the whole day and throughout dinner. The fact that Luke's ex-wife had come back to the house again today was none of my business. Except my heart refused to listen. What did she want now after all that time away?

Jealousy speared me. It didn't help that Penelope resembled a centerfold model for Playboy magazine. Standing next to her made me feel gaudy by comparison. Like a real-life Barbie with an exaggerated hourglass figure, gorgeous big blue eyes, and thick lustrous blonde hair that flowed in waves down her shoulders and back.

"Shouldn't you be wearing a uniform or something?" she asked with a disapproving look at my summery dress.

I straightened my spine. "Wearing a uniform was not part of my job description."

"I'll have to talk to Luke about that."

My eyes widened, but she had already flounced away, while calling out to Molly.

After dinner, as was our custom, Luke and I watched Molly playing with Bean before he was put into his crate and she was whisked off upstairs for a bath and bed.

Bean jumped on her and licked her face and hands thoroughly.

Dutifully, I laughed at all the puppy's antics for the next ten minutes, but my heart was truly not in it.

After Molly's bath, Luke came in and we tucked her into bed. Luke read a story to her. When the story was over, he closed the book. "Was it nice seeing Mommy today?" he asked her in a gentle voice.

Molly nodded.

"You don't have to see her if you don't want to," Luke continued.

I felt like an intruder, listening in on a moment that didn't belong to me. I quickly kissed Molly's forehead and padded softly out of the room. Then I returned downstairs. My muscles were tight with tension at the sudden change in our lives.

I had grown comfortable with my new life. That had been my mistake. I had started to see myself as part of the family. That's why having Penelope return came as such a shock. And I wasn't handling it so well.

Maybe it's because she had introduced herself to me as Luke's wife and not his ex-wife. Then she'd marched around the house with all the confidence of a woman who knew she belonged here.

I couldn't even hate her because she was Molly's mom. I just wished she'd stayed wherever she had been and left us alone. Then I instantly felt ashamed of my thoughts. I loved Molly, and I knew she needed her mom. It was unfair and nasty of me to wish that she hadn't come.

All of this was my fault. I had allowed my heart to become involved. But how could you not love Molly or feel something for Luke?

"I thought we'd have some wine," Luke said.

His voice startled me. I hadn't heard him return downstairs. A cold fear came over my heart. Despite the pep talk I had given myself, I felt frightened. What if Luke said he didn't need me anymore?

It wasn't about the money. I knew he'd pay me the full amount if he cut our contract short, because that was the kind of person he was. I realized as I walked to the window that I would be heartbroken if I was cast aside because Penelope had returned. I crossed my arms over my chest, inhaled deeply, and admitted it all to myself.

It was more than just feeling a little something for him. I simply wasn't ready to leave. Somehow, he had sneaked into my heart and I'd developed deep feelings for him. Then there was Molly. Such a little darling and I wanted to stay around to protect her. True, Penelope was her mother, but I didn't trust her for a moment. I'd only watched her with Molly for a few minutes, but already I noticed something false and forced about her feelings for the child. She acted too happy, her laugh sounded too high, and when she kissed Molly, it was a fleeting peck. Almost like one of those meaningless air kisses women who lunch together would give one another.

Now, a longing to be held and loved by Luke overwhelmed me. A longing I should not have been having. A relationship between us was impossible. How many times did I need to tell that to my brain?

I was Molly's nanny who just happened to be having an affair with my charge's father. An affair that could never be more than the physical. Penelope's return had really highlighted the fact that I needed to put some distance between us, both physical and intimate.

"Here you go," Luke said from behind me.

I turned around and took the glass from him. I took a sip and sighed as the icy cold wine went down my throat.

"I'm sorry there has been no time to ask you how you are doing," Luke said, staring at me with an intensity that made me tremble.

I chewed at my bottom lip. I thought of all the things I wanted to ask him. Did he have feelings for Penelope? Did he want her back in his life? Only I couldn't. We had made an agreement to enjoy each other without the burden of feelings and expectations. "Did Penelope talk to you about me wearing a uniform?" I asked.

Luke cocked his head. "No. Why?"

I shrugged. "It's just she said she was going to talk to you about getting me into a uniform."

"Did she now?"

I nodded.

"Hmmm… I think it's actually a very good idea."

My jaw dropped. I couldn't believe he thought it was a good idea. "What?"

"You wouldn't have to wear it all the time. Just sometimes in bed. I'd love to fuck you in a uniform."

I began to laugh with sheer relief… a sex thing. For a moment there, I thought he was serious and he would make me wear a dowdy uniform to please her. "Okay, I'll look for something. Would a nurse's uniform do?"

He grinned. "A nurse's uniform would be wonderful."

"I'll buy one tomorrow."

"Let's sit down," Luke said and touched my arm lightly to guide me to the couch.

We sat side by side with our thighs touching lightly. Arousal pulsed through me.

Luke shook his head. "I can't believe she's back."

My heart soared with hope. This wasn't the tone of a man who was excited or happy. The image of Luke's ex-wife leapt into my mind again. How could a man not want to be with such a gorgeous creature? "She's very beautiful," I noted cautiously.

Luke laughed humorlessly. "If you knew her character, you wouldn't say that. But I suppose I have to give her the benefit of doubt. She says that she's changed."

My euphoria had been crushed in half a second. What did he mean by giving her the benefit of doubt? I had to know. "Do you still love her?"

Luke turned to me, his eyes wide with surprise. "Love Penelope? Hell, no! It's a little hard to love someone who betrayed you and ran off with a man, and scarred your daughter for life."

His voice vibrated with emotion and my tension ebbed away. I had nothing to fear from Penelope. The person I needed to be careful about was Luke himself. If he found out I had developed feelings for him, it would be the end of us. I felt sure about that.

"I'd promised myself that if she ever came back, I wouldn't let her see Molly," Luke explained. "But a lot of things have changed. I'm not bitter about her anymore. All I am interested in is what Molly needs. Penelope is around because there is a chance she could be the thing Molly needs to heal completely. If she ever gives me the impression she is not making things better for Molly, she's out of here in a flash."

What he said made sense. I nodded. "It's worth a shot. Anything that can help Molly is worth it."

"I really hope she has truly changed and won't just up and leave again, making Molly worse," Luke said, voicing my own worry.

I turned to face him. What Luke needed from me was support, not pointing out all the things that might go wrong. "The only thing you can do is to give it a try and hope for the best. Molly is older and emotionally stronger now, and she has you and me that love her. She'll be fine."

A smile lit up Luke's face and he placed a hand on my bare knee. "How did we manage without you? Thank you."

"You're welcome," I said, keeping my voice light.

Luke took my glass from my hands and placed it on the table together with his. He pulled me onto his lap. "I've been wanting to do this all afternoon." I hiked up my dress as I straddled him. He raised his head and cradled my cheeks to kiss me. I tangled my hands through his hair. His hands circled my thighs, clutched my ass, and he gently pulled me forward.

His hard cock was the flame and my pussy was the tinder. And as soon as it pushed against me, my whole body became fire. Soon, I was moaning and rocking against his cock.

"You feel so good in my arms," Luke said, his voice husky and sexy. He gripped my thighs and bounced me up and down on his cock.

Our bodies created waves of delicious friction but I needed more. A sense of urgency came over us and I grappled with Luke's pants.

He moved my hands and undid his button and zipper himself. Holding me, he raised his hips and pulled down his pants and boxer briefs. His cock stood up proudly between us and I wrapped my hand around it.

Luke snapped my bra open and my breasts came free. He grabbed both of them then proceeded to lick and bite each aroused nipple while I fisted his hair and moaned loudly. Usually, I loved the foreplay part of our coupling, but today I needed Luke inside me. To make me feel whole again.

Seeing Penelope come into this house and behave as if she belonged here had hurt and disturbed me in a very profound way.

I got up and pulled down my panties, all the while Luke's hungry eyes were gazing at me as his hands caressed my thighs. I straddled Luke and he arranged the entrance of my pussy over his cock.

"I'm so hard for you," Luke growled.

My pussy clenched at his words. In one smooth motion, I impaled myself on his cock. I held his shoulders for leverage and rode him again and again. Luke's hands gripped my thighs and each time I came down, he thrust upwards, burying his cock even deeper inside me.

I looked down at his big cock glistening with my juices as it disappeared in and out of my pussy and moaned helplessly. Luke's gaze remained glued to my tits as they bounced up and down. This is what we were about. Great sex. Sex that could make me forget all my problems.

I had to remember that and enjoy it while it lasted. It was just sex. Nothing more. The sooner I got this fact through my thick head the better.

# ELLA

*B*ean's soft bark filled the air as he ran for the softball Molly had thrown. Luke and I had taught her how to throw a ball for Bean and she was loving it. Bean seemed to love it too.

For me, it just felt nice to sit on the grass and watch them.

It was a beautiful afternoon to be out. The sun felt warm on my skin and the skies were a gorgeous shade of blue.

Luke was cooped up in the library working on something he had termed to be a problematic project.

The sounds of a back door opening made me turn around.

Penelope stood in the doorway. Paul must have let her in on his way out. She looked amazing in a skintight pantsuit. I felt my stomach clench. Like it did every time I saw her.

Molly's face lit up and she looked over at me questioningly.

"Go on to your mom. I'll take care of Bean," I told her with an encouraging smile.

But she didn't go towards her mother. Instead, she stood staring at the house.

Penelope walked towards us. She had a frown on her face and stepped along carefully as if the grass might destroy her shoes. "My girl," she cried and opened her arms to Molly.

Molly went to her mom and stood inside the circle of her arms. "Do you want to meet my puppy?" she asked.

"Oh, no!" Penelope cried. "I hate the smell of dogs."

Molly's face fell.

What was wrong with this woman? Couldn't she see how important the animal was to Molly?

"I have a better idea. Why don't we go to the park? We could ask your dad to go with us?"

Molly nodded but the light had already gone from her eyes.

"Where's Mr. Meyers?" she asked without bothering with niceties.

"He's in the library," I said in an equally unbothered tone.

She patted her hair. "Well, I'll just say hello to your dad and then we can go. Do you want to take me?" She smiled at Molly.

Hand in hand, they walked towards the house.

I swallowed the lump in my throat.

Bean made mournful noises, lay on the ground, and buried his face between his front paws.

I went to him and patted his head. "She'll be back, Bean," I murmured.

As I usually did in the hours when Molly was with her mother, I went up to my room to work on my designs. My notebook was already more than half-filled with designs and I was excited about the new styles I'd come up with. I had no concrete plan of what I wanted to do with them when the notebook filled up.

I just enjoyed the creative process. With time, things would fall into place.

I plopped down on my bed, grabbed my notebook, and was soon lost in my work until I heard Luke call my name. I ran to the top of the stairs and looked down.

Penelope, Luke and Molly stood in the hallway.

I swallowed heavily. They looked like a real family.

"We're going out for a spot of shopping," Penelope said cheerfully.

"Okay," I said, coming down the stairs slowly.

Molly dropped her parents' hands and flew up the stairs to me. Meeting me halfway, she wrapped her little hands around my waist.

I kissed the top of her head. "See you later, sweetheart."

"Can you come with us?" Molly asked.

We all froze.

Then I smiled at her. "No, sweetie. I've got things to do. But you go ahead with your dad and mom. I'll be right here when you get back, okay?

"Let's go," Penelope said tightly.

I watched them walk down the hallway to the door.

Luke glanced back at me.

His stare was blank and I couldn't read any emotion in his eyes at all. I shivered and when the door shut, I slipped back into my room.

I tried to capture my earlier concentration, but failed. I kept thinking of Luke's expressionless eyes. What had he been thinking? Was he regretting what we had? Penelope was a beautiful woman and she was Molly's mom.

She had broken his heart, but human beings had a big capacity for forgiveness. Maybe he would try again for Molly's sake. I folded my legs and wrapped my hands around my knees. If Luke and Penelope managed to salvage their relationship, they would have no use for me.

From what I had gathered, Penelope had taken care of Molly herself when she and Luke had been married. I'd be out of a job, but that wasn't the issue. I had my own plans for the future which included taking some classes and looking for a part time job with a designer.

I was willing to take on a low paying job just to have the exposure of working in my dream industry.

No, losing the job was not the issue. It was losing Molly and Luke. They had become important to me and I couldn't fathom life without them.

I pictured Luke walking into the dining room to join us for breakfast, as he did every morning, his hair ruffled from forking his fingers through it.

The way he turned his gaze to me after greeting Molly, his eyes dropping to my mouth and I'd know he was thinking about kissing me. How he made impromptu visits to the playroom to check on us, and when Molly was distracted, he would kiss the back of my neck.

Restlessness came over me. I needed to talk to someone, or I would go crazy. I reached for my phone on the bedside table and called Ruby.

"Hi stranger," Ruby greeted in her cheerful voice.

"Hi you," I replied.

"What's going on? You sound down."

I explained to her about the way Penelope had inserted herself back into not only Molly's life, but also Luke's.

"Whoa, that's not good at all. She wants him back."

Dismay came over me. Ruby had just confirmed what I didn't want to believe, but knew was true. Penelope's real mission in coming back was to win Luke's heart. And she had went about it the right way, too. Through Molly. There was no way I could compete with the mother of his baby. Not to mention her looks.

"She said she came back to get to know Molly again," I said weakly.

Ruby made a dismissive noise. "Don't be fooled. She's after Luke. A woman who leaves her child for a man doesn't just develop a conscience. She misses the life she had with him. I mean, she was a fool to leave in the first place. God, she must have a head full of air to walk out on a man like him and her own child."

"People make mistakes, Ruby."

"Not those kinds of mistakes. Can you imagine running off with a man and leaving your husband and baby girl behind?"

I tried and failed. I couldn't.

"You have to fight for him, Ella," Ruby said fiercely.

How could I fight for someone I did not have? "We're not about that," I said miserably. "We're fuck buddies, that's all." Even saying it aloud sounded false. We had become more than that. We had developed a friendship and we cared about each other.

"Well, have you kept your end of the bargain?" Ruby asked.

I sighed deeply. "I don't know."

"Shouldn't that be a hard no? I'm looking at the photos from that night you went on a date with him right now, and you look like a woman deeply in love to me."

"I'm not deeply in love."

"Hey," Ruby said softly. "It's not a bad thing to open your heart, you know. All men are not like Stan. You're a good person Ella, and you deserve to be happy."

After we ended the call, I thought about what Ruby had said. What if I opened up my heart to Luke and he rejected me? What if he chose Penelope, where would that leave me?

Opening your heart to someone wasn't as easy as it sounded. People hurt you when you gave them that power. Had I not loved Stan? I would have walked away from that relationship the first time he put me down in public if I hadn't had feelings for him. He would never have had a chance to treat me like his boxing bag.

My self-esteem would not come close to being destroyed... not ever again.

# ELLA

*I* felt relieved when I heard Luke's car at three thirty in the afternoon. There would be time for Molly to catch a quick nap before dinner.

"Hi sweetheart," I said to a tired looking Molly as she trudged up the steps holding her dad's hand.

I kept my gaze on Molly, frightened of what I'd see if I looked at Luke. What if he'd realized how much he'd missed his ex-wife? Or maybe he knew I had feelings for him and would look at me with pity?

"Let's get you to bed," I said to Molly and took her hand.

"Did you have fun?" I asked, as I tucked a light blanket around her.

"Yes," Molly said sleepily, her eyes already half closed. Then she stuck out her hand and touched my cheek.

I melted. I covered her hand with mine.

Seconds later, she was snoring gently.

I kissed her forehead and tiptoed out.

I stood outside her room indecisively. I could have gone to my room to continue working on my designs, but a strong urge to see Luke came over me. I knocked softly on the library door before pushing it open.

His face lit up with a smile when he saw me and all my insecurities melted away. You couldn't fake such a reaction. Smiling, I went to him.

He stood up and pulled me into his arms.

All the tension in my body ebbed away as he held me tight. I inhaled his masculine scent and let my head rest on his chest.

"I missed you," Luke said, his voice gruff.

"I missed you too," I said and raised my head, needing to feel his lips on mine—to lose myself in his kisses.

Our kiss was gentle and probing, familiarizing each other with our tongues and mouths, though we'd only been apart for a few hours. From the corner of my eye, I caught a movement and broke the kiss. When I looked again, there was nothing.

"How was your afternoon? I'm sorry we couldn't go together," Luke said.

"It's fine, I got a lot—"

"Here you are," Penelope said and stepped into the library. "I promised Molly I'd stay for dinner, so I thought I'd take in a swim and catch some sun." She twirled around.

My jaw dropped.

She wore a skimpy bikini, if it could even be called a bikini. The bottom was a silver colored thong with the scrap of material disappearing into the crack of her curvaceous ass.

"Anyway, we had better let you get back to work," she said, favoring Luke with a sexy look. "Come on, Ella."

I had no choice but to follow her out.

She held the door for me and then shut the door. She faced me and smiled. Her lips curved and her teeth showed, but the smile didn't reach her eyes. "I've missed my family so much. Do you have any of your own?"

"No," I said stiffly.

She caught my meaning because her eyes narrowed. "Do you want to join me for a swim? We can continue with our girly chat."

The sudden interest in me made me suspicious. I suspected she had been the shadow I had seen when Luke and I were in each other's arms. I had just moved up from being part of the furniture to her main competition. I had no choice but believe Ruby's instinctive assessment now. Penelope was working her way back into Luke and Molly's lives. "Thanks, but I need to tidy up the playroom," I said and smiled politely.

"Fine," she said. "I'll be out in the back if you change your mind." She turned and sashayed down the hallway, her ass cheeks jiggling with every step.

I climbed the stairs wearily. I was at a loss about what to do. Penelope was Molly's mom and she needed to be with her daughter.

Molly had been opening up more day by day and that was all because of her mother's presence. I couldn't do anything about Penelope wanting to seduce her ex-husband. It would be up to Luke now what happened. If he wanted her back, I would have no choice but to bow out and give them their space. Even if it broke my heart into a million pieces.

For now, I would continue to do the work Luke had hired me for and enjoy what we had while it lasted.

# LUKE

o you always sit down to dinner with the staff?" Penelope asked with a sweet smile.

That smile could deceive someone who did not know her as well as I did. She had an acidic mouth but she always accompanied it with a smile, so whatever she was saying seemed innocent.

Ella was in my line of vision and I saw her turn to Penelope.

Before I could answer, Ella spoke up, "If you mean me, the answer is yes. We've always had dinner together since I started working here. Molly likes it."

I hid a smile. I wanted to cheer Ella for standing up for herself. Penelope was a bully, but she had picked on the wrong target.

Penelope's lips tightened.

"Ella has been a wonderful addition to our family," I added.

"That's nice," Penelope snapped. "Though, I don't know how long we'll need her now that I'm back."

I stared at her. "Back?" I asked.

She had the grace to look embarrassed.

"If you don't mind, I'll leave you two," Ella said, and pushed her chair back and turned to walk away.

I swallowed down my disappointment. I couldn't protest with Penelope there. If she got an inkling of something going on between Ella and me, she would try her damnedest to make life difficult for Ella.

"Have a good night," Penelope said to her and then smiled at me as she placed her hand over mine. "Shall we move to the living room and have a drink? I miss those cozy evenings, sipping wine, and dancing the evening away."

I snatched my hand away. *What the hell? Had Penelope lost her mind?* I used to put in a lot of hours at work and I had no time to sit around drinking wine. What she was saying had to be a figment of her imagination.

I wanted to set her straight but, even more importantly, I wanted Ella to know, I was there for her. She was walking away when I pushed my chair back and said, "Ella, may I take a moment of your time. I need to go over a clause in your contract. In the library, please."

I needed fuel if I was to spend another minute in Penelope's company. My fuel came in the form of having Ella's soft body molded into mine and her sweet tongue entangled with mine.

Penelope stood up and made as though to come with us.

"Could you wait in the living room," I said to her. Then I placed my hand on the small of Ella's back as we left the room.

In the library, I shut the door behind us.

Ella opened her mouth to say something.

I covered her mouth with mine and crashed her body against mine. I groaned into her mouth as our bodies were pressed intimately against each other. I swiped my hands over her hardened nipples and she gave a low sexy moan. I slid one hand between her legs and cupped her pussy.

"Please Luke," she cried.

The heat from her pussy seared my hand and I groaned, imaging my cock sheathed by that heat.

"More," Ella moaned against my mouth.

I dipped my hand under her dress and pulled her wet panties to the side. She was wet and ready for me. "Were you thinking about my cock during dinner?" I growled.

"Yes."

Animal noises came from my throat before I captured her mouth again, and slipped my fingers into her wet pussy. She clenched and unclenched her pussy against my fingers and I increased the pace until she was grinding against my fingers.

I wished we were alone. I would have thrown Ella over my shoulder and carried her to my room. She had become an addiction. Her pussy had entranced me. I needed it on a daily basis and if possible, several times a day.

A sharp knock came on the door, startling us apart.

"Luke!" Penelope's sharp voice called.

Her shrill, annoying voice penetrated my lust-soaked brain. I leaned into Ella and kissed her on the mouth. Then I arranged my cock and opened the door. "I needed to set Penelope straight and send her on her way. "Will you wait for me in my bedroom?" I asked Ella.

She nodded.

I kissed her lightly on the forehead and went out the door.

Penelope was waiting for me, a strange expression on her face.

*Fuck no, she's jealous?* "We need to talk," I said coldly.

We stood facing each other in the living room, her gaze locked on mine. Then she licked her lower lip and batted her fake eyelashes seductively.

I recognized the move. How could I have ever been taken in by her obvious ploys?

"It used to be so good between us, can you remember?" she asked.

Ella had gone up to her room by now, I mused. She was probably playing with herself to relieve the ache I'd left unsatisfied right at this moment. My cock started to stir at the image of her doing this in my mind. Ella sprawled on her bed with her legs thrown apart.

"Luke?" Penelope snapped.

"Huh?" I hadn't heard a word she had said.

"Weren't you listening?" she demanded, her eyes narrowed with irritation. "You used to do that a lot. Let your mind wander while we were talking about something important."

I snapped my attention back to her.

Her face had turned to an ugly shade of pink.

"Penelope, we need to talk about what's going on here."

She shrugged. "Nothing's going on. I'm just trying to be a good mother to my daughter.

I nodded. "Please don't think you can do any more than that."

Her eyes widened. "What do you mean?"

"I mean. Don't for one second, imagine that we could ever get back together."

"What if Molly wanted it?"

"Not even if Molly wanted it," I stated firmly.

She laughed. "Well, you sure told me. I got the message loud and clear. Do you mind if I finish my drink before I go?"

"Not at all. Since you've been drinking, I'll call an Uber ride for you."

"Thank you. I'll collect my car tomorrow."

I sighed and followed her into the living room. One drink and she was gone, but today was the last day I would allow this. After today, she would come in the afternoons to see Molly and be gone by dinner time.

It seemed like hours before Penelope finally left. I shut the front door and bounded up the stairs.

I stopped to check in on Molly.

She was sleeping peacefully with her thumb firmly stuck in her mouth. I was tempted to pry it out of her mouth, but the last therapist to see her had said to leave it. She would stop it on her own when she was ready. Besides, she never sucked her thumb during the day. Only at night, in bed.

I shut the door and stepped over to my bedroom, but Ella wasn't there. I went over to her bedroom and opened the door softly. The curtains were open and the moonlight cast a silver glow on Ella's face and hair. I edged closer and peered at her face. She wore a peaceful expression and a hint of a smile on her lips.

Ella could only be dreaming sweet dreams. Good people dreamed of good things. Regretfully, I turned away, internally cursing Penelope for ruining my evening. Had she not overstayed her welcome. Or even better, if she'd left us to our evening routine, Ella and I would have slept wrapped up in each other's arms.

In my own bedroom, I stripped off my clothes and slipped between the cool bed sheets. It would have been selfish of me to wake Ella up. Sleep didn't come easy, but as I drifted away, I felt a warm body press against my back.

I moaned, feeling sure it was a dream, but enjoying the feeling nonetheless. Until the dream wrapped its slim, soft hand around my cock and stroked it lovingly.

My cock roared to life from the loving attention. I inhaled Ella's scent before seeing her. My throat thickened as she stroked my rapidly hardening cock. I reached a hand behind me and grasped her thigh. It felt satiny soft. I needed more. I turned to face her. "If this is a dream, I don't want it to stop,"

I murmured as I wrapped her in my arms and pulled her close for a kiss.

I kissed her without rushing, tangling my tongue with hers, and nibbling softly on her lower lip. I dipped my head to her neck, kissing and nuzzling her until her moans became interspersed with giggles.

"I should punish you," I said to her while enjoying the sound of her giggles.

"What for?" she asked lazily, as she stretched luxuriously, her deliciously naked body teasing mine.

"For falling asleep in your own bed. We had a date." I played with her wonderful nipples as I spoke, palming them with my thumbs and watching them grow with my touch. I loved her sweet nipples.

"I'm here now," she whispered.

"Yes, you are," I said and sat up. I tugged at her legs and she slid onto her back. I caressed her inner thighs, going higher and higher. Her scent was intoxicating, a mixture of sex and heaven. Instead of caressing her pussy with my hands, I buried my mouth between her legs.

"Yes," she gasped.

And I went into starving beast mode. I parted her thighs wide open and teased her slit with long slow licks.

"Fuck Luke!" Ella cried. "I love your tongue."

I chuckled softly. I would make her love my tongue even more if it was the last thing I did. That way, she wouldn't go looking for another job. I could just keep her here with me

193

and Molly then we'd spend the rest of our lives pleasuring each other.

"I'm going to make you come hard, my sweet Ella," I said.

She cried out when I sucked her clit. Hard. I then soothed it with soft licks from my tongue and then went at it again.

"Please, no… yes!"

When Ella's words stopped making sense, I knew she was close to orgasm. I teased her with feathery flicks of my tongue, then without warning, I pushed my tongue into her pussy and slick wetness gushed out.

"Yes," Ella cried, raising her hips and burying my tongue deeper into her pussy. She grabbed my head with both hands as her legs shot into the air.

I replaced my tongue with my fingers, and as I pumped my fingers furiously in and out of her pussy, I sucked on her clit.

When she came, she screamed.

"That was out of this world," Ella said when her trembling subsided. "Now, I need your cock."

"You're an insatiable woman," I growled, arranging myself between her legs.

I slid my cock into her slick wetness easily and groaned as it was enveloped by an envelope of heat and wetness. The pressure built in me to unbearable proportions and I pumped furiously, conscious only of Ella moans of pleasure.

I held on just long enough for Ella to come, then I shot a load of cum into her pussy, a primal grunt escaping my mouth as I came.

Afterwards, Ella lay sprawled on my chest, her mound pressed against my thigh.

I smoothed her hair as we relaxed in the darkness. "Are you still working on your designs?" I asked.

"Yes. I have to draw. It's like a compulsion," she said.

It was the same for me. Even though the firm had employed enough architects, so I could just concentrate on the overall direction of the company, I still took on new projects myself. I loved coming up with the concept, drawing it on paper or computer and then liaising with the clients.

Without that, I felt lost. I understood what Ella meant. It also confirmed something I had been playing around with in my mind. I wanted to do something special for her. A small token to show our appreciation for what she had done for us.

She hadn't just taken care of Molly, she had made us a family. She had helped Molly and I become close. "You told me that your dream was to go to fashion school," I said.

She turned her head towards me. "You remember. Yes."

I felt her stare on me. "Well, I've been thinking that Molly and I would love to do something special for you, just like you've done for us."

"You're paying me to do it," Ella said.

"You know you do a lot more than that. You can't put a price on the love and attention you've given Molly."

"Thank you for saying that. It really means a lot to me, but you don't need to do anything extra," she whispered hoarsely.

She was an easy woman to fall in love with. How many women would say no to the offer of a gift like this? "Nope, saying no is not allowed. Molly and I want to pay your college fees for a course in fashion and design," I insisted.

She went absolutely still. "I can't let you do that."

I stroked her cheek. "It's already decided. There is nothing you can say or do that will change my decision. Your job is to identify a college and start the application process. Oh, and we'll cater to your expenses while you're studying."

Ella burst into tears.

# ELLA

*A*s I pushed Molly to and fro on the swing, her laugh filled my ears and made me smile. When I first became her nanny, she didn't even smile. Now she was laughing like a normal child.

I couldn't wait to see more of her emerging from her shell. So many good things had happened to me and sometimes, I felt like I was living a dream. Once, I had believed I was one of those people whose life never really aligned with their dreams.

Now, thanks to Luke-even though I hardly dared dream of getting into fashion-was about to come to fruition. I couldn't remember being as excited about the future like I felt now. Penelope's presence still grated on me, but now that I had something else to focus on, I tried not to let it bother me so much.

It also helped that Luke did not seem interested in the least to get back with Penelope. That ship had sailed a long time ago for him.

I had zeroed in on two colleges with intensive two year courses and sent applications to both. Now, I would just wait with my fingers crossed that one of them would accept me.

Meanwhile, I kept myself busy with Molly, my designs, and playing with Luke.

My phone vibrated against my thigh. I dug into the pocket of my jeans and pulled it out. I smiled with anticipation. Luke liked to send me dirty messages when we weren't together, or even when we were but someone else was with us.

I swiped the screen and raised it up at a better angle to read. Then stared at the message in dismay. A cold ice formed in the pit of my stomach and my blood went cold.

*Sorry I went silent.*
*Had a few things to take care of.*
*But now I can concentrate on you.*

"OH, GOD PLEASE," I murmured. "Not again."

I reread the message and searched around us. I saw no one watching us or behaving suspiciously. I tried to think rationally. The last time I'd gotten a weird message, Ruby had convinced me it was likely a wrong number.

This one destroyed that theory. Whoever was sending me messages knew exactly what they were doing. And they knew the recipient of those messages. Me. I forced myself to continue pushing the swing as if nothing had happened even though all my instincts were screaming at me to run like the devil was after me. No way, would I show him I was afraid of him.

*Fuck him. And his stupid messages.*

We stayed until it was almost lunchtime. Only then, did we walk back home. I kept Molly's hand in mine the whole way. As much as I tried, I couldn't stop myself from glancing back again and again, to see if anyone was following us.

Back at the house, Molly rushed to the backyard to say hello to Bean. We had taken him to the park once and he'd almost gotten lost. After that, we left him at home, free to roam in his enclosed space in the back.

Later, we ate lunch and then at exactly two in the afternoon, Penelope came.

She had a bag with her. As always, she did not bother greeting me, but she did throw in some information. She was planning on spending the weekend with us. In the hallway, she narrowed her eyes and stared at me. "You could take the weekend off if you want. I don't think we'll need you."

I knew what she wanted. She wanted to have Luke all to herself, perhaps even show him how it could be if they were a family again. Penelope wasn't a fool and she had probably sensed that there was more to Luke and me than employer and employee.

"I'd have to clear it with Luke," I said to her. "He's my employer, after all."

She cocked her head to the side. "You're an odd one. A lot of people would jump at the chance of a weekend off, but not you. Unless..."

"Unless what?" I asked, though I knew where she was going.

"Nothing," she said and strode off.

I took Molly up for her nap and while she slept, I tried to work on some designs, but I couldn't. I felt restless and jittery. I glanced at my phone every few seconds. At one point, I switched it off and then turned it back on again, a minute later.

*Maybe I should tell Luke.* My insides clenched at the thought. It wasn't fair to involve him in a matter that didn't concern him. Stan was my business and I had to find a way to deal with it, without involving Luke.

I jumped from the bed and strode across the length of my bedroom. I went to the window and looked out at the street. I knew Stan was out there, planning how to make my life a living nightmare.

I forced myself to look at the situation calmly. What was he likely to do? Probably nothing. Stan was violent, but after a bad stint in prison, I agreed with Ruby. He wouldn't risk anything that would put him back there. His plan was most likely to frighten me by turning my life upside down.

Well, if that was his plan, he had another thing coming. I might have been that person before but not anymore. He wasn't going to frighten me with text messages and subtle threats. I would ignore his messages until he got tired of sending them.

I wasn't going to let Stan drive me out of my mind. Not when my future had just started to look bright. For once, I had something to be excited about. I'd started to believe I could follow my dreams and make something of my life.

Being with Luke and seeing him follow his own dreams had inspired me. I had also learned how a man should treat a woman. He treated me with respect and he cared for my opinions. It sounded so simple, but that in itself had shifted something inside of me.

It made me believe in myself and I now believed I had the capability of being whatever I wanted to be.

These last few weeks working for Luke and taking care of Molly had opened my eyes to a new way of living and thinking. Like a curtain in my brain had been opened and showed me life could be paradise on earth. Human beings were like flowers. Flowers need water, and humans need encouraging words. I got that from Luke. He encouraged me to go back to college and most importantly, he made me believe I could do it.

I remember once confiding in Stan that I wanted to be a fashion designer.

He had stared at me open mouthed with disbelief, then burst out laughing. *"You've got to be kidding me! You, a fashion designer?"* He'd doubled up in laughter and then proceeded to mock me for weeks by sarcastically referring to me as Ella Wang because he knew I admired Vera Wang.

Needless to say... that had been the end of that and I had pushed my crazy dreams to the back of my mind.

I had allowed Stan to mess with my head once. I would not let it happen again, I thought fiercely. I smiled when I spied Luke's car coming up the drive. He was home a little earlier than usual. I was about to bound out of my room when I remembered Penelope was here.

I ran a hand through my hair and adjusted my dress. Not that it mattered. Luke had seen me at my best and my worst.

Minutes later, a knock came on the door and the doorknob turned.

Luke peered in, and all my worries evaporated.

I smiled back at him. He entered and shut the door and locked it. My heart pounded wildly as he closed the gap between us.

"My sweet Ella," he said.

"Hi," I said shyly.

He slipped his hands around my waist and lowered his head to kiss me.

I inhaled his scent and shut my eyes, enjoying the feel of his mouth against mine.

He pulled back after a moment. "I checked in on Molly. She's asleep. She must have been very tired."

"We went to the park," I told him.

Luke lowered his head again, and kissed my neck.

I giggled when he touched a sensitive spot.

"I didn't know you were ticklish there," Luke said and went for the same spot.

I tried to push him away and when that didn't work, I curled my body and slipped out from his grasp.

Our horseplay ended up with Luke lying on top of me on the bed. He smoothed my hair away from my face and stared down at me.

He looked so sexy in his work clothes. An expensive looking grey suit, a white shirt, and a tie. I imagined what his employees would say if they saw him now and giggled.

He touched my nose with a finger. "What's so funny?"

"I just wondered what the people at work would think if they saw you now," I said.

He chuckled. "They would think it's my clone. They probably don't think I know how to laugh."

I burst out laughing at the accuracy of his statement. I felt special since I got to see this side of Luke. The playful side.

I became aware of a bulge pressing into my stomach. The air between us changed from playful to heated. Luke's gaze dropped to my mouth and I parted my lips. He brought his mouth down and kissed me. Hard. Deep. I dry humped him, wanting to feel more of his rock-hard cock.

My hands dropped from his shoulders to his back and then to his tight ass. A wave of longing to be filled came over me but it wasn't the right time. Molly would be waking up and then there was the added complication of Penelope being in the house.

Our breathing grew heavier and I knew if we did not stop now, we would go all the way. I broke the kiss.

Luke stared at me questioningly.

"Molly will wake up any time," I said.

"She's not awake yet though and I can be very fast," he quipped and captured my mouth again.

For a few seconds, I allowed myself to get lost in his kisses, before I broke it off again. "And Penelope is in the house," I added.

Luke groaned and rolled off me. He lay on his back staring at the ceiling. "For fuck's sake. It's about time I set some rules with her."

Feeling sorry for the tent he sported, I reached out and cupped his cock. He groaned. Quickly, I unzipped Luke's pants and pulled out his cock. It pulsed heavy and smooth in the palm of my hand.

Luke lay back with his eyes closed but his heavy breathing let me know he surely enjoyed my touch. When I took him into my mouth, he let out a long happy groan. "I'll be done in a minute," he promised.

He was true to his word.

# LUKE

*I*t was Sunday and instead of feeling invigorated and rested, I felt exhausted. We had gone out for a meal the previous day, and even that had been tiresome. I'd forgotten what a diva Penelope was.

She had complained about everything, from the food to the service and the class of the restaurant. Molly, Ella and I had sat quietly and watched her, but she had ruined the meal for everyone.

It didn't help that my body was tight with sexual tension. All weekend, she kept popping back at the most inopportune times. And Ella didn't like to have sex with Penelope in the house. The end result... I felt horny and angry. All I could think of was how much I wanted to have Ella's soft body in my arms, but at the same time, I could see that Molly was starting to feel more and more confident. And as much as I hated having Penelope come in and out of the house as if she belonged here, I couldn't bring myself to hurt the progress Molly had been making.

I felt glad when bedtime came and the following day was Monday. Penelope could go back to her hotel and leave us to our normal peaceful lives. I slipped into the cool sheets, and waited patiently until...

I felt a warm body slip into bed. I grabbed her hips to pull her to me. She was naked as she usually was when she joined me in bed, but when my hands touched her skin, I froze. "What the—?" I pulled my hand away as though I'd been burned and reached for the bedside lamp switch. Light flooded the room and I turned my gaze to the person in my bed.

"What the hell are you doing?" I growled at Penelope.

She looked at me and smiled. "You weren't complaining a few seconds ago," she said, a knowing look on her face. "Don't stop."

I threw back the covers and got up. I grabbed my boxer briefs and slipped them on. Feeling more in charge, I faced her. "We need to talk, Penelope," I said. The most important thing now was for her to understand that it was truly over between us.

"Do we really have to talk?" she asked and pushed away the covers, exposing her breasts and pussy. Slowly, she opened her legs and showed me how wet she was. Then she did that thing she used to do when she wanted sex. She pushed her finger into her pussy.

I felt nothing. Absolutely nothing. I raised my cold gaze to her face.

She must have seen my complete disinterest because she pulled the covers up.

"There's something I need you to understand, Penelope," I said, my voice sounding like ice. "It's over between us. My only interest in you is as Molly's mother. Nothing else. I don't want to fuck you—"

"Must you be so freaking crude," she muttered.

"Call it what you like, but I'm simply not interested. I don't want you like that anymore. "

Her face twisted into an ugly grimace. "It's because you're fucking the nanny, isn't it?"

I inhaled sharply. I thought that we'd kept that private. It seemed not.

"You didn't think I knew, did you?" she said triumphantly.

I stared at her. "What does it matter if you know or not? I don't need your approval or disapproval."

That wiped the smug smile off of her face.

"Whether I'm sleeping with Ella or not, is none of your business, but since you seem to think it is important, yes, I am, and I like her very much. You and I are over. In fact, we were over long before you walked out. The only reason you are allowed in this house is because you could be good for Molly."

To my surprise, tears sprung to her eyes.

"I just wanted us to try again," she said. "For Molly's sake."

I shook my head. "Too damn late for that."

"I haven't been with a man for weeks. Remember how good we were together? How good I made you feel?" she said, speaking in that little girl voice I used to dislike even when we were together and I thought I was in love with her.

"Sorry, can't do," I said callously, before glancing at the clock on my bedside table. "It's late and I need to get to sleep."

"I'll go back to the hotel tomorrow," she said, sounding dejected. "But I'll be coming to see Molly."

Relief. It had finally penetrated her little brain that we were done.

"You can see her any time," I said. I wanted to say, *for now*, but I held back. Best to take it step by step. "Just be honest with her when you can, or cannot come. That's all I ask."

"I will," she said. "A goodbye kiss?"

I glanced at her and fought my revulsion. "Fuck off, Penelope."

She got up and sashayed to the door.

I frowned. Had she walked from the first floor stark naked? What if she ran into someone? Thankfully, it was just Molly and Ella in the house. But still, it made me feel violated somehow.

She blew me a kiss and shut the door behind her.

## ELLA

*H*eat and electricity raced through my body as Luke's hands caressed me. I arched my body to him, wanting to feel him on my skin. I'd never been this aroused before. I writhed, moaned, and called his name.

He silenced me with a deep kiss and nibbled on my lower lip.

"Oh Luke," I moaned. I'd never had a lover as skilled as Luke was. He made my body come alive with his hands and tongue.

He slid down my body and captured a nipple in his mouth while his fingers played with the other. "You're so beautiful, my Ella," he said in a low husky voice.

I arched my body so he could take more of my breast into his mouth. I could feel his cock on my thigh… rock hard and ready. My pussy clenched, needing to be filled and stretched.

Luke kept his hands on my breasts but continued planting kisses on my belly, going lower, and lower. He slid between my legs and raised them to his shoulders. Then he dipped his face to my pussy.

I screamed with pleasure.

His tongue pushed into my pussy hungrily, eating me like a starving man.

"Yes Luke!" I moaned, twisting my body.

He licked and sucked until I was begging for more. I was on the edge of orgasm but I wanted more. I needed his cock.

"Fuck me Luke," I said.

He heard the desperation in my voice and rose from his position. He moved up and angled his pulsing cock at the entrance of my pussy. I raised my hips to meet it. He grabbed the base and pushed his cock in. The ache in my pussy grew.

Despite Luke's cock being fully in, I felt empty and I writhed with agony. Why wasn't the ache in my pussy easing? Tears of frustration filled my eyes as I raised my hips in a desperate attempt to take in more of him.

My eyes popped open then and I found myself alone in my bed with my body raised in the air. Disappointment crushed through me. My body ached and I was aroused beyond belief.

I squeezed my legs together, trying to ease the desperate ache between my legs. Nothing helped. I needed Luke's cock. Now. I got up from bed, grabbed a robe and slipped into it, then tiptoed out of my room.

I peered into Molly's room. She was sound asleep. I made for the stairs and stepped softly, not wanting to wake Penelope up. Then I saw her just as I reached the landing.

She was stark naked and leaving Luke's room.

My blood became ice. The heat in my pussy evaporated. I pulled my robe tighter around me.

Penelope looked up and saw me. She didn't even bother to cover herself. She wore the look of a woman who had been fucked all night. Her hair was messy. Her lips curved into a victorious smile.

Humiliation washed over me. Dizziness swept me, as I turned and staggered back to my room. Tears blinded me but I made it safely back to my room.

I sat on the bed breathing hard and shaking. I couldn't believe what I had just seen. How could Luke do this to me? The pain I felt was incredible. Like a cold, steely hand had reached into my body and was squeezing my heart. I slipped into bed and curled myself into a ball. I'd been such a fool. I had believed him when he said he wasn't interested in Penelope. I had trusted him.

But he owed me nothing!

I was just the nanny. His side dish, conveniently living in his house. Penelope on the other hand was the mother of his daughter. I hated myself. Why did I always fall for the wrong type of guys? Why was I drawn to people who only hurt me?

I lost track of time. I kept seeing Penelope naked and skipping out of his room. Did Luke laugh at me after he finished having sex with Penelope? Did he think I was a fool to believe his interest in me could be more than just for my body? Penelope even knew that Luke and I slept together. So this had been a big coup for her.

211

He had just been using me while he courted her back into his life. I had so many questions and no answers. I cried until there were no more tears left. I'd never felt like this before ever in my life.

I felt like my new life had just been snatched away from me. It hurt to breathe. It hurt to think. I must have drifted off to sleep because when I woke up, it was to someone knocking on my door.

"Ella," a soft voice called.

I smiled at the sound of Molly's sweet voice. Then the events of the previous night came to me and fresh tears came to my eyes. "I'll be along shortly, Molly," I said as I forced myself out of bed and into the bathroom.

After cleaning myself up, I dressed and left my room. To my surprise, I found Molly still waiting outside my door. I'd expected her to go to Penelope's room. But in the last couple of days, she had stopped following her mother around.

Probably because Penelope always said no to everything. She didn't want to play with Bean because he would make her dirty or ruin her clothes. She hated playing on the floor because her knees would hurt. No wonder Molly had stopped trying to get her mother to do things with her.

Penelope expected Molly to be a little grown up. Someone to go to lunch and shopping with. I'd wanted to shake her until she realized Molly was a little girl, not a grown woman. To scream into her ear that Molly's interests were playing, reading, hearing stories and taking care of Bean.

Molly smiled at me and took my hand.

That simple gesture brought more tears to my eyes. She loved me and I loved her. Whatever else happened, I had to think of Molly. She was the reason I was here. I had to keep this in mind and not give in to my instincts of quitting. I would only leave when I was sure Molly did not need me anymore.

We said good morning to Paul in the kitchen and went to the dining room to wait for our breakfast.

"Did you sleep well?" I asked Molly.

She nodded.

I made a face. "I didn't."

"Why is that?" a voice asked from behind me.

My heart skipped a beat. I searched Luke's face. He was smiling as he came towards us. He showed no signs of being the cheater I knew he was. He looked fresh too. And why not? After spending half the night making love to his gorgeous ex-wife.

Anger coursed through me and I bit my lip to stop myself from saying anything.

"Good morning, Ladies?" he said, kissing Molly on the cheek.

I kept my gaze downcast. If I kept looking at him, I'd shout or worse, burst into tears.

"Ella?" he said softly, already sensing something was wrong. "Are you all right?" He even had a caring tone in his voice.

I couldn't believe what a good actor he was, pretending to care about my feelings. "I'm fine," I snapped.

Paul brought in our breakfast and I concentrated on helping Molly slather honey on her pancakes.

Breakfast was a strangely quiet affair. I could feel Luke's quizzical eyes on me as we ate, but I refused to meet his gaze. I was tired of playing games and if Molly hadn't been with us, I'd have told him so.

After breakfast, he pushed his chair back and stood up.

Penelope entered the dining room at the same time as Luke got up. "Are you leaving already?" she said and went to him. "Let me fix this your tie for you," she said and walked towards him.

It felt like I'd just been punched in the stomach. My insides felt as though they were being shredded apart.

I tore my glance away.

I could feel Luke's glaze on me. I refused to look up. I couldn't bear to look into his eyes, knowing he had been lying to me all along. He'd let me believe there could be something between us. I was on the verge of crying but I wasn't going to humiliate myself in front of Penelope.

"Don't," I heard him mutter to Penelope.

She giggled.

So he didn't want me to know they were back together again. I swallowed hard.

"See you later, Molly," he called.

"Bye, bye, Daddy," Molly said, slipping off her chair to go give him his kiss.

The whole time, I never lifted my head. I heard the sound of Molly kissing his cheek, then his footsteps faded away as he left the room. I breathed again, when I heard the slam of the front door. I fought to keep my face from crumbling.

"I'm going away today," Penelope said while pulling a chair next to Molly.

Molly's little face went white.

Penelope saw it too and spoke fast, "Not forever. I'll be coming to see you. I'll skip tomorrow and come the next day. Take care of your daddy for me, won't you?"

Pain shot through my heart like a sharp arrow. She didn't need to keep driving home the point that Luke was hers now. I knew this already. I was out of the ring. I just wanted to do my job to the very end and then go back to my own life.

"You can go and play while I have a word with Ella."

Molly left the dining room.

I stared at Penelope and waited for her to speak. What could she possibly have to tell me?

"I suppose you're wondering what's going on between Luke and me?" she asked, a sly smile on her face.

She was wrong. I wasn't wondering. I'd seen what I needed to see. But I didn't say it, knowing instinctively that she would tell me whether I wanted to hear it or not.

"We're together now, but I really need us to go slow," she said.

"Good," I croaked. I didn't know how long I could keep my tears at bay.

"Actually, I also wanted to reassure you that your job is safe for now. Molly really likes you and we want to do everything we can to make her feel secure and happy, but eventually..." She paused before carrying on, "So if you find anything suitable, just let Luke or me know, okay?"

"Okay," I mumbled.

"Good. I'm glad we're in agreement." She groaned dramatically. "God, my body aches," she said and let out a girlish laugh. She leaned forward as if to whisper to me even though there was no one else in the room. "I have to confide in someone and I know you can keep a secret, so I'll just tell you. My husband is such a beast in bed." She giggled again, then pushed her chair back and left.

I bowed my head and allowed the tears to flow from my eyes.

How was I going to do this? Would I be able to watch Penelope touch and kiss Luke when I wanted him for myself? I wanted to do right by Molly, but it hurt.

God, how it hurt.

The desolation I felt was all consuming and I had to force myself to get up from my chair and get on with my day. I had a job to do and I would damn well do it, whether my heart was broken or not.

## LUKE

*I* was in a good mood when I got home. Penelope was gone! I felt like I had been given a fresh lease on life. Now Ella and I could go back to our normal passionate lives. I missed sleeping with her in my arms and waking up to her sweet sounds of sleep.

But during the day at the office, it wasn't Ella's hot sexy body I thought of. It had been the sound of her laughter and the various expressions she wore. She hovered in my mind throughout the day and when I left work, she jumped at the forefront of my thoughts and I found myself smiling for no reason.

I pushed open the front door. "I'm home," I announced.

A patter of little feet sounded before Molly appeared and threw herself at me.

I laughed and held her close. "How was your day sweet-heart?" I asked.

She smiled up at me. "Good."

"Wonderful. Where's Ella?"

Rather than reply, Molly took my hand and led the way out to the backyard where Ella was playing with Bean. Molly dropped my hand and ran to join them.

I stood for a moment to watch the three of them. Molly's laughter rang out as Bean wrestled her to the grass and licked her face.

Ella knew I was standing there but she never looked up once. With a frown, I approached them. "Hi Ella."

She mumbled a response.

I stared at her in confusion. I couldn't even hold her gaze and ask her what the matter was. What the hell was wrong? She had acted odd even at breakfast. Obviously, it had something to do with me because she'd been laughing and playing with Bean and Molly, but I couldn't question her when Molly was there.

"I'll be in the library," I said curtly and strode off.

My plan had been to come home then spend time with Molly and Ella, but I'd gotten the unwelcome message loud and clear. Unexpected pain ripped through me as I made my way to the library. The strength of it shook me.

How I'd felt when Penelope left me for another man was nothing compared to this pain. Angry with myself, I hurried to the library and banged the door shut. I wasn't going to think about Ella. I was done with exposing my vulnerability to women I thought I could trust.

I turned on my laptop and though I was tired, I forced myself to work. It would wipe away the questions floating in my mind, demanding answers I did not have. All I knew was that I didn't want to play games. I'd thought Ella was different!

I stayed locked up in the library until it was dinner time. It grew dark and I stood up wearily, my body stiff from being seated in one position for hours. I found Ella and Molly already in the dining room eating.

"I hope I'm not too late," I said, inserting a cheer I did not feel into my voice.

Molly smiled, but Ella didn't even bother to look up at me.

When my food came, I ate without tasting any of it and kept a conversation directed at Molly. I felt relieved when dinner was over and I could escape.

In the living room, I sat with Molly and read from her story-book. Then when it was bedtime, I carried her to her bed and tucked her in. I kissed her goodnight and left. At the door, I almost bumped into Ella as she was entering Molly's room.

She jumped back as if I had seared her.

Our gazes met and to my shock, her eyes were red rimmed. She had been crying! To my dismay, her tears spilled over her lower lids and ran down her cheeks.

"Ella, what is it?" I asked, everything in me screaming for me to pull her into my arms. I slipped my hands around her waist.

She stepped back.

Her rejection felt like a slap to my face. Undeterred, I took a step closer. "I don't understand? Please, talk to me." I sounded desperate but I didn't care.

She wiped her tears away with the back of her hands and stared at me almost defiantly. Ella had become a stranger. "I'm fine," she said. "I just want to say goodnight to Molly."

I held her arm lightly. "You're not fine. Please," I begged.

"We can talk downstairs. I'll come and find you," she said, refusing to meet my eyes.

"Okay," I said with a frown and went downstairs to wait for her. No matter how much I wracked my brain, I couldn't come up with anything I'd done to hurt her. I truly hadn't done anything that I knew of.

I waited for over half an hour. She wasn't coming. My gaze bounced around the living room. I felt disjointed. Lost. As if my world had tilted. If she couldn't even talk to me—then it was over.

Whatever it was we had before was over. I looked up at the ceiling and refused to do what my instincts commanded—march up the stairs to her room and demand to know what had caused her change of heart.

But I didn't want to force her to have to tell me the words.

I felt too tired to go back to work and too tense to sleep. I grabbed the remote and turned on the TV. Maybe the news would distract me. I watched the action on the screen but my brain refused to process what I was seeing.

Instead, images of Ella played in my mind. I saw her laughing, sleeping with her lips slightly parted, and drawing, her brow creased in concentration.

All the memories led me back to wondering where it had gone wrong? Had I missed some signs of her getting tired of me? Then a memory came to me. Something that had been nagging me. Ella's distraction and her habit of checking her phone constantly.

I felt as though someone had doused me with icy cold water. Could I be so unlucky as to have two women cheat on me?

She'd spoken about an ex, a man she had been in a relationship with for a long time. Perhaps they were communicating again, and she wanted to get back with him. Could I really blame her?

What had I offered? The only thing I had offered Ella was sex. And she could get that from any man. Something stirred in me. Something I hadn't felt in years. Jealousy. The thought of Ella with another man made me want to growl and punch something.

I switched off the TV, turned off the lights, and trudged up the stairs. I strode across the hallway and stopped in front of Ella's room. What if I entered and told her how I felt? How did I feel?

I raised my hand and stopped just before I touched the doorknob. I couldn't do it. I knew I wanted her back in my bed but what if she didn't want to be there? What if she had found someone else to love her? I turned away and headed to the stairs.

I felt miserable, lonely, and sad. I longed for Ella. She'd become such a big part of my life in such a short time. Resolutely, I shed my clothes and slipped into bed. It was going to be a long night.

# LUKE

*I* was working from home the following day. I'd slept badly and finally managed to fall asleep at almost five in the morning. Which meant that I overslept and woke up at nine.

I felt moody. Angry with myself and the world when I went downstairs. I stopped on the first floor when I heard Molly and Ella's voices coming from the playroom.

I pushed the door open and peered in. They were on the floor playing with some sort of figurines. Ella looked up and when our gazes met, I felt a longing so strong that I almost went on my knees to beg her to take me back.

Instead, I smiled. "Good morning, ladies."

Molly jumped to her feet and ran to hug me. I held my daughter and kept looking at Ella.

She looked so sad. The thought that I might be responsible for putting that sadness there broke my heart.

"Morning," she finally said and managed a small smile.

Seeing her smile made me feel as if color had been splashed into my world again. "Is Penelope coming today?" I asked Ella.

Her smile faded and a haunted look came over her features. The change was drastic... I knew then that whatever had made her change had something to do with Penelope. Anger coursed through me. Had she said something to Ella? I needed to find out.

"She said she'll come the day after tomorrow," Ella said stiffly, confirming my fears.

I felt desperate to know but now was not the time. Not when Molly was in the room. Reluctantly, I withdrew and went downstairs. I asked Paul to serve my breakfast in the library and as I headed there, a glimmer of hope grew in me.

If it was about Penelope, I felt sure we could solve it. Penelope wasn't in my life and I had no feelings for her whatsoever.

I got the opportunity to speak to Ella in the afternoon while Molly napped. She came into the library to let me know she would be in the backyard.

"Can I speak to you for a moment?" I asked.

She looked hesitant, but stepped in and shut the door. She wore a dress that showed off her shapely legs. My eyes greedily devoured her, wishing the dress were shorter, so I could see more of her creamy thighs.

She stood far away from me as though I might hurt her. My heart squeezed. This was the woman who'd been comfortable sitting on my lap whenever we found ourselves alone. Now, she couldn't even stand to be close to me.

"What is it," she asked.

I took a deep breath. "Ella, my sweet Ella."

At my words, her lower lip trembled and she bit it.

Taking advantage of her vulnerability, I stood up and went to her. I made sure to get close but not to touch her. "Talk to me, I need to know what happened," I said.

Her eyes filled up. "I know about you and Penelope."

I narrowed my eyes. *Damnit, I was right.* "Did she say something to you?"

"She didn't have to. I saw it with my own eyes."

I was puzzled. "Saw what?"

Anger flashed in her eyes. "If you want me to spell it out for you, I will. I saw Penelope leave your room at night and she was stark naked. You've been sleeping with Penelope. That wasn't part of our agreement."

My heart felt like it was shrinking. I thought we had trust between us. That we understood each other and Ella knew me well enough to know I kept my word. "Is that what you think of me?"

She blinked rapidly. "What other explanation would there be of a woman leaving your room at midnight without clothes on? What was I expected to think? Please don't play games with me Luke. I'm fine with you wanting your ex-wife back, but don't lie to me."

I stared at her incredulously. If Ella didn't know me then I had no hope that any woman would ever know me. She had penetrated my walls. Become closer to me than any other woman ever had. And she thought I was fucking Penelope.

"So, you're going to stand there and tell me that I was hallucinating?" she asked, her tone sarcastic.

"Penelope was in my room. And yes, she was naked but I didn't sleep with her and I've never slept with her. I have never looked at another woman since you and I got together.

I could see the battle going on in Ella. She wanted to believe me but she was frightened. I put myself in her shoes and imagined seeing a naked man tiptoeing out of her room at night. The conclusion would be that they were sleeping together.

Except that I'd gone through enough things in life to know things weren't always what they looked like.

"Then what was she doing leaving your room naked at that time?" Ella asked, her voice trembling.

I wanted to take her into my arms and kiss her insecurity away. But I needed to give Ella a permanent sense of security. Penelope would be in my life for a long time and if our affair were to continue, Ella needed to learn to trust me. "She had come to seduce me. I told her that nothing would make me sleep with her or get together with her again. Ella, I'm with you now, and I don't cheat! I told you that before."

She shuddered as she inhaled.

"You have to trust me Ella, or she will play mind games with you until you are broken," I said. "Will we have a fight every time Penelope says something to you? Come to me, ask me and I promise I'll always tell you the truth. Can you do that?"

Tears streaked down her cheeks. She nodded.

I opened my arms. "Come here."

Ella came to me and buried her face in my chest.

hat night, I burrowed deeper into Luke's chest unable to believe we were back together again. Tears sprung to my eyes when I thought how close I had come to losing him. And all because I had jumped to conclusions and believed Penelope rather than go straight to Luke and ask him.

"Are you asleep?" Luke murmured.

"No," I said, a smile in my voice.

It probably was way past midnight but time had lost all meaning from the moment we locked ourselves in Luke's room and stripped off our clothes. Our lovemaking had been different too. More tender, slower. And we'd made love over and over again, as though to make up for the time we had wasted.

"We need to talk," Luke said.

My heart skipped a beat. He sounded so serious. My skin prickled with fear. "Okay."

"I've never met a woman like you, Ella. Perfect for me, in and out of bed," Luke said, his voice heavy with emotion.

My chest filled with syrupy warmth. I felt the same about him. When I was alone, I'd started to picture the three of us together as a family. Luke, Molly and me. I'd even gone as far as imagining us married and adding to the family.

"I guess, what I'm trying to say is, I have... um... feelings for you, Ella," Luke admitted.

My heart began to race. I wanted him to go on. To say the words that had been playing in my mind... desperate to know that he felt the same way I did. Because I'd fallen in love with Luke. A new fear trembled through me. That hadn't been our deal.

It seemed as if Luke could read my mind, because he said the same thing, "I know this was not part of our deal, but Ella, you're special... and I want you for myself. Does that frighten you?"

I inhaled deeply. "A little."

"It frightens me a bit too," Luke confessed. "When you withdrew from me, I thought you had gone back to your ex and it was killing me."

His admission infiltrated my bloodstream, rendering me unable to speak. Then I took a deep breath and told him, "That will never happen," I said and let out a trembling breath as memories of my past came back. "Stan liked to hit me," I admitted softly, ashamed that I could have let someone do that to me.

Luke's body stiffened as his arms tightened around me. "Bastard," he hissed violently.

"I feel like such a fool now for staying, but he had manipulated me into believing that he would kill himself if I ever left him. I thought I could rehabilitate him, you know? He said he was like that because his father abused him. I believed him, but I don't know anymore. I met his father and he seemed like a really nice guy. Anyway, in my arrogance, I thought I could help him. That maybe one day, because of my unstinting love, he would stop being a psychopath and become a normal human being."

"He was the problem Ella, not you," Luke said harshly. "Any man who lifts his hand to a woman should have his balls cut off."

I giggled. "Why the balls? Why not the hands, they're the ones doing the hitting."

"Because balls are the things that inflate his stupid ego. Cut them off and he'll shrink like a deflated balloon. "

I felt safe, wrapped in Luke's arms.

"So… shall we try and see if a relationship can work between us?" Luke asked.

I almost couldn't believe that something I had dreamed about, but thought was impossible was finally happening. True, there was no declaration of love but this was enough. The fact that Luke wanted to have a relationship beyond just sex *was* unbelievable.

"Don't make me sweat. Say something Ella," Luke teased.

I chuckled. "I'd like that."

Gently, Luke flipped us around, so that he lay on top of me. He caressed my face and lowered his head to kiss me. "I never thought I'd be saying something like this again," he confessed.

"Me too," I whispered, his scent surrounding me, his breath fanning my face. He brought his lips to mine again, and we kissed deeply.

Luke broke the kiss. "I want you in my bed every night," he growled.

"You won't get any arguments from me." Luke was everything I wanted and I intended to go with it and see where it led us.

I parted my legs and Luke guided his rock-hard cock into my pussy. I wrapped my legs around his waist, drawing him deeper into me.

"Please," I begged as those magnificent sensations came over me.

*M*olly and I were in the backyard, playing with Bean. We took turns throwing a small stick and he would run off and get it, a triumphant look on his little face.

Every time there was a sound from inside the house, Molly went still and listened. It was half past two, Penelope hadn't shown up yet, and she hadn't even called to say she wasn't coming.

My chest ached each time I saw the hope flair in Molly's eyes and then go off again.

Her eyes drooped, as it was her nap time.

"I'll take you for your nap," I told her gently. "I'll wake you up when your mom comes, okay?"

She nodded.

Hand in hand, we walked back to the house and up the stairs to Molly's room.

She fell asleep the moment her head hit the pillow.

I smoothed her hair back and kissed her forehead.

I tiptoed out and shut the door behind me. I stood outside the door seething. What was so urgent that Penelope couldn't have found the time to call and say she would not be coming?

To me, nothing could be worse than disappointing a child. What was worse was that Penelope had been aware of the damage she had caused Molly the first time. I shook my head and went to my room. My phone vibrated from the bedside table just as I entered and a cold sweat formed on my skin.

So far, I hadn't received any more threatening messages but waiting was another type of hell. I knew it would come and so, I was always bracing myself to it.

With slightly trembling fingers, I swiped the screen. The message was from Luke. My legs grew weak with relief.

*Hi sweetheart, has Penelope come?*

I typed back a reply. *Hi, not yet. Molly was very disappointed.*

A pause went by before another message came in. *I'm so angry right now. She'd better have a good reason why she lied to Molly.*

We texted back and forth a few times before we said goodbye. I grabbed my notebook and pencil then immersed myself in creating new designs, until Molly woke up and came knocking on my door.

We spent the rest of the afternoon in the playroom drawing but Molly wasn't herself.

I tried to comfort her. "You know sometimes urgent things come up," I said.

She looked up at me with large hopeful eyes and nodded.

I didn't want to offer her false hope but at the same time, I wanted the forlorn look gone from her face. "Your mom might come tomorrow." I hated myself for saying it. What if she didn't?

She managed the first smile of the afternoon and she went back to coloring.

While Molly was playing, I straightened up the playroom.

My phone vibrated with a message and I smiled as I picked it up. My heart took on a faster beat when I saw the message wasn't from Luke. He was back at it again, and dread filled my chest.

*I've been thinking about you a lot. I miss you. We were good together.*

Sweat gathered in my armpits. The person writing the messages was Stan. I felt sure about it now. Despite my earlier bravado and decision not to let him get to me, every part of me trembled.

I noticed that Molly had stopped playing and was staring at me. She wore a worried look.

I smiled at her automatically.

This seemed to reassure her and she went back to her toys.

Another message came in.

*What do you say to us getting back together?*

I couldn't ignore the messages any longer. My finger flew as I typed a response

*Please leave me alone.*

Thirty seconds later, a new one came in.

*I'm trying to be really nice here. After what you did, I should be mad, but I'm giving you another chance.*

Nausea rose up my throat. He was mad. Insane, if he thought we could ever get back together. The next time my phone vibrated, I contemplated not picking it up to read the message. But that wouldn't make them go away.

*You had me locked up.*

My fingers flew into action. I didn't want to get into a conversation with him but I simply couldn't let this go.

*You got locked up because you got into a fight with someone in a bar. NOTHING TO DO WITH ME!*

I stared at the screen. Sure enough an answer came right back.

*If you hadn't left me, I wouldn't have been at that bar. I blame you.*

I was trembling again. I couldn't do it. I shouldn't have given in to the temptation to try and justify myself or communicate with him in any way. He was criminally insane. I switched off my phone.

Then I sat down and I held on to the rational side of my brain. His aim was to torment me. He was probably far away, living his life and if I completely ignored him from now on, he would go away.

He had to.

I contemplated calling Ruby, then changed my mind. I didn't want to burden her with my problems and besides, she would urge me to go to the police.

I didn't want to. Not yet, anyway. I didn't want to cause a fuss when I hoped it would blow over with time. Stan had a tendency to grow bored quickly and I knew he would eventually tire of texting me when something more exciting came up. In the meantime, I just needed to keep my cool.

But I kept remembering the murderous look in his eyes the night when he'd kicked me again and again, in the ribs while I was on the floor. I'd felt alone and scared.

An hour later, Luke came home. "I'm home!" he announced, in his usual loud fashion.

It always got Molly giggling. She jumped to her feet.

I followed her.

Downstairs, Molly ran to him and threw her arms around his legs. She held him tighter than she usually did and for longer.

Luke kissed her head and murmured loving words to her.

I could have hugged him. She needed this so much. A reassurance telling her someone loved her and had been thinking about her. Penelope was a bitch. And that was me being kind.

My turn came next to say hello. Still holding Molly, Luke pulled me in with his other arm and held me tight against his body.

I inhaled his scent and when I leaned on his chest, it felt like I was home. And safe. With Luke home, my fears ebbed away. I was safe from Stan and his threats.

"How was your day?" Luke asked while shepherding us all to the living room.

"It was good," I said cheerfully. "We played a lot with Bean, and we ordered a sleeping basket for him. He's chewed his until it looks like a rug now."

Molly and Luke both laughed.

"That sounds like a fun day. I have meetings all day tomorrow. Otherwise, I'd have loved to spend the day with both of you. You have all the fun."

We spent a pleasant evening catching up before Luke excused himself to take a shower.

Molly and I went out to the backyard to play with Bean.

A bit later, Luke joined us and got down on the grass to play with Molly and Bean. "He's growing so big. You're really good at taking care of a puppy," he said to Molly.

The smile she gave him could have split her face.

"Has she forgotten about being let down by her mother?" he whispered to me later, when Molly was engrossed in Bean.

"I think so, but she took it hard. She almost didn't want to have her nap."

A hard look came over Luke's features, but he didn't say anything.

My heart went out to him. Penelope was putting him in an impossible situation. It was important for Molly to see her mom, but at the same time, Penelope had shown herself to be unreliable and uninterested in Molly.

I leaned in and kissed Luke on the mouth.

He looked at me, pleasantly surprised. "Not complaining, but what was that for?"

I laughed. "Just because you're a wonderful man."

Luke didn't say anything, but he looked pleased.

# LUKE

*H*i, *sweetheart... missing you.*

I'd never been one to text before but Ella had converted me. I had never thought of texting as fun, but with Ella, it was.

*I miss you too. Last night was awesome.*

My body heated up at the reminder of the night and suddenly, I couldn't wait to go home. I felt like the luckiest man on earth to sleep next to a sexy gorgeous woman every night.

*How's Molly?*

Her response was instant.

*Crushed. Penelope didn't show up.*

Hot searing anger washed through me. What was the matter with Penelope? Didn't she know she held a little girl's heart in the palm of her hands? I typed a quick reply.

*See you soon and give her a kiss from me.*

I turned off my laptop, packed it and several minutes later, I headed out to the parking lot. Penelope wasn't going to get away with such behavior, I thought as I drove towards The Sheraton hotel.

My mind worked out a plan as I drove. If I announced myself at the reception, Penelope would bolt. I needed to catch her by surprise. Except, I didn't have her room number. I drove my car to the underground parking of the hotel. I fished out my phone and searched for the phone number then hit call. "Good evening, my name is Luke Meyers and I'd like to be put through to my wife's room. Her name is Penelope Meyers and she's in room..." I let my voice trail off as though I was trying to remember.

As I'd thought, the clerk put me out of my misery, "Room 204, Sir. I've put you through. Have a nice day."

When the phone rang in Penelope's room, I disconnected the call and got out of the car. I walked through the lobby to the elevators. Room 204 was on the second floor and seconds later, I strode down the heavily carpeted hallway.

Penelope's room was at the very end. I put my ear to the door and heard muted voices coming from inside. One voice sounded deeper, like a man's voice. My insides clenched. I raised my hand and knocked as softly as I could, not wanting to alert her that it could be anyone else other than the hotel staff.

I heard soft steps and then the door swung open.

Penelope emerged wrapped in a white towel. Her hair was messed up and she had the *just-fucked* look that was hard to miss. Her mouth fell open when she saw me.

I didn't give her time to react and pushed my way in.

I stepped into the room and stared at the blond-haired young-looking man in the bed.

He looked back at me, his mouth falling open with dismay.

Silly boy! He probably thought I was a husband who had caught his wife cheating. And he was in for it.

"What are you doing here?" Penelope hissed, coming to my side.

"Why didn't you come and visit Molly? You promised her you would." I could barely control my anger.

She shrugged and looked away.

"I thought so!" I snapped. "You chose a man over your daughter, yet again!"

"It's not like that, Luke," she said. "Why do you always have to make such a big deal of things? I was going to come tomorrow."

I shifted my glance to the man again. He didn't look old enough to have a job or the ability to keep Penelope in the lifestyle she liked. She was probably just using him to satisfy her itch until something better came along. It meant that he wouldn't be around for long. I raked my fingers through my hair in frustration. Why was she lying to Molly then? Even a half hour visit would have pleased Molly.

"Get dressed!" I barked. "You're going to see Molly now, if you ever want to see her again, that is."

She opened her mouth to protest and then shut it. "Can you excuse me?"

I didn't intend to leave the room. I walked to the window and stared out. Behind me, Penelope clicked her tongue and I heard the rustle of clothes.

"Are you just going to leave me here and go with him?" the young man in bed asked a petulant note in his voice.

I snorted in disgust. He was just a kid. How could Penelope stand to be with such a young person? Didn't she get irritated by the child like behavior? Then I remembered how Penelope herself behaved like a child.

There were two words she hated. Responsibility and Commitment. Why hadn't I seen it before I married her? Had I been so infatuated with her good looks to see the real person underneath? And yet, I couldn't regret marrying her. She had caused me a lot of pain but she had also enriched it by giving me Molly. For my daughter alone, I refused to think of Penelope as a mistake.

"Well, you can wait for me," Penelope said to the kid in a cajoling tone. "I'll have something good for you when I come back. I promise."

That seemed to satisfy him and he didn't say another word.

I shook my head. They deserved each other.

"Okay, I'm ready," Penelope announced minutes later.

When I turned, the young man was engrossed with his phone. When he wasn't looking at me, I could truly see how young he was.

Penelope and I walked to the car wordlessly.

"I don't understand you," I said to her when we got into the car.

She let out a dramatic sigh. "You're going to start on the lectures again."

"You sound like a child!" I snapped. "And you're a grown woman with a five-year-old child."

Penelope sniffed.

Even if she cried, her tears wouldn't move me. "Molly waits for you every day and you keep disappointing her. Can't you make time for her when you say you will?"

She didn't respond and stared outside the window instead.

I hadn't expected her to respond but I had a plan B. I intended to resort to threats. I'd do anything I had to do to get her to do the right thing.

Clearly, Penelope wasn't wired like other parents. She saw no big deal in disappointing her daughter over and over again.

I waited until we got home and parked the car.

She made to open the door.

"Wait!" I said.

She turned her head to glare at me.

"I'm giving you one last chance to do right by Molly. If you tell her you'll be here tomorrow, you damn well better be."

She thrust out her chin. "That sounds like a threat."

I nodded. "Well done for catching on so fast. It is a threat. If you disappoint her one more time, I'll get my lawyer to work out a new settlement seeing as you won't need all that extra money I deposit into your account that the judge had felt you would need to take care of Molly, since you claimed you wanted joint custody. I can show the judge two years' worth of evidence proving that you have no intention of ever taking care of her. I'm sure he'll have no hesitation in deciding that you have no need for all the extra money I pay into your account for childcare. If you look carefully, that comes to almost half of what you get."

Her eyes widened in shock. Now, we were speaking a language that Penelope understood clearly. *Money.* "You can't do that!" she cried.

"Try me!" I replied grimly.

She searched my face, and then nodded resentfully. "Okay, but this is not necessary."

"One more time, Penelope. You do it one more time," I warned as I walked behind her to the front door.

It swung open before I inserted my key.

"Mom!" Molly cried and threw herself against her mother.

My chest squeezed painfully. I really hated Penelope sometimes.

Ella stood behind Molly and we exchanged a look.

Penelope took Molly's hand and they walked into the house. Molly led her up the stairs.

I pulled Ella into my arms and held her close.

"How did you get her to come?" she whispered.

"I forced her," I admitted grimly, and told Ella about going to the hotel.

"She hasn't been coming to see Molly because she has a new man?" Ella asked, her voice coated with disgust.

"Yes," I said. "I could do with a coffee."

"I'll make some," Ella said and left me in the living room.

I did feel pleased that Penelope and I had reached an understanding. With her monthly stipend at risk, she wouldn't play around with Molly's heart again. It was a shame that I had to coerce her into seeing her own daughter.

Ella returned moments later with two mugs of coffee.

Staring at her, I couldn't believe that I could now introduce her as my girlfriend. It felt good to call her *my woman*.

"You look happy," she said as she sat down next to me on the couch.

I shifted close to her, draped my hand around her shoulder, and pulled her to me. "That's because I am. Have I told you today how beautiful you are?" I asked and slid my other hand under her jaw. I brought my mouth to hers and kissed her soft lips. "I've been thinking of doing this all day," I said to her, our eyes boring into each other.

"Me too," Ella murmured.

I nibbled on her upper lip and then swept my tongue into her mouth. She tasted like she smelled. Vanilla and spice. I cupped her breast and squeezed tenderly.

Ella let out a groan.

Her sounds of arousal turned me into a beast and I pulled her into my lap in one movement, without breaking the kiss. My hands were everywhere. On her ass, breasts and creamy thighs. I stopped short of sliding my hand under her dress to feel her pussy.

Her fingers threaded through my hair as she moaned my name repeatedly. Ella peeled her mouth from mine and we stared at each other as our breaths came out fast.

Ella then slid off my lap just as we heard Penelope's voice coming our way.

She and Molly walked into the living room, a huge smile on my girl's face.

"I was just telling Molly that I won't make it tomorrow, but I'll be here the day after," Penelope said, all the while staring at me.

I nodded. That was all I needed. For her to be truthful to Molly about when she would be able to visit and when she couldn't. It wasn't a lot to ask.

She left shortly after, so Molly and I went out to the back to play with Bean while Ella excused herself to make a call.

"Were you happy to see your mom?" I asked Molly when we were outside.

She nodded happily.

"Good. She loves you very much," I said. "And so do I, and so does Ella." I wanted Molly to know she was loved by everyone.

It felt like my life had a semblance of order now and we were back to our normal routine.

After dinner, I went up with Molly to the playroom. I picked up one of her notebooks and scrolled through it. To my surprise, Molly came to where I was and sat down on my lap. She wasn't given to impromptu displays of affection. The exception to this had been in the evenings when I came home from work.

We looked at her drawings together.

"You're really good at drawing," I said to her.

"Ella taught me," Molly said.

I smiled. "It's good she came to live with us, isn't it?"

Ella nodded happily. "Yeah, it's very, very good."

## ELLA

"Molly is so happy," I said as I scrubbed Luke's wide shoulders and expansive back. "You did well to blackmail Penelope."

Muscles rippled underneath his skin as I spread shower gel all over his back. I made circles on his skin and then dipped my hands to his tight, gorgeous ass. It was pure muscle.

"It was worth it just to see Molly's joy," Luke said.

"Turn around," I said and stood up.

He turned and as I washed his chest and front, his fingers idly played with my nipples. I could feel myself getting thoroughly turned on. I wasn't the only one. Luke's cock stood erect and bobbed against my hand when I gripped it.

The idea had been to shower together and then slip into bed for a night of sweet lovemaking. But my pussy throbbed with an ache that couldn't wait until after the shower. I raised my right leg and wrapped it around Luke's waist.

Seeing the look in my eyes, he gripped my thigh and with the other hand, held the base of his cock then brought it to my entrance. We were always in sync that way. He knew when I needed him pronto, when my pussy urgently needed something to clench around.

"I want you. I've always wanted you," I whispered.

He pushed into me with the blunt head of his cock.

When he plunged all the way in, I threw my head back and let out a cry, "Yes, please," I said as his cock traveled deeper into me.

His thrusts were powerful, making a storm rage through me. I became a wild woman, screaming and demanding for more and more of him.

Luke stopped thrusting and withdrew but before I could protest, he turned me around. "Bend over," he ordered.

I leaned forward and I pressed my palms against the wall. Panting, I waited for his cock to fill me up again. When he did, I pushed my ass back against him and with one lunge-he drove all the way in-stealing my breath away.

Luke then held me in place by gripping my hips with his large hands. He alternated between slow thrusts and fast, hard thrusts. Every time I was at the edge, he'd pull back. Until I was so desperate to come, I clawed at the bathroom wall.

"Do you want to come?" he growled.

"Yes, oh God, yes," I whimpered.

This time he was merciful. He thrust hard until my body exploded into a thousand splinters and for a brief while, all I saw was stars. Beautiful stars.

Luke growled and pumped faster, emptying his hot cum deep inside me.

Afterwards, we rinsed off and Luke turned off the shower. He held the towel for me and when I walked into it, he wrapped it around me. I padded into the master bedroom and finished drying myself off as he brought the hairdryer and dried my head. It all just seemed to be so perfect and I felt wonderful too. When he switched off the hairdryer, I slipped into the bed naked.

The sheets were crisp and cool and I let out a sigh of satisfaction. Just then, my phone vibrated and I reached for it.

*You've been ignoring me. Is someone else taking what is mine?*

The cool sheets suddenly became stifling. My body became hot and then cold. I looked at the message again, and wanted to weep. Why couldn't he leave me alone? I pressed the turn off button just as Luke walked into the room, a towel wrapped low on his hips.

"Are you okay?" he asked.

I realized then I had pushed away the covers. "I'm fine, I just felt hot for a few minutes, but I'm good now." I pulled the light duvet up around me.

Luke loosened his towel and proceeded to dry his own hair.

Stan fought to occupy my mind, but I resolutely pushed away those thoughts and concentrated on the gorgeous man in front of me.

Luke turned around to hang his towel and I ogled his ass. His fine ass was wasted in official suits when it should have been on display in one of those billboard ads, advertising men's underwear.

My body grew hot as I watched him unconsciously walk to the bed, his cock semi hard. "You, Luke Meyers are a temptation to all women," I said.

He gave me an amused smile. "I'm glad you think so and I hope you always will," he said as he gathered me into his arms.

I needed to occupy myself to keep from thinking about that last message from Stan. I crawled on top of him and aligned my body with his. His cock rested in between my legs and I made little rocking movements to rub it against my pussy.

Luke's hands went to my ass, kneading it and then sliding a finger down the crest between my ass cheeks. His hands went lower to the curve of my butt cheek, down to my hips. He placed his hands on my inner thighs and parted my legs then dipped his fingers to my pussy. "I love how wet you always are," he said.

I brought my mouth down to his and kissed him softly. "I'm always wet for you." I rode his hand and rubbed my nipples along his chest.

"You trying to kill me, woman?" Luke growled. "I haven't recovered from round one."

"How long do you need to recover?" I asked.

"Clearly, I'm not going to get any time," he said, sounding pleased about it.

Luke's expert hands played with my pussy, teasing my clit, until I needed more from him. I raised my hips and snaked a hand between our bodies to guide his cock inside me. I halfway sat up and when his cock was in, I slid back into my earlier position. We moved our bodies gently, our gazes locked.

We moved in sync, our bodies meshing together and then pulling apart before coming together again. When we reached our peaks, it became intense and beyond the physical. It felt like we had bridged another wall between us and we had become as close as two human beings could be.

*I*'d noticed how Molly was short on tops. She'd probably grown in the last couple of weeks and outgrown some of her clothes. Luke had put a credit card at my disposal, he wanted me to go out and get myself something lovely. At first, I had refused, but he had frowned and asked me why he couldn't buy me a dress if it made him happy. So I agreed.

I decided to take Molly shopping while getting a few things for myself. Specifically, a dress. I hadn't had time to sew myself one, like I normally did, and Luke had seen all my dresses, several times over, in fact. I decided to treat myself to a short, sexy number. Something that would make him want to strip it off and take me there and then. The thought made me grin.

Just as Molly and I were getting ready to leave, Ruby called. I recognized the tune I'd chosen for her ring. I fished for my phone in my bag and swiped to answer, "Hello stranger."

"I know. I'm sorry, we got a little busy with a wedding at work. How are you, and how's Molly?" Ruby asked.

"We're fine. We're actually on our way out for a bit of shopping."

Ruby squealed. If there was anything she loved more than beauty, it was shopping. "Can I come? I'm bored at work and it's my lunch hour."

"Sure," I said.

We arranged to meet in an ice cream shop on Fifth Street.

"Ruby will meet us there," I told Molly.

She grinned in response. "I like Ruby."

"Yes, she's lovely, isn't she?"

Molly nodded enthusiastically.

The Uber was already waiting. I got Molly in and we were on our way. I'd opted to use an Uber for the ease in leaving, plus it was difficult for someone to follow you when you were using an Uber.

Still, I turned back to look out the back window.

At first, I didn't even want to go out of the house because of my fear of meeting Stan, but I told myself I couldn't live like that. I wouldn't allow him to turn me into a mouse. I relaxed when I saw no suspicious cars following us and leaned back in the seat. "Is pink still your favorite color?" I asked Molly.

She shook her head. "No, I like blue now," she said softly.

I smiled happily. Before too long, no one would be able to differentiate between Molly and any other five-year-old girl.

Fingers crossed, it wouldn't be long before she would be chatty, cheerful, and carefree.

Just like a kid should be.

We got off on Fifth Street and I held Molly's hand as we hurried into the ice cream shop.

Molly spotted Ruby first. She called her name and dashed between tables to where Ruby was seated.

Ruby jumped to her feet and enveloped Molly in her arms. "I have missed you so much, beautiful girl," Ruby was saying when I reached them.

"I missed you," Molly said shyly.

"Molly is doing so well," Ruby said to me.

I reached out and stroked Molly's hair. "Yes, she's doing awesome."

We sat down and ordered ice cream. Vanilla for me while Ruby and Molly ordered a rainbow mixture of ice cream flavors.

"Yuk!" I said.

"You don't know how to choose ice cream," Ruby said while she and Molly giggled.

We kept our conversation mild and included Molly. Ruby was good with kids and she kept Molly giggling throughout. When the ice cream came, Ruby and Molly laughed uproariously as they dotted ice cream on each other's noses.

Afterwards, we went to a kid's store and had a ball picking cute outfits for Molly. With Ruby for company, the outing became a dress up party. We laughed until our stomachs ached.

"I wanted to get a dress as well," I said to Ruby. "It might be a bit boring for Molly."

"Say no more." Ruby nodded. "I saw a kids' play area downstairs. Find us there when you're done."

I paid for the outfits and we said goodbye outside the store. I knew exactly where to get the dress I had in mind. The store was on the third floor of the mall and I took the elevator. I loved clothes stores and I forced myself not to linger as I ogled all the outfits. One day, maybe, just maybe I would see my own designs in some of these stores.

I saw *my dress* from a distance, hanging from a hanger away from the rest, as if it had been waiting for me. Leafy green and sexy as hell. I grabbed it and carried it with me to the changing rooms.

I grinned as I stripped, imagining Luke's reaction when he saw me. It fit me like a second skin, but it was the plunging neckline that stole all the attention. It made my breasts look even bigger than they were and squeezed my tits into a deep valley of cleavage.

I adjusted it and stared at myself in the mirror. The leafy green color went well with my red hair. My phone vibrated and I reached for it. Probably Ruby, asking why I had taken so long.

As I read the message, my blood went cold.

*Beautiful girl. Whose daughter?*

My eyes darted around the changing room. He had seen me, and I had no doubt in my mind about it. My legs trembled. I needed to get out of the mall. Fast. I gripped the hem of the dress and as I was about to pull it up, the doorknob turned and a figure entered.

A scream rose up my throat, but before it could come out, he clamped his hand on my mouth. Fear gripped me and I couldn't think.

With his other hand, he pulled me against him, squeezing my chest, so my breasts were pushed half out of the dress. His eyes dropped to my cleavage. "You've become even sexier than I remembered," he growled.

I tried to dislodge the hand clamped on my mouth. It wouldn't move an inch. I tried to calm myself down. To recapture my cool. We were in a public place. He wasn't going to hurt me. Except he could break my neck and leave me slumped on the ground and no one would know.

Until Ruby raised the alarm and they searched for me all over the mall, no one would be the wiser. I thought of Luke. I thought of my sister and her family and I made a promise. If I got out of this, I would call her and make more of an effort in keeping touch.

Tears sprung to my eyes. I didn't want to die. I was just beginning to live. For the first time ever, things were looking up. I had a chance at making a success of my life and being happy.

"Tears? Have you missed me?" Stan whispered in my ear. "I've missed you too. Soon, very soon, we'll be together. Just like we used to be."

Instead of playing along like I should have, I instinctively shook my head.

His eyes bulged almost right out of his face with rage. "What? You think you're too good for me now?" he snarled. His hand went around me and grabbed my ass. He slammed me against his cock and rubbed himself against me.

Nausea swirled in my stomach as I tried to get away from him.

"Can you feel how hard I am for you? You must miss how I used to fuck you. If there's one thing I remember about you Ella, is that you love cock. A real whore, you were. Remember that one time I forced you to keep my cock in your mouth like a baby's pacifier until I fell asleep? I still haven't found a woman that would do that for me." He chuckled.

Tears spilled from my eyes when I remembered the pitiful creature I was when I'd been with him.

A sound came from the entrance of the changing rooms.

"I have to go now," he whispered. "But if you know what's good for you and the child, you'll keep this little visit to yourself. Okay?"

I nodded quickly. I just wanted him to leave.

He grinned, exposing a front broken tooth and as quickly as he had come—he left.

I covered my mouth to stifle the scream. I took a few terri-fied breaths, then I quickly stripped off the dress and got back into my own clothes. Pulling open the curtain of the changing room, I raced out of the shop.

I found Ruby and Molly by the escalators.

"What happened to you?" Ruby asked with a frown as she studied my face.

I almost burst into tears, but managed to contain myself since Molly was looking at us. I wanted to tell Ruby everything, but she would insist that we go to the police. Stan's words replayed in my mind.

*...if you know what's good for you and the child, you'll keep this little visit to yourself.*

I wouldn't do anything to put Molly at risk. I didn't know what to do but I wasn't going to go to the police.

At least, not yet.

# LUKE

*I*'d been working in the office the last couple of days due to an important project proposal. I whistled as I wound up for the day, knowing that in the next few minutes I would be on my way home to *my girls*.

A knock came on my door.

"Come in," I said.

My secretary Janice peered in, her eyes wide. "Uh… Mrs. Meyers is waiting to see you."

I frowned. I couldn't understand why Penelope insisted on keeping her married name. "Send her in."

She came in, her heels clicking on the floor. Penelope did look smart and pretty, if you didn't know what was behind the beautiful facade. "Hi, I hope I'm not disturbing you," she said sweetly. This woman was so utterly narcissistic she had never cared about anyone else's time, or whether she was disturbing them.

"What is it?" I asked rudely.

"Thank you, yes, I will," she said sarcastically, and sat down.

I sighed tiredly. God, how I hated playing games. "What do you want, Penelope?"

She twisted her fingers in her lap. "I just want to let you know that I may be going away soon. On a long cruise, actually. To see the world." Her eyes sparkled as she spoke.

I stared at her incredulously. "What about Molly?"

She thrust out her chin. "Of course, I love Molly. She's my daughter, but I deserve a life too. Jack loves me and I love him and we want to get to know each other better without distractions."

"Molly is a distraction?" I asked her, doing my best to reign in my anger.

"That's not what I said. You always do that Luke! Put things in my mouth," Penelope accused.

"How long is this cruise?" I asked her.

"Three months," she said in a barely audible voice.

"You've only just come back into her life and you want to leave?"

She glared at me. "Don't lay that guilt trip on me! I have to live my life too," she said. "You're busy fucking the nanny and what do I have?"

Penelope could say what she wanted about Ella and me. It didn't matter. What mattered was what we felt for each other.

"Jack said that when we get back from the cruise, we'll get married," she continued.

I guessed it must be the boy who'd been in her bed at the hotel. She must have fallen really hard for this Jack boy if she was contemplating marrying him. "How old is Jack?"

Her face colored. "Old enough to know what he wants and he wants me."

"Can't you go sometime next year? Give Molly a bit more time with you?" I pleaded.

She shook her head. "I can't keep Jack waiting for that long."

"But you can keep Molly waiting!" I exploded.

Her face closed up and her mouth became a thin line of rebellion.

I could tell by the tilt of her chin that she had already made up her mind. I would even bet she had already paid for the cruise... with my money.

There was no point in getting angry. I don't know why I'd thought Penelope would change. That she could stick it out this time and be there for Molly. She was selfish and that would never change. "What will you tell Molly?" I finally asked her.

"I was thinking that maybe you could tell her—"

I banged on my desk with my fist. "No! You are going to do it yourself. And you're going to let her know how much you love her, and that you'll call her every day."

Penelope bowed her head and when she looked up, tears were in her eyes. "I'm sorry that I'm not the kind of mother Molly deserves. Maybe…" She sniffled. "Maybe… you should marry Ella. She'd make a good mother for Molly."

All the air left my lungs. I leaned forward to make sure this was actually Penelope speaking. Her words rendered me speechless for a while. Her admission that she wasn't a good mother shocked me. But for once, Penelope had been honest.

"I'll tell her when I come tomorrow," Penelope said and then stared at me with real fear in her eyes. "You're not going to cut off my money, are you?"

I held her gaze and shook my head. No matter what she did, I'd never leave her penniless. She was the mother of my child. My responsibility, whether I liked it or not. "I won't."

She sagged with relief. "Thank you." She pushed her chair back and stood up.

I got up too and went around to her side. "Take care of yourself and I hope you have a good time on the cruise," I said.

Penelope looked surprised by my words. "Thank you." She reached out and touched my cheek. "You're a good man Luke and Ella is lucky to have you." After one last look at me, she left.

# LUKE

e had a nice evening, though I did notice Ella seemed quieter than usual and pensive. Molly had really come out of her shell and during dinner, she told me about their shopping trip, albeit in halting sentences. I couldn't believe how far she had come. I hoped Penelope's leaving wouldn't impede her progress.

After dinner, Molly and I went to the playroom.

Ella joined us a few minutes later.

"Are you all right?" I asked Ella.

She scooted closer to me, so Molly wouldn't hear us. "I'm fine. It's you, I'm worried about. You look a bit sad."

Her perceptiveness astounded me. I'd thought I'd done a pretty good job of hiding my feelings. "I'll tell you about it later."

Later, after we'd put Molly to bed, we decided to go up to our room and talk there, rather than sit in the living room.

IONA ROSE

We slipped into bed and Ella curled up in my arms. "Tell me," she said, "what happened?"

I sighed. "Penelope is leaving on a three-month cruise."

Ella went still. "What about Molly? She can't just leave her?"

"Apparently, she can. She's going with her new man," I told her while I stroked her hair.

"You're going to let her?"

"I can't stop her. She's a grown woman, and to be really honest, I don't want to. I actually find it to be a huge burden having her around, but I was prepared to put up with it for Molly's sake. This might work out for the best. I believe this will be the pattern and eventually, Molly will get used to it. I made her promise to speak to Molly about it tomorrow."

"Molly will be heartbroken," Ella said slowly.

"Maybe not," I said.

I'd never stepped in properly after Penelope ran away with another man. I hadn't been there for Molly like I should have. I retreated into my own shell and became my father. If I had attempted to fill in the void left by Penelope, Molly wouldn't have reacted so badly. "She has me and you now. We'll shower her with love and although, she won't forget her mother, she won't feel cast aside this time. Especially, if she knows it just for a vacation cruise."

"I think you might be right," Ella said, her hand splayed across my chest. She traced a pattern on my skin with her fingers.

Soon, my breath was coming out faster. I tipped her chin up and brought my mouth to hers. We kissed slowly, exploring each other's lips and then mouths.

I lost myself in Ella's kisses, kissing her leisurely even though what I really wanted was to devour her immediately. I'd learned that savoring everything left me more satisfied after it was all over. I enjoyed the sweet taste of her mouth and the softness of her body as she melted into me.

I felt her tremor as my hands cupped her curvy ass and squeezed her against my cock. "You're so beautiful," I whispered to her.

"Then what are you waiting for?" Ella prompted.

I shifted us around, so I was on top. Then I kissed her cheek and trailed kisses down along her neck to her breasts. I thumbed her perfect nipples.

Her hands caressed my back and hair, and then held my head in place as I sucked her nipples.

She rubbed her pussy against my stomach, her wetness coating me like a second skin. I dropped further, trailing kisses all the way, until I was looking at her sweet pussy. I inhaled her sweet scent of arousal.

Usually, I would have dove straight in, licking, and eating her pussy, but I was in the mood to tease her. I nibbled on her inner thighs. She clutched at my head and tried to steer me back to her pussy. But my head remained like an immovable block of cement. She let out a moan of frustration as I continued licking and biting her thighs.

"Please Luke," she said. "I'll do anything."

I chuckled. "What do you need?"

"I need you to eat my pussy," she cried.

Her words went straight to my cock. I let out a ragged breath and swooped down on her. I dragged my tongue along her slit, as she raised her hips up to meet the onslaught. She thrashed her legs as I devoured her tasty little pussy.

Before she could come, I moved over her, my cock throbbing painfully for some part of the action. I wrapped my hand around my shaft and shoved it into her pussy.

"Yes!" she gasped. "Fuck me, Luke. Please?"

She thrust her hips upwards as I pumped into her. She let out a cry every time my cock hit a certain spot, deep inside her. We moved as though we were born to mate together.

I stared down at her as her orgasm started to tear through her and in that moment, I knew that I loved Ella Cooper.

# ELLA

*A*s I ironed my dresses, I glanced at my phone fearfully, then remembered I had switched it off. Luke had been going to the office every day this week and it was a good thing he had, because he definitely would have noticed that something was terribly wrong.

I wasn't as strong as I'd thought I was. I felt like an animal trapped in a cage with nowhere to run. Even the house had started to feel unsafe. I closed the curtains during the day when I was in my bedroom.

Stan was succeeding.

I could feel myself unraveling. I was becoming crazy and barely holding it together. I needed to turn on my phone in case Luke had called or texted. He would get worried if he found my phone switched off.

With trembling fingers, I reached for it and turned it on. As soon as the screen came alive, messages started coming in, one after the other.

Dread filled me. They were all from Stan.

*You're my woman.*

*I know you miss me just like I miss you.*

*You're going to keep ignoring my messages, as if I'm not important to you.*

*I was ready to give you another chance. A chance to right what you did wrong.*

*Do you fucking understand that I was locked up because of you?? And you won't answer my messages.*

*BITCH. BITCH. BITCH.*

*You'll pay for all this. For getting me locked up. For thinking you're better than me and all you are is a whore!!!!!!!!!!!!!!*

I dropped the phone and sank to the floor. I buried my face in my hands. What could I do? I lost all track of time as I tried to think about my options. But my brain refused to function. All I could feel were his hands wrapped around my waist and his hot breath on my neck.

A knock on the door jolted me back to the present and I scrambled to my feet. I yanked the door open, heart pounding. I sagged in relief when I saw Paul, the chef.

He narrowed his eyes at me. "Are you all right?"

I arranged my mouth into a smile. "I'm fine."

"Why are the curtains closed?"

"Uh… I was uh changing."

"Right. I want to ask for a favor," he said. "Could you go to the grocery store for me? I'm in the middle of making a pastry and I need a couple of things, but I can't leave the oven."

"Sure," I replied with a nod. "Just keep an eye on Molly for me, will you?" I wasn't worried about leaving her with Paul for half an hour at the most, since Luke had told me it was okay to leave her with Paul when I had to run out for a few minutes.

"Thank you," Paul said. "You're a lifesaver."

I followed him to the kitchen where he gave me a list of stuff he needed. I popped into my room to grab my handbag and changed my shoes. Then I went to stand at the window and peered out.

I had no doubt that Stan already knew where I lived, but he'd probably seen Luke and Paul, so he'd stayed away. When I was sure no one was lurking about, I sneaked out of the house like a thief and hurried down the street.

I walked fast, checking over my back constantly. I felt exposed. As if Stan would appear any time. I hated what my life had become. In a matter of weeks, I had gone from a happy, carefree woman to a nervous mess.

The grocery store was a ten-minute walk but it felt like half an hour before I was in the safety of the shop. I stood for a moment to catch my breath, then grabbed a shopping basket, and proceeded down the aisle.

I was being paranoid, I told myself. He couldn't follow me everywhere. I refused to think about those text messages and what they meant.

I shopped fast, grabbing the things on the list without inspecting them for flaws as Paul liked to do. When I was done, I went to the cashier and paid. Then I began to walk back home.

It happened when I was crossing the road. One minute, I was standing on the sidewalk and in the next, a blue sedan veered off the road and came straight at me. My instincts took over and I jumped back just as it swerved in my direction.

I stared at it horrified and caught a glimpse of the driver.

Stan's grinning face stared back at me.

Terror took over as it hit me that Stan was not kidding around. He actually intended to kill me. I ran across the road and sprinted all the way home, stopping every so often to see if I could spot the blue sedan again.

I rushed into the house and slammed the door shut. I leaned on it and tried to come to terms with what had just happened. *Stan had tried to kill me!* I felt sick and dizzy. My phone vibrated in my handbag and I jumped. It took a moment to collect myself and answer it.

"Luke." My voice sounded different even to my own ears.

"Ella, what is it?" Luke asked.

"It's a long story, but I'm fine now," I said and then burst into tears.

"Are you home?" he asked, almost shouting down the phone.

"Yes," I managed to say.

"I'm coming. Sit tight. Everything will be fine, I promise," Luke said and disconnected the call.

I pulled myself together and took the groceries into the kitchen. Surprisingly, everything inside the bag was intact.

After everything that had happened, I'd at least expected the eggs to be broken.

"Thank you," Paul said. "I owe you one. Molly is still napping. That puppy does a good job of tiring her out."

"You're welcome," I said and added, "I'll just go check on her anyway."

I needed to see for myself that Molly was safe. If anything happened to her, I'd never forgive myself. My heart pounded as I pushed her door open even though Paul had assured me she was fine.

She was snoring gently with one hand hanging from the bed. I tiptoed in and tucked it back into place. I stared at the innocent image she was for a moment longer, then left.

I stayed in my room and peered out through the slit in the curtains. I kept reliving the moment when the car had veered off the road and climbed up onto the pavement. If I hadn't jumped back, I'd be dead or seriously injured now.

Clearly, I didn't know Stan or what he was truly capable of.

*Murder!*

Did he hate me so much that he wanted to kill me? The sound of Luke's car coming into the drive brought me back to the present. Weak with relief, I hurried downstairs and opened the front door for him.

"Ella!" he said and took my hand.

I led him to the living room.

"Tell me what happened," he said when we sat on the couch.

He kept my hand in his as I told him everything, leaving no detail out.

"Why didn't you tell me when he started?" Luke asked in astonishment.

I searched his eyes and saw no hint of what he was thinking. A feeling of dread filled my stomach. I was about to lose my job. I hadn't given one thought to my job all that time but now, it hit me afresh that my being here, taking care of Molly was putting her at risk.

It didn't matter if I lost my job. As long as Molly was safe.

"I truly thought if I ignored him, he would go away," I defended. "I knew Stan could be violent, but I didn't think he would become a dangerous stalker."

"My poor baby. You've been carrying this burden alone," Luke muttered and massaged my hand.

His kindness brought fresh tears to my eyes. I didn't want to take advantage of the kind of person he was and I didn't want to make him say it. "I'll understand if you don't want me to continue working for you," I said, my voice shaky.

He frowned and looked confused. "What?"

"I don't want to put Molly at risk," I said.

He took both my hands into his. "Listen to me Ella, I'm going to take care of you. Both of you. Bullies make you believe that no one can help you. Their tactics are to make you feel helpless and alone. You're not alone. I'm here. He has no idea about the kind of man he has picked as his opponent. No more talk about leaving your job."

Tears flowed furiously down my cheeks. I could hardly believe he wanted to protect me. I'd never felt like I did in this moment. So completely safe and protected. Was that how people felt when they were in a loving relationship?

If so, I had missed out on so much during the time I'd been with Stan.

Luke pulled me on his lap and held me close. "Everything will be fine, but first, we need to go to the police station and report this."

My heart skipped a beat. I remembered what Stan had said about Molly. If I told anyone, something would happen to her. "He said he would hurt Molly if I told anyone about him," I whispered with a shiver of dread. Even the thought was too frightening to contemplate.

"That's exactly the kind of reaction stalkers want you to have. The first rule is never, ever give in," Luke stated. "I'm glad you told me and now, we'll tell the police. That bastard cannot get away with such behavior." His jaw was set and a white line of fury appeared around his mouth.

I felt sure that if Stan had been nearby, he'd have gotten his face punched into a pulp.

LUKE CAME to my room that night rather than me going to his. I was paranoid and wanted to sleep close to Molly even though I knew the house was secure. Stan had no way of entering the house. I wore a negligee and slipped into bed to wait for Luke.

The sound of his breathing seemed amplified and his manly scent was everywhere. I let out a sigh of contentment.

"Feel better?" Luke asked.

"Much better. Thank you."

We kissed and caressed each other unhurriedly. I found out there was something so sensual about knowing that your man could take care of you. I had no doubt I was safe in Luke's care. This knowledge added another layer of sensation as we made love.

I was his woman and Luke took care of his own. I wasn't the vulnerable Ella I had been earlier. I felt free of all the fears I'd had. Stan had another thing coming if he thought that he could take my life from me.

I heard myself urge Luke to take me.

I needed him more than I ever had. I needed to feel like his completely. I clawed his back and whimpered as he lifted me to new heights of passion. We made music together and when we came, we made cries of surrender, as though finally —it was official.

We belonged together.

## ELLA

*I*n the days that followed, the knots in my stomach slowly loosened, and I stopped looking over my shoulder every time I was out of the house. The police had gotten back to us. Stan had been given a warning. He'd denied that it was him who had been in that car and they found no evidence that he owned a blue sedan.

Still, he'd gotten off with a stiff warning and as one day melted into the next, I became convinced that the stiff warning had worked.

Luke had been working from home for the last few days, but I knew he was needed at the office. I urged him to go and if anything happened, I would call him. Paul had gone off to the grocery store to stock up on food and the lady from the cleaning service had been in and left already.

It was just Molly and me in the house and we were in the backyard playing with Bean. The sun was out and we were both dressed in matching sundresses I had made myself. Luke had convinced me that if I allowed myself to live in fear, then Stan would win. There was no way I would let that happen now.

Molly's laughter rang out every time Bean caught the stick while in midair. He had grown bigger too, and more attached to Molly.

My phone sang that familiar tune in my pocket and I picked it up without a second thought.

"What are you up to?" Ruby asked.

I smiled when I heard Ruby's voice on the other end. "Molly and I are in the backyard, enjoying the sun and playing with Bean."

"That's some life you have there," Ruby said.

I laughed.

We caught up on each other's news.

Bean sprinted off towards the house, with Molly hot on his heels.

"I gotta go," I said to Ruby. Ending the call, I sprinted after Bean and Molly.

"Molly," I called as I entered the house.

They weren't in the kitchen and I went to the living room. As I walked through the door, a hand appeared from nowhere and clamped over my mouth. A familiar sickening stench rose up my nose.

Fear gripped my chest. I looked around, wildly twisting my head this way and that way until I saw Molly on the couch, her hand on Bean. I was glad she was restraining him. He was a puppy and there wasn't much he could do to save us.

"Don't get any ideas," Stan said and pressed cold metal against my neck.

I knew even without even seeing it, that it was a gun.

"Did you think me and you were done?" he said and let out a bark of a laugh. "That will never happen. We're bound for life. You made a big mistake by telling the police. "

"Please," I tried to say. All I could think of was Molly. How could I get her out of the house? I thought about Paul. I didn't want him to come back soon. Not when Stan was still in the house. I had no doubt that he would shoot him.

Oh God, what was I going to do? I knew he wasn't going to kill me. His interest was in me. I had accepted that. I needed to make sure he did not hurt Molly or anyone else.

"Let's go," he said abruptly and pulled me toward the door.

Molly made as if to stand.

"Make her stay!" Stan barked. "Unless you want her to come with us."

"Molly, I have to go out for a while. Sit and wait there for Daddy, okay?"

She looked confused and unsure about what was happening, but to my relief, she nodded and sat back down.

Stan spoke in my ear, his breath hot and already reeking of alcohol, "I'm done playing games, so listen to me very carefully. I have a car outside. We'll walk together and enter as if we're old friends. If you do anything stupid, like scream or run, I'll go back in there and put a bullet into that kid's head."

I stifled a cry. "I promise I won't do anything."

He opened the door and we stepped out. I did as he had instructed and slipped into the blue sedan. The one he had tried to run me over with.

"Good girl," he said, when he got into the driver's seat. He stared at me. "If you had cooperated this well from the beginning, it would not have come to this. We would have been so happy." A mad glint came into his eyes. "But you had to go and report me to the police. Do you know what you've done?" His voice rose in rage.

I shank away from him.

"Don't worry I won't touch you," he said, lowering his voice. "Not here anyway. Not when there are nosy people looking out their windows, poking their noses into other peoples' business." He switched on the child locks in the car.

I jumped at the clicking sound. Any thoughts of throwing myself out of the car were gone. As he drove away, I prayed silently that Paul wouldn't be too long and Molly would do as I said… just sit there quietly.

"How have you been?" Stan asked conversationally, as if we were old friends who hadn't seen each other in a while.

I knew then that he was now completely insane. He had lost his mind. Being bullied in prison must have done that to him. My insides turned to water.

He sensed my stare and stared back. He smiled. A friendly smile. But it did not reach his eyes.

Dread came over me. I knew without a doubt that he intended to rape me first then probably kill me. I had to fight. I wasn't going to let him win. Whatever it took to survive, I would do it.

We were leaving the city and panic was mounting in my chest. I fought the urge to lash out, knowing it would just make him mad. It would be better to stay calm and wait for an opportunity to get away.

My blood went cold when Stan turned off the highway. I suddenly saw another car and sucked in a breath as it slowly went by, I mouthed, *"Help me,"* silently at the driver. I didn't even know if the man behind the wheel saw it, but I had to try.

Stan drove down the sandy rutted road. I gripped the dashboard of the car and fought down a primal scream rising up my throat. When I saw the desolate area we were in, courage failed me. "Please let me go?" I begged.

"Shut up, Ella!" he said harshly.

The tires of the sedan screeched as Stan brought it to a stop in front of a dilapidated looking house. Weeds had overgrown and climbed onto the porch.

He killed the engine and grinned at me. "Welcome home!"

I looked around and shivered. No one would ever find me here. There were no neighbors and no one to hear me if I screamed.

His grin disappeared. "Get out and don't think of doing anything stupid. I'm not averse to putting a bullet through your head."

I didn't doubt it. Besides, where would I run to? There seemed to be nothing for miles and Stan had a gun. I grew frantic.

"Walk," he ordered.

I trudged up the wooden steps, afraid they would give way. I didn't know what would be worse—to be stabbed by a piece of wood or to be shot by Stan.

Stan pushed the door open and I stepped into a dark interior. As my eyes got used to the dim light, as I made out two straight backed chairs and ropes on one of them. I took a step back at the realization that the rope was for me.

Stan placed a hand on the small of my back like a lover would and then shoved me across the room so hard, I lost my footing and fell. I inhaled dust and coughed hard.

"Get up!" Stan yelled.

I hurriedly scrambled to my feet, knowing he would kick me if I didn't.

"Sit there." Any pretense at friendliness was now gone.

When I sat down, he came behind me and proceeded to tie my hands behind the chair.

"Please don't do this Stan," I said to him.

"This is just the beginning," Stan sneered. "I'm going to do things to you that are going to make you wish you were dead."

The sound of my heartbeat thrashed in my ears. Fear coursed through my veins. I didn't want to die. I thought about Luke. We had something special and I wanted to see what we could be together. I had never told him that I loved him. I would die and he wouldn't know how much I had loved him.

"I'm going to cut away every stitch of clothing on you and then fuck you all night. In every fucking *hole*." He emphasized the last part.

I shuddered.

He came around the chair and stared at me before striding off.

I had to free myself. He could shoot me in the back as I was running away. I didn't care. I wished I'd tried to run when I got out of the car. I fought with the rope, twisting my hands this way and that way.

I must have moved too much because in the next moment, I toppled over.

The noise brought Stan hurrying back. "Were you trying to get away?" he said, and made a clicking noise with his mouth. "Now, I'm going to untie you, but you had better behave yourself. I'm going to fuck you just like I used to and I expect you to make appreciative noises. Tell me what a great lover I am. Can you do that?"

I bit my lower lip. I had to wait for the right moment when he was vulnerable. Then I would make my move. Meanwhile, I would play dumb.

I nodded.

He glared at me with that evil grin. "That's the Ella, I know. Whore to her dying breath."

## LUKE

*M*y hands were shaking as I drove home. Paul had called me and said in a barely controlled panic that he'd found Molly alone with Bean and no sign of Ella. He had tried to ask Molly what had happened but she wouldn't respond. She had just stared at him mutely. She had gone back into her shell, but the immediate problem was Ella.

In my gut, I knew something had happened to Ella. And that something—was Stan.

I called the police as I drove and when I got home, a police car was already parked outside. I brought the car to a screeching halt and jumped out. I sprinted up to the house and found Molly in the living room with Paul and two policemen. "I'm the one who called you," I said by way of explanation, and went straight to Molly.

I knelt down in front of her and she threw her arms around my neck. I held her tight and listened to the rapid beat of her heart. "It's okay sweetheart," I crooned. "You're safe now."

We stayed that way for a while and then I gently pulled back. "Tell me what happened. Where's Ella?"

Tears filled her eyes and her lips trembled.

"Please tell us so that these good policemen can go and find her and bring her back to us," I said to her, keeping my voice low and soothing.

She glanced at the two policemen and then back at me. In halting sentences, my Molly told me everything from when they had been playing in the garden to the man with the gun, taking Ella with him.

Even before she finished speaking, one of the policemen was on his phone giving instructions about CCTV footage.

"You've done well sweetheart," I said to Molly when she finished and held her in my arms again.

"We're looking at the CCTV footage of this street," one of them told me.

Whatever happened I needed to go with them to find Ella. I fished out my phone and called Ruby. I gave her a short explanation and before I could ask her to come be with Molly, she was already saying she was on the way.

I stayed with Molly until Ruby came and took over. Paul promised to stay in the house with them.

Outside, our house looked like a crime scene. There were policemen walking up and down the street, knocking on doors.

One of the policemen who had first responded came to me. "We have the car registration number," he said. "We just got a report from a man seeing a woman mouthing 'help me' to

At my insistence, he was out doing one more check around the house, double checking that the windows and doors were locked. He came in a few minutes later. "Safe," he said grimly. He came and knelt on the floor close to me. "I'm sorry."

"For what?"

"For the fear that madman has created in you," Luke said with feeling. His face was close enough that if I moved an inch, our noses would touch. "I want you to feel safe Ella. I promise I'll keep you safe. I'll work from home from now on, until this mess is over."

I threw my hands around his neck and pulled him to me. He slipped into the bed and we held each other. It meant so much to me that he would be working from home.

The police had been non-committal though earlier today, they'd said they would call him in for questioning. Luke had been as frustrated as I was and had raged at the policemen who had taken down my statement.

"Thank you," I murmured into Luke's ear.

He got into bed, propped himself on his elbow, and looked down at me. "You are so special and so beautiful. I'm not losing you just when I've found you."

If I'd been standing, for sure, my legs would have buckled from under me. No one had ever spoken such words to me. Luke made me feel special. He turned us around and held me as if instinctively knowing-that what I needed right now-was comfort.

As I lay on his chest, he stroked my hair and murmured sweet words. It worked. Every worry dissolved and soon, all that remained in my mind was how perfect it felt to lie there.

him from the passenger seat of a blue sedan. We have the location. He thought it was suspicious because the car turned off down a dirt track, leading to a derelict farmhouse."

"I'm going to come with you," I said to him.

"We'd rather you waited here," he said. "It could be dangerous."

"I'll stay out of your way."

He contemplated me, and then nodded.

Ten minutes later, we were on the way to a location outside the city. I was in the back seat of the third police car and kept my hands fisted, just praying we wouldn't be too late.

I felt the kind of terror I had never experienced before as we drove down a rough road. *Please. She has to be alive. She has to live. For us. For me.*

I loved Ella with all of my heart. She had broken down all my barriers. Without her, my life would become empty and meaningless again.

"Please stay in the car," one of the policemen said, parking the car a long way from the dilapidated house ahead.

When the two policemen started moving towards the house, I instantly got out of the car and ran along the tall grasses. I crept around the back and heard the sounds of scuffling. Then I heard Ella scream, and I burst into the house.

Stan was on top of Ella. He looked up in surprise then fired his gun wildly and missed me. I ran to him, grabbed him, and threw him off my baby. Then I was on him. Punching his head, his neck, his chest. I was like a mad man. I had lost control. I didn't stop until I was roughly grabbed from the back and pulled away from him.

"Calm down," one of the policemen yelled as he held my arms.

I was breathing so hard I was panting like an animal.

Stand had his hands twisted behind him and the other cop was handcuffing him.

I turned my head towards Ella.

She still laid on the floor half-naked in the same position I had found her when I came in. I took off my shirt and quickly wrapped her in it. Then I picked her up and carried her out of that stinking house.

Ella wrapped her hands around my neck and cried like her heart was breaking.

She was alive. That's all that mattered.

"You're okay now. You're safe now. He'll never hurt you again. I promise."

# LUKE

*I* was haunted by thoughts of what would have happened if that driver hadn't reported seeing Ella mouthing 'help me' just as they turned off onto the dirt road. What if Stan had succeeded in killing Ella?

Later that evening, I walked into Ella's room, carrying a bowl of soup that Paul had made. I found both Ella and Molly curled together in bed asleep.

For a moment, I just leaned against the doorway staring at them both.

My heart swelled with gratitude. I hadn't thought it possible to love a woman as much as I loved Ella. My gaze shifted to Molly. She lay in the crook of Ella's arm, her face upturned to her. A stranger looking at them would think they were mother and daughter.

I wanted to stand here all night just looking at them while feeling this amazing love in my heart, but thc soup would have gotten cold. So, I tiptoed into the room and placed the bowl on the bedside table. Then I went to Molly's side and as gently as I could, I lifted her from the bed.

Ella's eyes shot open, her head jerked up and she looked about her wildly.

It broke my heart to see her like this. I knew it would take a while to heal from the trauma she had been through, but I would be here to see her through it. "It's okay," I murmured. "It's only me. I'm carrying Molly to her bedroom."

She flopped back onto the bed as understanding dawned on her.

"I'll be back. Start on your soup," I said with a smile.

Then I carried Molly next door to her room. She didn't wake up as I tucked her into bed and kissed her forehead. "My brave girl," I murmured to myself while staring at her sweet, little face.

When Ella and I returned home, she had held on tight to Ella's legs and wouldn't let go. They'd both cried as Ella told her over and over again that she was fine and nothing bad had happened to her.

We'd gotten to Ella in time before Stan could do any real damage to her. I would make sure he wouldn't be leaving prison in the next couple of decades. Besides, I intended to go all in with regards to security.

Suddenly, the world had become a more threatening place and I would not take any more chances where my girls' safety was concerned. The first thing I intended to do was to consult a security company and get their recommendations on how to further secure the house.

When I returned to Ella's room, she was propped up against the pillows eating her soup. "Thank you for this," she said. "I was hungry." She hadn't been able to eat earlier, but the emergency room doctor had warned us that she was still in shock and would be for a few more hours.

"How do you feel now?" I asked her, sitting on her side of the bed.

She smiled. "Relieved to be alive."

This was my opportunity to tell her how I really felt. I had allowed a bad marriage to come between me and happiness. I refused to allow it to rule my life anymore.

"What?" she asked. "You're staring at me without speaking."

"I'm trying to come up with the right words," I explained. "I don't want to mess this up."

Ella's eyes twinkled with amusement. "The right words for what?"

"The right words to tell you how much I love you and what happiness you've brought into my life. You've turned me from a man who was cynical about love and happiness into one who now knows that love exists."

She placed the bowl on the side table.

"My sweet Ella, I love you more than life itself. If I'd lost you…" I choked on my words.

She leaned forward and cupped my cheeks. "You didn't and I'm here now. I love you too, Luke." She laughed softly. "I don't know how it happened. But I love you with all my heart. You and Molly."

I slipped into bed where Molly had lain and gathered Ella into my arms. I must have held her too tightly because she started wriggling like an eel.

"You'll squeeze the life out of me," she said with a laugh.

I laughed too, and loosened my hold.

She tilted her gorgeous face to mine. "Kiss me Luke. Make love to me."

"Yes ma'am," I said and lowered my head to kiss my woman and soon to be wife, even if she didn't know it yet.

# EPILOGUE

## TWO YEARS LATER

### Ella

"That's it. I'm done. I'm not speaking to Michelle anymore, she's not my friend," Molly announced as Luke and I tucked her into bed.

I hid a smile. Recently, every day was a big drama with Molly and her friends, although they did have weeks when everything went smoothly.

"Can't you all just get along?" Luke asked her.

I'd told him countless times that this was part of a girl growing up, but he always shook his head in bafflement.

Surprisingly, Penelope had gotten married to her boy toy and they came to see Molly when they were around and then disappeared for months at a time. The good thing was that she kept in touch with Molly via email and sent her countless pictures.

Molly seemed pleased with that arrangement and never seemed sad when her mom went off again.

"Maybe she's sorry she refused to give you a pencil," I said to Molly and smoothed her hair back. She was becoming so big so fast. It was easy to forget how she was when I first arrived at this house. Now she was a regular chatterbox, surpassing all the hopes we'd had for her.

She looked at me, her eyes wide with wonder. "Mommy, how did you know?" She'd taken to calling me Mommy and Penelope was mom.

I never tired of hearing her say the name. I chuckled mysteriously. No point in spoiling her awe by telling her it was always one of two. A pencil or an eraser. I'd just taken a lucky guess.

We tucked her in and said goodnight.

"I don't understand little girls," Luke said as we went downstairs. "But thankfully, I understand women. *My* woman… to be clear."

"Yes, you do," I said with a laugh.

The last two years had been full of wonder and joy. Luke had insisted on us getting married immediately. As he'd said it, he didn't want to risk losing me and being married ensured that I would be bound to him for life.

Like there had been a chance of that happening.

I'd gone to college and finished faster than I had anticipated by doing the crash program. I was now working as an apprentice for a well-known designer and I loved it.

Luke as a husband was everything I dreamed of and never thought I'd ever find. He was thoughtful and kind as he showered me with more love than I deserved.

With his love, I'd been able to forget that awful day two years ago when Stan kidnapped me with the intention of raping me and then killing me. He'd been sentenced to thirty years in jail after the police found evidence that he had killed another woman before me and hidden her body on that same property he'd taken me to.

I trembled every time I thought of how close I'd come to losing my life. Luke had ensured that I felt safe by making the house super secure. A person would have to be superman to enter our house.

I'd found no real way to repay him for the life he had given me and the love he showered on me every day, but I knew my news would please him. Soon, Molly would have a little brother or sister. Luke thought he'd kept it from me, but every so often, I saw him staring at my belly with a wistful look on his face.

Now, I was about to gift him with another little human to love. I'd been bursting to tell him my news, but I waited until we were comfortable on the couch. We lay facing each other with Luke massaging my legs.

"Do you know how much I love you?" he asked while staring at me intently. "Sometimes, I think I love you so much my chest feels like it might just burst."

"Oh, dear. Does that mean there's no more space to love another little person besides Molly?" I asked with a look of fake horror.

Luke's eyes widened. He glanced down to my flat belly then back up to my face. "Are you…?" he faltered, his voice full of hope.

I grinned. "Indeed, I am."

He sat up, scooped me into his lap, and kissed me. "Oh my God, Ella! You're the gift that just keeps giving."

My grin got wider. "I am a bit of that, aren't I?"

"Another little girl, I hope?"

"Or a little boy who looks just like you," I said.

He cupped my cheeks and kissed me deeply. "You made me the happiest man on earth when you loved me back and agreed to marry me. Now, there's no way to describe how I feel."

I kissed him gently on the lips. "Then describe it with your body."

THE END

**Chapter One**

**Leah**

"Leah..." Anne groaned. "Shut that thing off!"

I came to from my light doze. The crowing from my phone's alarm finally pierced my subconscious. My eyelids lazily fluttered open.

"Leah!" She groaned again.

It took me a few more seconds to process what her complaint was about. I reached for the phone on the stool by my side and cut the ringing.

"We'll burn, Leah," Anne complained. "Set it for another half hour."

I turned from my front, and rested on my back. I ignored her for a moment as I tried to recollect myself. My eyes opened fully then, squinting a little at the daylight's sharp reception beyond the shade of our wicker parasol.

There were now hordes of people in the ocean and around the sandy beach, much more than had been present when we'd arrived about two hours earlier.

I picked up my phone, and reset the alarm.

Slender, but hostile hands reached out to repeatedly tap my arm. "Change the sound from that damn crowing cock. It's driving me crazy."

I turned my gaze to my pestering friend.

Laid out by my side in an orange gingham bikini, Anne's blonde hair looked matted wildly on top of her head, akin to a bird's nest. Her expression looked drowsy as her face contorted irritably.

"You're becoming a nightmare," I growled as I lifted my hands above my head. The stretch was almost magical, the creaks and soreness I hadn't even been aware of smoothened out of my overly rested bones.

She sighed and went back to sleep.

I turned to the beach bed by my right, to see that the third member of our party was missing. "Where's Tracy?" I drawled.

I didn't get a response so my gaze roved across the expansive stretch of sand and people, hoping to spot her one-piece Coca-Cola swimsuit somewhere amongst it all.

I had no luck, so I gave up and was about to shut my eyes when I heard her high-pitched call. I looked over at the shout.

Tracy was waving excitedly from the distance with one hand, while the other supported a basket of snacks as she headed over to us. Behind her was Mehmet, the genie from the beach's snack bar we had acquainted ourselves with since our arrival two days earlier.

He was approaching with a tray of colorful fruit garnished cocktails.

This sight instantly made me sit up.

"Anne, I brought you a Mai Tai," Tracy announced as she arrived. "Leah, the Hurricane's for you."

"Thank you," I cheered as I reached out with both hands for the red gradient drink. "Thank you, Mehmet." I smiled at the gaunt, bearded server.

"You're welcome ma'am," he said, his eyes lowered to the ground, his response was somewhat shy.

I couldn't blame him. We were all half-naked.

I took a good long sip of the fruity rum punch, and it made me feel like I'd been resurrected from the dead. A moan escaped my throat, as I thanked the gods for a good life.

Tracy settled into her bed as Mehmet placed the remaining cocktail on the stool by her side. "Anne, I'm taking yours," she said.

Our presumably sleeping friend got up instantly. With a sharp look at Tracy, she rounded our beds and picked up her drink. Then she grabbed some cookie packets from the basket, and returned to her corner.

It was amusing enough.

We all soon settled in, watching the vastness and flurry of activities beyond as we consumed our light refreshments.

"I want to lounge there tomorrow," Tracy said.

I turned to see her longing gaze on the beds and parasols on the pier extended over the sea.

"Keep dreaming," Anne said. "In order to get a spot there you have to be up at the crack of dawn to make the reservation."

"I'll do it," Tracy said brightly and picked up her phone. "I'll set the alarm for 6 am."

Anne shared a look with me.

I couldn't help snorting with laughter into my drink. "We came here to get away from alarms, Tracy," I said. "Not continue to set them."

She was adamant. "Well, I want to lounge on the pier, so I'm going to get up to reserve it."

"Good luck with that," Anne said. "By the time we get back from Pirates today, who knows if we'll even be able to walk."

Tracy and I both turned to her.

"What do you mean?" I asked.

"We're going back there?" Tracy complained.

"There's a foam party tonight," Anne replied. "The hot bartender told me."

"Foam party?" Tracy spat, her tone laced with disgust.

I remained indifferent because no matter how crazy things got I planned to stay on the sidelines.

"Yup! Foam party," Anne repeated unapologetically.

"What are we, nineteen? Foam parties are ridiculous!" Tracy huffed.

"No, they're not!" Anne countered. "They're a helluva lot of fun, and did you miss the part about 'the hot bartender'? I have a grinding appointment with him tonight."

"His mouth was in yours half the night yesterday, and you still don't know his name?" Tracy countered.

Anne set her empty glass down and leaned back on her bed, her arms behind her head, eyes shut with a massive smile across her face. "I don't need to. What's important is that the entire floor is going to be steamy... and wet... and he's going to be there..." She gave us a glance, bright with perversion. "Preferably behind me. I'm wearing white and no bra."

I smiled. "I've never been to a foam party before," I said to Anne. "Heard about them though. Are they really that bad?"

Tracy's eyebrows shot up. "Really? Not even in college?"

I shook my head.

"Well, you're not missing anything. They're disgusting. The entire floor is covered with soap suds that may or may not blind you before the end of the night. Everyone is wet and stepping on you and pushing each other out of the way. And the falling? Ugh, that's the worst part. You'll most likely be sliding and slipping into vomit and pee. People even have sex in there so you can add a floor full of cum to that mix."

"Oh my God. Tracy!" Anne scolded. "Leah, don't listen to her. It's gonna be fun."

"Hate to burst your bubble," Tracy countered, as she couldn't hold back her smile at the pun. "You're going to wish you came with me to the Fire of Anatolia dance show." Tracy nodded.

I smiled with her. "Dance show?"

Tracy sat up excitedly, eager to sell her agenda. "Yes, and it's going to be fabulous."

"Isn't that held at the Aspendos Arena?" Anne asked.

"Yeah, it is."

"Leah, that's a two hour drive."

"Oh hell no," I refused. "I got carsick on the way here from the airport. I'm not riding in anything until we're leaving."

Tracy settled back on her bed with a defeated sigh.

Anne chuckled in victory. "Don't worry, Leah," she said, "the actual foam dispensing will only begin at about 2 am."

"Oh, I'm not worried," I said. "I plan to watch from a very safe and dry place."

Tracy's gaze turned fiery. "I will kill you." She turned to Anne. "And you."

Anne tapped my hand. "Great choice, Leah. Great choice.

~*~

Just before midnight, we arrived at the Havana club in the center of the city.

We were dressed accordingly-me in a leather miniskirt, a black tube top and knee-high alligator sandals.

300

Tracy wore baggy jeans and a fitted graphic tee with the words, don't talk to me, printed across the front. She was long over what had been our routine since our arrival of partying until sunrise and then heading back to the hotel to deal with the resulting hangovers and exhaustion for the better part of the following day.

Anne however, was the star of the night. She wore a smile she hadn't been able to wipe off all evening at the prospect of her night. She had come as intended, braless and in a white cotton dress.

"You're already nipping," Tracy pointed at her chest as we headed down the dimly lit stairs towards the club's main entrance.

"I'm also already wet," Anne said unashamedly.

"Wow!" Tracy responded.

"Exactly," Anne said. "I'm choosing to have fun. You can hang out in the corner with your flats and sip water." The club's stamp was pressed to the inside of her wrist then she shimmied to the rhythm of the deafening electronic music as she made her way into the club.

I put my hand around Tracy's reluctant frame and led us both along.

"Why does she have so much say over our itinerary?" She grumbled.

"Because she arranged the trip," I said.

"If I don't get a say in what we do tomorrow, I'm going home." Tracy pouted.

"Let's just give her a few more days," I said. "She'll tire of the clubs soon and we'll be able to get to all the other fun stuff."

After this, we couldn't speak without having to lean in and scream into each other's ears, so we saved our energy and headed straight to the bar.

Two glasses of dirty martinis were already waiting for us, and Anne's beloved bartender's tongue already down her throat as she leaned across the counter.

"Makmad!' Someone yelled at him.

He pulled away from his frolicking enough to notice myself and Tracy as we took our seats. "Ladies," he greeted.

We gave him a nod before turning condemning looks to our lust stricken friend.

It was then I first spotted him.

Somehow, it was as though I felt his eyes on me and was compelled into turning my gaze specifically towards him.

He was quite the distance away at the curve of the circular bar and just as I picked up my glass, he did the same to his tumbler of golden liquor.

He was speaking to the man by his side, his gaze fixated on him and the vibrant hues from the lights around the club dancing in his seemingly translucent eyes.

He looked handsome, more handsome than any man I'd seen in a long time, and I found myself unable to look away. His structured face was clean shaven, a particularly rare sight for people on vacation on this side of the world. I'd spotted the occasional stubble, but a clean shave seemed quite rare.

He appeared to be confident, but it took absolutely nothing away from the raw, masculine aggression I could almost feel from where he sat. A chiseled jawline and silky hair brushed away from his face in perfect waves. His lips… they were just the perfect curve to compliment his features. His eyes looked so intense that they could literally make me combust if they were to ever settle on me.

And then they did.

He turned as though fully aware of my staring and rested his gaze on me.

I immediately turned away, my hand almost missing my glass as I dove for it as cover. I lifted the rim to my lips, ignoring the thudding of my heart against my chest and faced Tracy. "Texting Jared?" I asked, glancing at the phone in her hands and the worried look on her face.

"Yeah," she said. "He was sick today. He couldn't even go to work."

I sucked in my breath. "That sucks."

"Yeah," she said.

Then I noticed Anne was missing.

"She went to the bathroom," Tracy told me.

Nodding, I turned around to watch all the fun people were having on the dance floor beyond. I tried to push away the thought that perhaps the man had noticed me just like I had him, but I didn't expect this to be likely, given the plethora of women who paraded near us in even shorter skirts and dangerous stilettos.

I chatted and laughed lightly with Tracy, but my mind was no longer with her. It was across the room, with the hot looking stranger I so desperately wanted to come up to me to introduce himself.

I set my empty glass down to my left and didn't bother ordering a refill. I hoped to God that he would take the hint and come over with an offering to buy me another.

The minutes ticked away... and nothing happened.

My hopes fell, as I fought with myself about turning towards his direction to catch another look, but my head refused to move, especially since I'd already gotten caught staring. So I continued speaking to Tracy, "What's the best way to get a man to come say hello to you?"

Tracy rested her gaze on me. "What man?"

"No one," I shifted on the stool. "I'm just asking."

"I have no idea," she answered and returned her attention to her phone.

"Didn't you meet Jared at that French coffee shop?"

"He came up to me on his own. I had nothing to do with it."

"Ah, so I'm screwed."

She paid attention then. "Where is he?" she asked and started to look around.

My heart almost gave out. "I will punch you," I threatened.

She laughed. "Seriously, where is he?"

I turned in my stool to face the bar. "Nine o'clock."

She faced it too. "Yours or mine?"

"Mine," I groaned. "Towards the end of the curve, he's talking to someone."

She looked, discretely enough I hoped.

"There's no one there," she said.

My brows furrowed. "Are you sure?"

She nodded.

I shot my gaze over to where he had been sitting.

Tracy was right.

He was gone.

## Chapter Two

### Leah

The hours that followed were completely uneventful.

Loosened up after a few drinks, myself and Tracy eventually went down to the dance floor. But we remained in a safe corner, moving in comical spurts with each other and then pausing when we got tired to watch the rest of the crowd.

They all seemed to grind and twist their bodies against each other to the rhythm of the deafening music.

Anne was in the midst of them somewhere, as we had long set her free to experience the night in the very wild way she wanted to.

Soon enough, Tracy was itching to return home and so was I, but a corner of my heart still held out the hope that perhaps I would see the hot guy again. So I stalled, refusing to take her suggestions of leaving to heart. "When the foam machines begin, we'll leave," I said, so we pressed on.

Soon enough, the machines started.

After an announcement that no one could make out amidst the deafening blare of music, the lights went out for a moment, plunging the entire club into a frightening darkness. Then the sound of running machines sounded across the room. The lights came back on and from the ceiling, soap foams were blasted down.

The crowd went wild!

"Time to go," Tracy said and held my hand as we tried to get off the dance floor, but people thrashed around in wild excitement. Everything and everyone seemed to have chosen to stand in our path, so getting around the railing to the exit steps got harder and harder.

My stomach roiled with the concern that we would eventually be trapped in the midst, unable to get away before the bubbles made everyone wet. My heart also went out to my sandals. They were low heeled and comfortable, but had cost me quite a ridiculous amount, so having them ruined was not part of the agenda tonight.

A cloud of foam began to drift towards us but thankfully a group of half-drunken people attacked it. The middle of the club was fast becoming completely covered in foam and we were running out of time.

"Get out of my way!" Tracy yelled as she pulled me along.

I went amusedly along with her.

We eventually made it to the steps before things could get out of hand, and I released a deep sigh of relief.

Tracy let go of my hand, and I held onto the railing, but then suddenly I slid on something wet and I started to go down.

A hand suddenly locked around my arm, holding me upright and I was able to regain my footing. "Thank you so much," I said, and lifted my gaze to see who'd saved me.

It was him.

Every external noise seemed to fade into the background, and for the longest time I couldn't speak until I heard Tracy call out my name. "I'll be right there," I called back to her, and tucked my curly hair behind my ears as I glanced at him. "Thank you."

"You're welcome," he said and retreated till I was on solid ground. I turned to walk away, my knees wobbly.

He called out to me, "Can I buy you a drink?"

My legs almost gave away again as I turned and nodded much too eagerly and had to catch myself.

He smiled in response, perhaps finding me endearing. I hoped.

"But I have to speak to my friend for just a moment," I said. "I'll come join you."

"Sure," he said and went on his way.

I returned, dazed, to Tracy.

She had ordered herself another drink and was waiting. "Who was that?"

"The guy that disappeared earlier," I said.

For a moment, her face remained blank. Then it hit her. "Ahh... Oh."

"If you turn to look at him, I will smack you," I said with gritted teeth.

She laughed, but still peeped at him. "That's the second time tonight you've threatened to deck me because of him."

"I'm sorry," I muttered. "I'm just so nervous. I don't know why."

"Oh, I know why." She nodded. "He's fucking gorgeous. Those broad shoulders and long legs are enough to mess with a girl's head."

I couldn't help my amusement. "Well, I'm going over. He's buying me a drink. I'm sorry for leaving you alone."

"It's fine. I'll keep an eye on you..." She looked out towards the still enlivened crowd... "and try to see if it's still possible to spot Anne. You know this scene makes me wonder if any of us really grow up, because all I see right now are a bunch of five year olds. They're fucking going crazy over bubbles. I don't get it."

"You're an old soul Tracy," I told her.

"What? You don't get it either."

"I do, I just don't want to get wet."

"Well with him now in the picture I'm sure you already are."

I smacked her arm.

"Ow!"

"How does my face look?"

"Stunning," she said.

"Lipstick on my teeth?" I asked, and grinned just enough to flash her my pearly whites.

"You're all good," she assured me.

I let out a deep breath. "See you later."

"Have fun," she called after me.

I walked away and headed towards him. With every step I took, it felt like I was heading towards a significant moment.

A moment that could quite possibly change everything and it made me not want to proceed, but then I reached him.

He got off his stool. "Hi," he said.

I couldn't get myself to respond, so I just focused on settling as gracefully as I could on the stool, which was quite the task given how easily it swiveled around.

He on the other hand, set his foot on the ground as he took his seat.

I realized then just how tall he was. I calculated that the top of my head would barely reach his shoulders.

He called the bartender over and turned to me, a smile on his face. "What do you want to drink?"

I decided to be confident. I wasn't one who felt irrefutably convinced of their own charm, but since he had noticed me, there was undoubtedly something here I could work with. Somehow, being in his presence made me feel sexier and more desirable than I ever had. The tip of my tongue softly rimmed the inside of my upper lip as I took a second to think, and then the words slid out of my mouth like butter, "Sex on the beach, would be great."

He didn't blink.

His gaze lingered boldly on my lips, painted a stark red, and then he lifted his eyes to mine.

At first sight I had thought his eyes were grey, but as it turned out, they were green. An aqua shade of green and mesmerizing.

"Sir..." the bartender called.

He peeled his gaze away from mine to place our orders. "Just a Macallan for me, and Sex on the Beach for the lady."

I relished the husky tone of his voice. It sounded so smooth and quiet, but the underlying authority was unmistakable.

He resettled his gaze on me. "My name is Carter Edwards." He held out his hand.

I paused, realizing we hadn't even introduced ourselves. I accepted the offered hand and replied, "I'm Leah... Leah Peters."

"You're American, I suppose," he said.

My gaze lingered on the joining of our hands as I slowly pulled mine away, almost convinced they were beginning to sear from the contact with him. "I am." I thought about mentioning that I was from Indianapolis, but I didn't think it was needed. Tonight was about two strangers meeting in a different part of the world, choosing to be in each other's company for a little while.

Perhaps it would be just tonight, so the less we knew of each other, the better off we would be, but exactly what was I expecting to happen between us tonight? I had never had a one night stand. I never believed I could pull one off, but right now as I stared at the insanely gorgeous man before me —it was all I wanted. We could spend the remaining hours of the night together, and then before the sun rose, we would be out of each other's life, just as quickly as we had come into them.

I loved the sound of that.

"I'm from Minnesota," he said.

"Oh, I'm from Indiana," I replied, choosing to just follow his lead and take each moment as it came.

Our drinks were delivered then and he lifted his tumbler to his lips for a sip.

I noticed when our legs touched, his jean clad knees brushed against the exposed skin of mine. It sent tiny prickles of excitement coursing through my body.

"So what brings you all the way to Turkey?" he asked.

"Just a quick vacation," I replied. "With friends."

"And how long are you here for?"

"About two weeks."

"Hm. And you've been here…"

"Two days," I replied. "What about you?"

"I'm here on business. It's my first time here, so I have been struck by how beautiful this city is. I might just extend my stay for a proper vacation. Now that I'm here I think I need one."

I smiled. "Don't we all?" I lifted my glass, the liquid wetting my lips as my gaze lowered to the sliver of rich, olive, skin beneath his white dress shirt. I couldn't seem to look away. The way the material molded to his torso was nothing short of art. It wasn't tight, but fitted enough to show the ripped build of his frame underneath. I looked towards the dance pit of adult kids and now wanted to be in the midst of them, with him.

Quite a lot of people had taken layers of their clothing off. What a great excuse it would be for him to do the same. But somehow, I couldn't picture him being there. He seemed too... respectable for playing in bubbles. This fact made me feel happy and sad at the same time.

"So what do you do in Indiana?" he asked.

I just wanted him to kiss me already. The information exchange just seemed too slow for me, especially since I'd just gotten out of a non-relationship with a guy I'd met online. We'd talked off and on for about three weeks before deciding to meet. I'd later come to find out after a few more dates that compulsive lying to cover his wilting confidence at being thirty-five and unemployed was a trait he'd forgotten to share.

So my enthusiasm for a love that would go the distance was currently nonexistent, especially given the breathtaking man sitting next to me. My body was currently brimming and humming for him, and I wanted to give it what it wanted-his mouth on mine-on me. "I work in marketing," I answered.

"Oh," he said. "I'm involved in marketing too. We're actually out here handling the new campaign for the Splash brand."

"Oh, I'm aware of them but aren't they majorly in Dubai? They're opening a branch here?"

"They are. We're in charge of the marketing and advertising for their year-end launch. What agency in Indiana do you work for?"

"Steer Point. You've probably never heard of it, we're really small. We're involved in digital marketing around the metropolitan area."

"Interesting," he said. "I've never been to Indiana, but maybe one of these days I'll stop by for a visit since I now know someone there."

"You'll be welcomed," I said, unable to control my smile. Damn, he was so magnetic.

He leaned in.

I paused, especially when his eyes bored into mine and I didn't dare breathe. Something about his gaze was so arresting and I couldn't quite place a finger on it.

"You're incredibly beautiful, Leah," he said.

"Thank you," I breathed the words out. "You're um—you're beautiful too."

He leaned back and laughed. "Nothing compared to you, but message received."

"I mean it, you're beautiful too—oh God. I didn't mean like pretty... I meant you're handsome."

A massive smile showed on his yummy lips as he placed his hand over mine on the counter, and once again leaned towards me. "Well, I'm glad to know you think so. I hope you don't have a boyfriend, Leah. Because, I don't think I can go any longer without kissing you."

I stopped breathing.

His gaze remained on my lips, focused solely on my mouth.

Simply frozen, my mind going blank. I know that I responded along the lines that I definitely did not have a boyfriend. But otherwise, I couldn't seem to focus.

His left hand slid around the side of my neck.

Instantly, I dripped between my thighs.

He gently drew me closer to him.

My startled gaze roved over his unbelievably beautiful face as his forehead met mine. My eyelids fluttered shut as I inhaled the exotic scent of his skin… a heady mix of lemon and some kind of woodsy scent, and I knew I would never forget it. The warmth of his breath tickled my face, and then our noses met, stroking lightly.

His mouth captured my lips and for a moment—my heart stopped.

It all came at once… something warm started in my belly and seemed to spread out to my limbs. It seeped into the crevices of my body, and rendered me completely limp. I struggled to hold on to his waist for some semblance of balance.

His tongue slipped into my mouth, bold and velvety as it tasted me with long, leisurely licks. His hold around my neck tightened, and so did my grip at his waist. He tasted like heaven. The flavor of the scotch he'd consumed right before, an elegant mix with his unique taste, clean and heady with the promise of primal fucking, drew me closer and closer to the edge.

I never wanted him to stop and kissed him back like my very survival depended on it.

My breasts felt heavy and tender from the dizzying arousal, my sex throbbed and pulsated with excitement. If he could do this to my mouth, I wondered in awe at just what he could do to other parts of my body. The possibilities made me almost choke with a gasp.

He broke off the kiss and it was punctuated with a low smacking sound. He pulled away, his hand released my neck.

Incoherent, I almost fell off the stool. His hands grabbed my arms to save me. I came back to my senses enough to process what had just happened. I was almost shocked at now hearing the chaos we were surrounded by. Like the sound had just been turned on after the mute button had been on. In the last few minutes with him, the entire world had faded away, just the two of us existed.

What the hell just happened?

I avoided his eyes as I tried to get myself together. I busied myself with adjusting my clothes and brushing off nonexistent lint.

"Are you okay?" he asked.

I lifted my gaze to meet the genuine concern in his, a welcome surprise from the amusement I had been expecting. "I am," I replied. "Thank you for the uh… kiss. It was nice."

He smiled.

I felt like smacking my palm across my head. In situations like this, the less said was always better, but I couldn't seem to stop babbling.

"Let's go somewhere a bit more private," he said, and lifted his gaze towards the rooms on the second floor. "Would one of those do?"

Yes, it was a worn out line, but I so did not care. "Sure," I replied, as I tried not to grab him up and drag him out of his seat. I needed to not act so darned eager, but wow… if that kiss was any example—I was in for the hottest sex on the face of this earth.

Pre-order your copy here:
CEO's Secret Baby

# ABOUT THE AUTHOR

Thank you so much for reading!
Please click on the link below to receive info about my latest releases and giveaways.
NEVER MISS A THING

Or
come and say hello here:

Printed in Great Britain
by Amazon